INTEGRATED ENGLISH
LANGUAGE ARTS

Currents in Literature

Genre Volume

Mary L. Dennis • Harold Levine
Norman Levine • Robert T. Levine

AMSCO

Amsco School Publications, Inc.
315 Hudson Street/New York, N.Y. 10013

Reviewers
Krista Chianchiano, English Teacher, Indian Hills High School, Oakland, NJ
Rachel Matthews, Social Studies Teacher, Passages Academy, New York, NY
Erin M. Stowell, English Teacher, Huntington Beach High School, Huntington Beach, CA
Howard Withrow, Reading Teacher, Ida S. Baker High School, Cape Coral, FL
Melissa White, Instructional Specialist Secondary Reading and English Language Arts,
   Montgomery County Public Schools, MD

Cover Design: Wanda Kossak
Text Design: A Good Thing, Inc.
Composition: Publishing Synthesis, Ltd.
Illustrations: Anthony D'Adamo
Cover Art: Microphone © Hemera/Images.com

Please visit our Web site at: *www.amscopub.com*

When ordering this book, please specify:
either **R 062 W** *or* CURRENTS IN LITERATURE, GENRE VOLUME.
ISBN: 978-1-56765-147-8
NYC Item 56765-147-7

Printed in the United States of America
5 6 7 8 9 10   11 10

To the Student

Most famous writers say that while they were growing up they read the work of many different authors, and that they continue to be insatiable readers. Reading good literature as young people provided them with examples they could follow as authors, and gave them inspiration and motivation to write their own stories, poems, articles, and plays.

With this book, you can do the same. In each unit, you'll find four carefully chosen selections by authors from the United States and other countries. Each one is linked to its own unit theme: "The Power of Love," "Alienation and Identity," "Writers on Writing," or "Imagining a World."

Along with each selection, you'll find a strategy to help you become a better reader. Using these methods will lead you to deeper understandings of literature and of life as you think about the unit themes and your own experiences.

With a bit of effort, you will soon find yourself becoming a better writer. You'll build a more powerful vocabulary and learn to correct common mistakes. You'll feel the pride and satisfaction of writing an essay, story, or poem that represents you at your best.

In addition, you will enjoy the work of sixteen different authors who all have something interesting for you to think about, write about, and discuss. They are the inspiration for everything this book has to teach you.

Enjoy your journey into the fascinating world of language!

The Authors

Contents

Introduction

What Is Genre Study?

You probably make tons of genre decisions every week without thinking about it. Should you go see the new blockbuster comedy, or are you more in the mood for an action-adventure? Should you download that catchy rock song before your big game, because you know the beat will get you going, or would you rather listen to something soothing like an R & B ballad? Are you a *Harry Potter* fan, or is a sports biography more up your alley?

The word "genre" sounds like a difficult academic term, but it basically means a "kind" or "sort" (of literature, music, art, or other form of expression) that is characterized by a certain form or style. For example, what are the different genres, or kinds, of music, and what distinguishes each one? How do we know rap is rap? And how is hip-hop different from country-western?

In this book, the Genre Volume, you'll be reading a variety of genres of writing, such as short stories, memoirs, an interview, a play, and a poem. While doing so, think about what characterizes each genre. How do the different forms have different effects on the reader, and which types are more effective for certain purposes? What genre would best help you explain your feelings to someone? What genre would help you best persuade people to recycle? These are just some of the questions you will begin to ask as you delve into this volume.

Our Look at Genres

The readings in this volume represent diverse genres, but are organized by themes and ideas. This organization will enable you to compare the effects of different genres, and thus enhance your critical thinking skills. In addition, looking at themes will help you find personal meaning in the pieces, and make connections between them.

The first unit's theme is "The Power of Love." We begin with the short story "Loretta and Alexander" by Budge Wilson, about two people who find love when they are not looking. Then you'll read an excerpt from the Laurie Colwin novel *Happy All the Time* (1978), which also centers on people looking for love . . . but in this case, are they ready? Next, we move to a classic work, Sonnet 29 by William Shakespeare, in which the narrator speaks of the power love has over him. The following selection, a newspaper article from 2001, shows that Shakespeare's ideas are indeed timeless—love still has powerful effects on people. The article, "Young Love: The Good, the Bad and the Educational" by Winifred Gallagher, focuses on the effects love has on adolescents in particular.

Unit Two is titled "Alienation and Identity." The first reading is an excerpt from *My Forbidden Face,* a diary written by a young Afghani girl named Latifa. How does the political and social climate in which she lives affect her sense of self and of security? The next piece is from the nonfiction book *The Death and Life of Great American Cities* by Jane Jacobs (1961). Jacobs also talks about living environments—in her book, she discusses the impact of small neighborhoods. Then you'll read an excerpt from Ralph Ellison's 1952 novel *Invisible Man*. The narrator speaks of feeling invisible. Why don't others see him? Then the unit wraps up with an excerpt from the

1955 Arthur Miller play *A View from the Bridge.* The protagonist, Catherine, wants to go out into the world on her own and form her own sense of self, but faces opposition from her uncle, Eddie.

Unit Three is "Writers on Writing." James Baldwin, in an excerpt from his essay collection *Notes of a Native Son,* talks about what it means for him to be an African-American writer. The next selection is from *Letters to a Young Poet* (1929), in which the poet Rainer Maria Rilke gives a young writer advice on his work. Then we go back to 1678 and examine a poem from Anne Bradstreet, "The Author to Her Book." How does the writer feel about her own work? The final piece in this unit also explores the relationship between a writer and his or her writing and audience: contemporary Asian-American writer Amy Tan, in an interview, discusses the responsibilities she feels she should and should not have to her readers.

The theme of Unit Four is "Imagining a World." We begin with an excerpt from a science fiction novel *Ecotopia* (1975) by Ernest Callenbach, in which a journalist describes life in a new ecologically stable state. How does this new world function differently from our own? Then you'll read Primo Levi's poem "Almanac" (1992)—in this work, the narrator expresses his outlook on the future of our world. How are humans responsible? Next is a visual art selection, "Letter from Overseas," painted by Thomas Hart Benton in 1943. You will be asked to read this lithograph as you would a verbal text. What is the story behind the letter in the picture? Finally, the unit ends with an excerpt from Leonardo da Vinci's *Notebooks,* in which he discusses the differences between poetry (the written word) and painting (visual art) in how we imagine and represent things. Which transmits a message more effectively—a painting or a story?

As you read the selections and consider the authors' genre decisions, we hope you'll become more aware of your own choices as a writer. You have the ability to shape your work in different ways, and the more you are conscious of your options, the more you will get out of the writing experience. After all, the reason reading and writing fall under Language *Arts* is that expressing yourself is an art—you, as the writer or artist, have many different ways of bringing your work to life. Think about the tools at your disposal and enjoy the creative process.

The Power of Love

Chapter One

Prereading Guide
Words to know and ideas to consider before you jump into the reading.

A. Essential Vocabulary

Word	Meaning	Typical Use
centered (*adj*) SENT-urd	directed toward one goal or thought; focused	All of Kayleigh's thoughts were *centered* on making the cheerleading squad.
conceivable (*adj*) cun-SEE-vuh-bul	able to be imagined or believed; possible	It is *conceivable*, though unlikely, that an asteroid will hit our planet.
dexterity (*n*) deks-TARE-uh-tee	cleverness and skill in using the hands or body; agility	Thanks to Josh's *dexterity*, we had the desk put together in less than two hours.
exquisite (*adj*) eks-KWIZ-it	especially lovely or fine; stunning	He could not forget the girl's *exquisite* face.
indeterminate (*adj*) in-dee-TUR-mih-nut	vague, undecided, or uncertain; indefinite	He'll be out sick for an *indeterminate* period of time.
inept (*adj*) in-EPT	lacking in skill or competence; awkward	Kristen soon found that she was a rather *inept* tai chi student.
intact (*adj*) in-TACKT	remaining whole or unchanged; undamaged	To my great surprise, we emerged from the roller coaster with all our limbs *intact*.
neurotic (*adj*) nu-ROT-ik	suffering from unstable behavior; disturbed	My little brother is *neurotic* about monsters under his bed and has to be convinced every night they aren't there.
unassuming (*adj*) un-uh-SOOM-ing	down-to-earth and without airs; modest	Although she has a high GPA, she is quiet and *unassuming*.
variance (*n*) VARE-ee-unce	a difference or irregularity; discrepancy	There was a *variance* between his ragged appearance and his highly paid profession.

B. Vocabulary Practice

Exercise 1.1   Sentence Completion

Using your new vocabulary knowledge, choose the best way to complete the following sentences. Circle the letter of your answer.

1. The movie star we met _____ and was completely unassuming.
   A. was a snob
   B. seemed like one of us

2. I _____ tell you how long he will stay; the length of his visit is indeterminate.
   A. can't
   B. can

3. Ahmed has _____ and is very centered.
   A. decided to be a lawyer
   B. no ideas about a career

4. The _____ I earned on this test is at variance with all the hours I spent studying for it.
   A. high score
   B. low score

5. Mallory was so inept at sewing that she _____.
   A. made her prom dress
   B. could not sew on a button

6. The _____. It's conceivable that spring is coming.
   A. snow is melting
   B. forecast calls for more snow

7. The driver handled the package _____, so we were sure our new lamp was intact.
   A. with care
   B. roughly

8. Matthew's dexterity with the basketball means he _____ scores.
   A. rarely
   B. often

9. I'm afraid my dog is neurotic. When it thunders, she _____.
   A. hides under the bed
   B. takes a nap

10. I was _____ by the exquisite bracelet my friend gave me.
    A. revolted
    B. delighted

Exercise 1.2 Using Fewer Words

Replace the italicized words with a single word from the following list. The first one has been done for you.

centered   conceivable   dexterity   exquisite   indeterminate

inept   intact   neurotic   unassuming   variance

1. She is so *lacking in skill and competence* that I can't understand how she made first-chair violin.

   1. __inept__

2. The restaurant will be closed for a(an) *undecided, uncertain* time.

   2._____

3. Hannah is definitely *directed toward one thing*: She wants to be a model.

   3._____

4. This antique china is *especially lovely and fine*, and Grandma is saving it for me.

   4._____

5. A characteristic all good gymnasts have is *skill in using their bodies*.

   5._____

6. I suppose an earthquake here is *able to be imagined*.

   6._____

7. There is a(an) *disparity or irregularity* between all her accomplishments and her lack of self-confidence.

   7._____

8. I was sure I'd hurt myself when I slipped on the ice, but when I stood up everything seemed *whole and unchanged*.

   8._____

9. My friend is *suffering from unstable behavior*—every morning, he sets five alarm clocks to ensure he's not late for school.

   9._____

10. Kyle is *down-to-earth and without airs* despite his extreme good looks.

    10._____

Exercise 1.3   Synonyms and Antonyms

Fill in the blanks in column A with the required synonyms or antonyms, selecting them from column B. (Remember: A *synonym* is a word *similar* in meaning to another word. *Autumn* and *fall* are synonyms. An *antonym* is a word *opposite* in meaning to another word. *Beginning* and *ending* are antonyms.)

	A	B
_____	1. synonym for *disturbed*	centered
_____	2. synonym for *modest*	conceivable
_____	3. synonym for *discrepancy*	dexterity
_____	4. antonym for *damaged*	inept
_____	5. antonym for *plain*	intact
_____	6. antonym for *definite*	neurotic
_____	7. synonym for *awkward*	unassuming
_____	8. antonym for *unimaginable*	variance
_____	9. synonym for *agility*	indeterminate
_____	10. synonym for *focused*	exquisite

C. Journal Freewrite

Before you begin the reading on the next page, take out a journal or sheet of paper and spend some time responding to the following prompt.

TIP: Don't worry about grammar and spelling; just write what comes to mind. The purpose of freewriting is to explore ideas, not to produce a polished work.

Perhaps you've heard the expression, "There's someone for everyone," used to refer to people who become friends or fall in love. What does this mean to you? Do you think it's true?

Loretta and Alexander

by Budge Wilson

About the Author
Budge Wilson (1917–) grew up in Nova Scotia, Canada, where many of her stories and novels are set. She worked as a teacher, commercial artist, photographer, and fitness instructor for more than 20 years before publishing her first book at the age of 56. Since then, she has published over 29 books. She writes primarily for children and young adults, and has won numerous awards for her work in those fields.

Loretta was lumpy in what most people would have regarded as all the wrong places. Her stomach was large and visible, and a second bulge—firmer and of less bulk, but nonetheless there—was situated between her waist and her breasts. Her face was not ugly, but its features were not noticeably much of anything else, either. Her cheeks did not cave in like Katharine Hepburn's, but rather puffed out, like a young child's. But Loretta was not a young child. She was eighteen years of age.

However, Loretta did have a couple of enviable qualities —apart from her soul, which we are not considering here. It is true that few people reached far enough beyond her lumpiness to notice them, but they existed. Loretta had <u>exquisite</u> skin. And not just on her face. All over. Her hands—dimpled, fat—looked as though they were made of the finest of creamy porcelain. Her legs, although large, were as smooth as the petals of some rare and delicate flower. The skin on her face looked as though it were lit from within, and was of a fragile and subtle transparency.

Loretta's eyes, her second physical asset, were not unusually large but they were a remarkable teal blue color, bordering on green. The whites were uncommonly white and dependably so. She'd been known to cry for twenty consecutive minutes, then emerge with those whites <u>intact</u>. And around these lovely eyes was a fringe of splendid dark lashes—long, thick—bearing no relation whatsoever to her sparse, unruly hair of <u>indeterminate</u> shade, with its meandering center part.

Loretta had brought her beautiful skin and her blue-green eyes and her unlovely body to Gray Cliff Campground. Markedly uncoordinated, she was struggling now to pitch her tent. She had come alone, because her closest companions were either married or else making merry with their boyfriends. But it was July, and she had wanted to go camping. Loretta lacked the willpower to stick to a healthy diet, but in most other areas of her life, her will was <u>centered</u> and firm. If she wanted to go camping, she would go, and she would arrive early enough in the day to get the site with the best view. Deep down, she knew that someone her size should never wear shorts. But it was hot, so she wore them. She did not defiantly thumb her nose at potential disapproval. She simply did not care. She was equipped with a peaceful and <u>unassuming</u> self-confidence. Even in her struggles with the tent, there was an air of quiet acceptance.

Two sites to the north, Alexander drove his small truck into a parking space and turned off the ignition. He had been to this campground before. He knew which was the best site. And he missed it again, just as he'd missed it every one of the nine times he'd been here. He sighed, squinting through his thick glasses to assess the people who had beat him to that sensational view. But from this distance, even with those telescope glasses, he couldn't make out more than a dim form doing something with a tent. And you can't feel exasperated for very long with a dim form.

However, it was easy for him to feel annoyed with himself. If only he hadn't taken the time to put out the garbage; it hadn't been even marginally smelly, and there was nothing in there to poison the cat. But he hadn't been sure. And he hadn't needed to check the stove and the windows and the front door—*four times*. He closed his eyes against this apparently permanent form of neuroticism. Other people just closed their doors and left their houses. Not Alexander. He left his house time after time, returning repeatedly to check something and then something else. Could the cat get at the litter box? Had he left the basement door open so that she could reach it? Was the coffee pot unplugged? (Mind you, he hardly ever used that pot. Still— all the more reason to be uncertain as to whether or not it was unplugged.) Had he turned off all the faucets, particularly in the bathroom sink, where there was no overflow opening? Yes, he had. Were the matches safely stowed in closed containers? Yes, they were. Had he put the chain on the back door? Yes, he had. When he left the house for the last time, he'd kept his eyes on the driveway, not wanting to see his neighbors staring at him from behind their curtains, tsk-tsking.

Alexander sighed again as he lifted his pup tent out of the trunk. What was in that house, anyway, worth stealing or burning or losing? Just a pile of dreary furniture from his nervous (and dead) mother, and cupboards full of unused staples (cream of tartar, paprika, vanilla) as well as a large can of WD-40. What did people use those things for anyway? And his files.

His files! Alexander's hands paused in midair. He'd forgotten to bring his box of files. If there were a fire, all his poetry would go up in smoke. His mind raced through his precautions to avoid fire. Yes, he was *sure* he'd unplugged the electric kettle. (But *had* he?) and he really could remember checking the stove tops and oven, placing the flat of his hands (for good measure) on top of each burner. (Or had that been this morning, before work?)

Alexander swallowed carefully. Should he go back? Would his uncertainty spoil the whole weekend? Chewing his lip, he put up his little tent without enthusiasm, his hands working mechanically and skillfully through all the motions. Then, with the same casual grace, he unpacked his other needs. Over supper, he'd make up his mind whether or not to return for his files. It was only a twenty-minute drive. Still, he'd love to feel really settled in. A trip back to town was an intrusion upon his peace. What peace? He took a deep breath and let it out slowly. It was his mother's fault. She'd been a chronic door and stove checker, and she'd been given to frequent bouts of anxiety. Savagely, Alexander drove the can opener into a tin of corned beef, cursing his genes.

Alexander's <u>dexterity</u> as he set up his Coleman stove, assembled pots and pans and bags of food, was at <u>variance</u> with his appearance. Bony and slightly stooped, he had the look of someone who was destined to trip over cracks and get tangled up in his own two feet. But no. With training, with eyes less myopic, with a shorter frame, he had it within him to be a great dancer. But life for Alexander was full of a lot of if-onlys. If only he were more handsome, less nervous, more practical, less absentminded, more confident, less hesitant. Then, oh *then*, things would be different.

However, Alexander could be happy in this place, even with the wrong view. Poems just dropped out of the sky into his lap when he was here; in Gray Cliff Campground he felt as though he were plugged into some sort of poetical hotline. Even as he hungrily attacked his canned peas, he could feel a poem coming over him. Reaching into his pocket for a pencil and paper, he groaned aloud. Empty. It was <u>conceivable</u> that he might be able to cope with the absence of his file box. Without paper and pencil, the weekend was impossible.

In a state of mind bordering on panic, Alexander searched through the truck for pen, pencil, paper of any kind. Nothing. The world, it seemed, was composed of plastic. There were enough plastic bags stuffed under his seat to accommodate a novel, but even if he'd had something to write with, he couldn't have written a poem on *them*. And there was not a single paper bag in sight, nor envelope, nor even a stray used grocery list. He looked at the sites to the right and to the left of him, but the tenants had gone—to swim, to dine, to drive, to do anything except stay put, the thing that Alexander was so longing to do. He would approach the owners of the spectacular view. Maybe they would have a few sheets of paper they could spare and perhaps a stubby pencil they would be willing to lend.

As Alexander approached Site 15 (he knew the number by heart; had he not, after all, set up the number, the location, as a sort of cosmic and apparently unobtainable goal for himself?), he was no wiser about its tenancy. The large khaki tent was in a heap on the ground, and judging from the visible movement, at least one of the occupants of the area was underneath it.

When he reached the site, he waited beside the heaving tent and coughed carefully. Then a hand appeared, followed by a head. Alexander did not see any other part of the head except the eyes. It was as though a disembodied pair of eyes had appeared out of a khaki background. Marveling at the color, the profusion of lashes, he forgot for a moment why he had come.

"Hi," said Loretta, voice cheerful. "Looking for someone?"

"Yes," he said. "I mean, no. I'm looking for some*thing*. But I see you're busy. I'm sorry to have disturbed you. What a beautiful view."

"That's OK," said Loretta. "I was just putting up my tent." She laughed, her voice throaty and languid.[1] "Or trying to. I'm all thumbs. I can't put a nail in a wall without getting bruises on every single one of my fingers. What are you looking for? And yes, the view's great. That's why I hotfoot it out here the *minute* I'm through work on my summer job. To get it before some other clown beats me to it."

Alexander sighed yet again. "May I help you?" he said. "Paper and pencil."

"What?"

"Paper and pencil. That's what I'm looking for. I need something to write with. And on. I write poetry. May I help you?" he repeated.

She looked at him. Poetry! And he didn't look as though he could help anyone or anything. A towering composition of unrelated bones, she mused. This is someone who obviously could break a leg getting out of bed. Still, four awkward hands might be more effective than two. "Yes, thank you," she replied. "The tent's kind of big. It was my father's from the days before tents got simple."

He was already picking up the scattered tent pegs, sorting ropes, lifting the center pole. "Here," he said, "hold this," and she took the pole, blindly obedient to something new in him. Speechless, she watched him go from task to task, moving with unerring smoothness and accuracy. No change of position was excessive or <u>inept</u>. Every physical thing he did had a kind of easy rhythm that was a pleasure to watch. He should be accompanied by music, she thought.

"OK," he said. "You can leave that now. Stand here while I fix the guy ropes and hammer in the pegs." Bending down to work on the pegs, he found himself cheek to cheek, as it were, with her leg. Words, images, metaphors, attacked him, as he let his eyes wander to that leg again and again, between hammer blows. Soft. That was certainly the key word. A hill of freshly fallen snow. No. Wrong color. A virgin sand dune.

"What happens to it when you get some sun?" he asked, reaching for another peg.

"What happens to what? The tent?"

"No. Your skin." Then he realized what he had said, and blushed.

She did not blush. "It gets brown. Sort of like strong coffee. I never burn."

He shut his eyes and let himself visualize the tanning of that skin.

"How do you get here so fast after work?" he asked.

"Well," she said, "I just tear home, get my stuff, feed the cat, and leave. I drive over the speed limit," she added.

---

[1]slow and without energy

"Tell me about your leaving," he asked, brows contracted. The tent was up now, and he was sitting on the ground, leaning against a tree, hugging his knees, watching her eyes.

"My what?"

"Your leaving. How do you leave?"

"Your house?"

"Yes."

"Oh. Well . . ." She paused. "I just go. You know . . . *leave.* Check the stove . . ."

"Aha!"

Loretta stared at him. "Aha?"

"Yes. Aha! You check the stove. How many times?"

"Once. Why?"

He frowned. "And lock the door," he said, voice bleak. "Once, I suppose."

"Yes. *Why?*"

"Forget it. It's just that if you're <u>neurotic</u>, you kind of hope that maybe everyone else is, too." He told her why it was always impossible for him to get to the campground in time to get the best view. Then he stopped. Foot in his mouth again. *She,* after all, had the best view.

"Never mind." She grinned. "It's not like you beat dogs or steal paper clips or anything."

"Wow!" he said. "Do you mind if I write that down?"

"On what?" She grinned again.

"Right!" His face was relaxing, his brows unknotting. "Do you have some paper?"

She did. He might have known she would. "May I?" he asked, and settled down in her lawn chair to write a poem. It had just descended on him in one chunk when she'd mentioned dogs and paper clips. He glanced up for a moment, and she was sitting beside him.

"Oh!" he said. "Two chairs. Has your boyfriend gone for water?"

"No," she replied. "But I always bring two chairs. Just in case."

After writing for a while, he looked up from his poem, contemplating her eyes and her astonishing skin.

"I just bet," he said, "that you know exactly what to do with cream of tartar and paprika and vanilla. And WD-40."

She felt a warm peace pass over her and then settle deep into her chest. "Yes," she said. "As a matter of fact, I do."

He watched her, smiling quietly. "Beautiful view you've got here," he said.

"Yes," she said. "Haven't we."

Understanding the Reading

Complete the next three exercises and see how well you understood "Loretta and Alexander."

Exercise 1.4 Multiple-Choice Questions

Answer the following questions about the reading. Circle the letter of your answer.

TIP: Don't try to answer the questions from memory; go back to the text as often as necessary.

1. Loretta's enviable physical qualities include her
   A. dimples.
   B. small waist.
   C. beautiful face.
   D. skin and eyes.

2. Alexander did not get the campsite he wanted because
   A. his eyesight was poor and he overlooked it.
   B. he felt he had to check and recheck things at home.
   C. he had trouble getting his truck started.
   D. someone else had reserved it in advance.

3. Three words that best describe Loretta are
   A. beautiful, self-confident, and coordinated.
   B. overweight, self-conscious, and embarrassed.
   C. unassuming, self-confident, and uncoordinated.
   D. overweight, uncoordinated, and self-conscious.

4. Alexander surprised Loretta when he
   A. effortlessly set up the tent.
   B. asked her if her skin got sunburned.
   C. told her why he could never get the best site.
   D. asked her if he could share her campsite.

5. The narrator implies that Loretta and Alexander
   A. are hopeless misfits who will never be happy.
   B. both find the other ridiculous.
   C. may develop a romantic relationship.
   D. will probably never meet again.

Exercise 1.5 Short-Answer Questions

Respond to the following questions in one to two complete sentences. Go back to the text, as you did on the multiple choice.

6. What characteristics do Loretta and Alexander have in common?

   _____

   _____

   _____

7. In what ways are Loretta and Alexander different?

_____

_____

_____

8. Which character do you relate to more, Loretta or Alexander? Why?

_____

_____

_____

9. Do you believe that opposites attract? Why or why not? Consider the story and your own experiences.

_____

_____

_____

Exercise 1.6   Extending Your Thinking

Respond to the following question in three to four complete sentences. Use details from the text in your answer.

10. The theme of this unit is "The Power of Love." Assuming that Loretta and Alexander do fall in love, how might their relationship change both of their lives?

_____

_____

_____

_____

_____

_____

Reading Strategy Lesson
Using Context Clues

Context literally means "with text." It is the text that surrounds a word and helps to make its meaning clear, even if you've never seen the word before.

If you encounter a word you do not know, be sure to check for a footnote where the word may be defined. If there is no definition given, you can use context clue strategies to determine what the word means. On the next page are four ways to do so.

Four Ways to Use Context Clues

1. Read the words and phrases before and after the unknown word. They can provide clues to the word's meaning.

Read the following example. From the text before and after the word *sparse*, what can you determine about the meaning of the word?

> And around these lovely eyes was a fringe of splendid dark lashes—long, thick—bearing no relation whatsoever to her *sparse*, unruly hair of indeterminate shade, with its meandering center part.

The author tells us that her splendid, thick, long lashes bear no relation to her *sparse* hair. Therefore, her hair must be neither long nor thick nor splendid. So *sparse* must mean short and thin, and not very pretty. Other words like *unruly* and *indeterminate shade* also describe Loretta's hair and help us picture what it is like.

2. Check for restatements of the word in question.

How can you tell what *disembodied* means in the following example?

> Alexander did not see any other part of the head except the eyes. It was as though a *disembodied* pair of eyes had appeared out of a khaki background.

Disembodied is defined by restatement in the sentence right before it: Alexander could see only Loretta's eyes. So *disembodied* must mean "without a body." If someone spoke to you in a completely dark room, his or her voice might seem disembodied.

3. See if the word is defined by an example.

What example helps you understand what the author means by *splendid* lashes?

> And around these lovely eyes was a fringe of splendid dark lashes—long, thick . . .

Eyelashes that are long and thick are generally regarded as a good thing to have—beautiful and striking, so *splendid* must describe something that is especially good, lovely, or beautiful. You could have a splendid day or live in a splendid house—or your teacher could write "Splendid!" at the top of your next essay. Wouldn't that be splendid?

4. Look for word-within-a-word clues.

Are there any clues within the word *markedly* that help you determine its meaning?

> *Markedly* uncoordinated, she was struggling now to pitch her tent.

Have you ever used a highlighter to *mark* something that you wanted to stand out? You can find the word *mark* in *markedly*. The author could have written, "Marked by lack of coordination . . ." but she chose to use the adverb form of the word *mark—markedly* to modify the adjective *uncoordinated*. *Markedly* tells how uncoordinated Loretta was: extremely.

HINT: No matter which context clue method you use, always reread the sentence, replacing the word in question with the definition you have decided upon. It should still make sense.

Review:
Using Context Clues

- Read the sentences before and after the word in question.

- Check to see if the word is restated in different terms.

- See if there are any examples that lead you to the meaning.

- Look at the word's parts. Do you know a word within the word you are trying to define, or one that sounds or looks like it?

With context clues, you should be able to arrive at definitions of many words without having to look them up in a dictionary.

Exercise 1.7   Practice the Reading Strategy

The words in the table on the next page are from "Loretta and Alexander." Find each word in the selection and use context clue skills to write a brief definition. Then split up the words with a partner and check their meanings in a dictionary. If your definition is a close match to one of the meanings in the dictionary, give yourself a check mark. If not, cross out your answer and write the correct one in the check-or-revise column.

Word	My Definition	Dictionary's Definition	✔ or Revise
1. enviable (p. 7)			
2. asset (p. 7)			
3. uncommonly (p. 7)			
4. meandering (p. 7)			
5. defiantly (p. 8)			
6. exasperated (p. 8)			
7. marginally (p. 8)			
8. myopic (p. 9)			
9. disembodied (p. 9)			
10. unerring (p. 10)			

Exercise 1.8   Apply the Reading Strategy

Read each passage. Use context clues to determine the most likely meaning of the italicized word. Then choose the matching definition from the choices below and write its letter on the line. The passages are from "The Open Window," a short story by H. H. Munro.

A. horrifying   B. illnesses   C. hurried
D. dangerous   E. about to happen

_____ 1. It was a relief to Framton when the aunt *bustled* into the room with a whirl of apologies for being late in making her appearance.

_____ 2. "In crossing the moor to their favourite snipe-shooting ground they were all three engulfed in a *treacherous* piece of bog. It had been that dreadful wet summer, you know, and places that were safe in other years gave way suddenly without warning."

_____ 3. To Framton it was all purely horrible. He made a desperate but only partially successful effort to turn the talk on to a less *ghastly* topic.

_____ 4. "The doctors agree in ordering me complete rest, an absence of mental excitement, and avoidance of anything in the nature of violent physical exercise," announced Framton, who laboured under the tolerably widespread delusion that total strangers and chance acquaintances are hungry for the least detail of one's ailments and *infirmities*, their cause and cure.

_____ 5. Framton grabbed wildly at his stick and hat; the hall door, the gravel drive, and the front gate were dimly noted stages in his headlong retreat. A cyclist coming along the road had to run into the hedge to avoid *imminent* collision.

Writing Workshop
Identifying Audience, Purpose, and Task

Audience

What sort of reader do you think Budge Wilson had in mind when she wrote "Loretta and Alexander"? Who would enjoy reading this story? The answer is just about anyone from teenagers to senior citizens. She had a wide **audience** for the story.

When you respond to written questions in class or on standardized tests, your audience may be very specific. For example, you might be asked to write for

- your class
- your teacher
- a group of readers who score essays written for tests
- the entire student body
- members of your community's library board
- readers of your school newspaper
- readers interested in your class project
- your parents or other relatives
- your best friend
- a scholarship committee
- members of the school board
- your principal

Think about the differences in these audiences. You don't talk to your best friend the same way you talk to your teachers or your parents, and your writing style should also differ for various audiences. Keep reading to find out how your audience connects to your purpose and task.

Purpose

Authors write for many different reasons, such as to **inform**, to **persuade**, or to **entertain**. Budge Wilson's **purpose** when she wrote "Loretta and Alexander" was to entertain her readers. She created two characters who are lonely and brought them together in an entertaining story.

When you are the writer, you should identify a purpose for your writing before you begin planning. If you do not have your purpose in mind, it may be difficult to accomplish what you want to.

Now, how are your purpose and audience connected? Look at the following examples. Your purposes are listed in boldface. Your audiences are in italics.

Topic:	Homecoming Dance
Possible Purposes:	To **persuade**

- *students* to show lots of school spirit
- *your parents* to let you go
- *your friend* to go with you

To **inform**
- *graduates* of the dates, activities, and locations
- *students* of the expected way to dress
- *the band* what time it should set up and what equipment will be provided

Task

As you've seen in the examples, you can have many different purposes and audiences related to one topic. Budge Wilson's topic in "Loretta and Alexander" is love, her audience is readers from 14 up, and her **task** was to *write a short story*.

A **task** is merely a form of written material. Here are some of the many possible writing tasks.

essays	poems	Web sites
speeches	short stories	flyers
letters	plays	brochures
research papers	film scripts	glossaries
book and film reviews	novels	posters
memos	interviews	advertisements
e-mails	newspaper articles	song lyrics
magazine articles	children's storybooks	blogs

Now think about what type of writing you would need to create to accomplish the goals listed in the examples. The results are your tasks.

For example, to accomplish your purpose of getting students to show school spirit, you might write a speech or skit for school TV, make posters in school colors, or hand out flyers with the words to cheers and songs. Since your audience is your fellow students, you will be able to use informal language that will appeal to them in a friendly, upbeat way.

On the other hand, if your purpose is to inform graduates of the dates, activities, and locations, you will be more formal. You might compose a letter inviting them to return to their alma mater and include a schedule explaining what events will take place over the weekend, with times and locations noted. If they need to make reservations, you'll want to include a reply form or an e-mail address where they can reach you.

Exercise 1.9   Practice Identifying Audience, Purpose, and Task

Read each item. Then fill in the main audience, purpose, and task.

1. A flyer posted on a soda machine says:
   Do you *really* want that soda can to go to the landfill? What if everyone in the world who is drinking a soda right now tosses the can in the trash instead of into a recycling bin? Take it with you if there is no recycling can close by, and keep it until you find one. Recycling is good for your community, your country, and your world.

Audience: _____

Purpose: _____

Task: _____

2. An e-mail you wrote reads:
   Dear Customer Service: I ordered this DVD more than three weeks ago. My order number is QX4590876. I have not received it. Please let me know when it was shipped. If it has not been shipped yet, please cancel my order.

Audience: _____

Purpose: _____

Task: _____

3. The script for a soap opera:
   Nick: But darling, you know I wouldn't lie to you.
   Ashley: I wish I could believe you. You've done it so many times before!
   Nick: Not this time. We'll be together forever this time. (*kisses her*)

Audience: _____

Purpose: _____

Task: _____

4. A newspaper editorial reads:
   This mayor has repeatedly made promises to the citizens of this community that have not been kept. What ever happened to the new playground equipment? Where is the teen center? Does this mayor really care about our children? I urge you not to vote for him on November 2.

   Audience: _____

   Purpose: _____

   Task: _____

5. A story reads:
   The little garden snake could not understand why the children screamed. Why did they run away? He was such a little snake. He didn't bite, but he ate nasty bugs that did bite! He just wanted to get a better look at humans. Sadly, he wriggled away to find his mother.

   Audience: _____

   Purpose: _____

   Task: _____

Exercise 1.10 Apply the Writing Lesson

Choose five tasks from the examples in the lesson (p. 18) and write them in the task column below. Then create an audience and purpose for each. The first one has been done for you.

Task	Audience	Purpose
e-mail	*yearbook editor*	*to inform editor that I have attached the list of names for the freshman photo section*

Grammar Mini-Lesson
Building Sentences with Adverbs and Adjectives

A **complete sentence** can be as simple as a subject and a predicate:

Alexander sighed.
SUBJ   PRED

In this example, the subject (the person doing the action in the sentence) is a proper noun, *Alexander*. The predicate (the action in the sentence) is a verb, *sighed*. In most cases, a complete sentence must have a subject and a verb. The exception is when the subject is understood. For example, in "Get out!" it is understood that the subject is "you"—You get out!

A story or essay made up of simple sentences of one noun and one verb would lack details and probably not be very interesting.

How do you make a simple sentence more descriptive and lively? The answer is, you add **adverbs** and **adjectives** (also called **modifiers** because they help describe something).

Adverbs

- tell how or when the action in the verb took place:

  walked *speedily* (*Speedily* describes *how* the person or animal walked.)

  an article that appeared *recently* (*Recently* tells *when* the article appeared.)

- add to the way an adjective describes something:

  The redwoods were *incredibly* tall. (*Incredibly* tells *how* tall.)

- tell to what degree an adverb applies

  quite clearly (Both words are adverbs; *quite* tells *how* clearly.)

Let's go back to our sample sentence:

  Alexander sighed.

- The verb in our sample sentence is *sighed*. We can use an adverb to tell *how* Alexander sighed.

  Alexander sighed *loudly*.

Some other choices are *softly*, *sadly*, *happily*. Notice how each choice changes the meaning of the sentence.

- Adverbs can also be used to tell when the action took place. Let's add a "when" adverb.

  Alexander sighed loudly *again*.

  We could also use *then* or *now*.

- Let's add another adverb. We'll tell *to what degree* the adverb *loudly* applies.

  Alexander sighed *somewhat* loudly again.

  Some other choices are *extremely*, *rather*, *fairly*. They all change the degree of Alexander's loudness.

  We told the reader more about what Alexander *did*. Now we need to tell the reader a little bit more about Alexander himself. We need words that describe *him*, so we'll add in some adjectives.

Adjectives

- describe or modify nouns.

  The story told us a lot about Alexander. He is *tall*, *bony*, *stooped*, *nearsighted*, *neurotic*, *nervous*, and *poetic*. All of these words are adjectives that describe Alexander. We'll choose one that will be especially interesting and fit the sentence well:

  Neurotic Alexander sighed somewhat loudly again.

  If you read this sentence, you would want to keep reading to find out what makes the author describe Alexander as *neurotic*, as well as why he sighed loudly.

  When you write, add adverbs and adjectives to wimpy simple sentences to give them muscle and keep your readers interested.

Exercise 1.11 Practice Adding Adverbs and Adjectives

Add an adverb or an adjective to each simple sentence. Rewrite the sentence on the line provided.

1. The dog barked.

   _____

2. The bird flew.

   _____

3. Andrew laughed.

   _____

4. The rain poured.

   _____

5. The mail arrived.

_____

6. I'm leaving.

_____

7. Aaron voted.

_____

8. Kerri finished.

_____

9. Austin left.

_____

10. The gates opened.

_____

Exercise 1.12 Building Interesting Sentences

In Exercise 1.11, you added an adverb or an adjective to each sentence. This time, add *more* than one modifier to each sentence. You can change some words in the sentences if you need to.

1. Your turn will come.

_____

2. We had to wait.

_____

3. The bookstore closed.

_____

4. My bike is broken.

_____

5. I lost my ticket.

_____

6. The door is locked.

_____

7. We won the game.

_____

8. We loved the movie.

_____

9. The snow fell.

_____

10. Megan dances.

_____

Polish Your Spelling

Adding Suffixes

A *suffix* is a word part added to the end of a base to form a new word.

WORD		SUFFIX		NEW WORD
hope	+	ing	=	hoping
hope	+	ed	=	hoped
hope	+	less	=	hopeless
hope	+	ful	=	hopeful

If a suffix begins with a vowel (*a, e, i, o, u*), it is called a *vowel suffix*. Noticing whether the suffix you want to add begins with a vowel or a consonant will help you spell the new word correctly. It will also help if you check how the base word ends and whether the next-to-the-last letter is a vowel or a consonant.

Adding Suffixes to Words Ending in -Y

- In general, when you add a suffix to a word ending with a *y* preceded by a consonant, change the *y* to an *i*.

  Examples: victory + ous = victorious
  easy + er = easier

  Exceptions: dry = dryly, dryness, dryer
  spry = spryly, spryness, spryer

- If the letter before the final *y* in the word is a vowel, you usually don't change the *y*.

  Examples: play + er = player
  buy + er = buyer

  Exceptions: day + ly = daily
  pay + ed = paid

- You also keep the *y* when the suffix you are adding is *-ing*.

  Examples: rely + ing = relying
  stay + ing = staying

Exercise 1.13 Practice Adding Suffixes

Write the words with their suffixes correctly on the blank lines. Refer to the rules and examples if necessary.

1. outrage + ous = _____

2. noise + y = _____

3. study + ous = _____

4. probable + ly =_____

5. tasty + est = _____

6. crazy + ly = _____

7. happy + ly = _____

8. compete + ing = _____

9. ridicule + ous = _____

10. calculate + or = _____

Chapter Two

Prereading Guide

Words to know and ideas to consider before you jump into the reading.

A. Essential Vocabulary

Word	Meaning	Typical Use
administrator (*n*) ad-MIN-ih-stray-tor	a director of a school, business, agency, or foundation; manager	The principal is the chief *administrator* of our school.
benign (*adj*) be-NINE	of a benevolent nature; kind	Mrs. Martinez is always smiling; she has a very *benign* disposition.
civic (*adj*) SIV-ik	having to do with a government; public	It is your *civic* duty to vote.
deliberation (*n*) de-lib-ur-AY-shun	thoughtfulness and careful consideration; forethought	After considerable *deliberation*, the Senate approved the new bill.
indelible (*adj*) in-DEL-ib-ul	not able to be removed; permanent	Items you bring to camp should be marked with *indelible* ink.
perspective (*n*) pur-SPEK-tiv	a view showing things in relationship to one another; aspect	The artist had painted the street scene with perfect *perspective*.
peruse (*v*) pur-OOZ	to look over; examine	I need to *peruse* my notes one more time before the test.
refined (*adj*) ree-FIND	showing good taste and manners; cultured	My aunt and uncle are very *refined*; they belong to a gourmet supper club.
relegate (*v*) RELL-uh-gate	to assign to a lesser or more remote category or place; demote (usually used with *to*)	The quarterback was angry at being *relegated* to the bench by the referee.
subject (*v*) sub-JEKT	to expose or open; to undergo	They were *subjected* to a background check before they were hired.

B. Vocabulary Practice

Exercise 2.1   Sentence Completion

Using your new vocabulary knowledge, choose the best way to complete the following sentences. Circle the letter of your answer.

1. The administrator of the foundation will have to _____.
   A. make the final decision
   B. consult his supervisor

2. Residents of the Gulf and Atlantic coasts are most likely to be subjected to _____.
   A. blizzards
   B. summer hurricanes

3. Mr. Huang always _____ people with his benign smile.
   A. terrifies
   B. reassures

4. When his _____ were discovered, the sergeant was relegated to another rank.
   A. unethical activities
   B. brilliant skills

5. Most people who are prominent in civic activities say they _____.
   A. like to socialize
   B. want to serve the public

6. My aunt is very refined and always _____ at dinnertime.
   A. uses fancy silverware
   B. talks with her mouth full

7. With great deliberation, the prisoners _____.
   A. made elaborate escape plans
   B. got into a fight

8. Working with children had left its indelible mark on Nicole's _____.
   A. new dress
   B. career plans

9. We'll discuss this further _____; being away will give us some perspective.
   A. when we go on vacation
   B. in a few minutes

10. Wanting to go out with friends, Danielle perused her _____ quickly.
    A. history assignment
    B. fingernails

Exercise 2.2 Using Fewer Words

Replace the italicized words with a single word from the following list. The first one has been done for you.

administrator   benign   civic   deliberation   indelible

perspective   peruse   refined   relegated to   subjected

1. Katie is very good at showing things in *relationship to one another*.

    1. <u>perspective</u>

2. I asked my mom to *look over* my final draft.

    2. _____

3. Emily is sweet to everyone. No matter how the conversation goes, she always remains *of a benevolent nature*.

    3. _____

4. The *director of the agency* will see you shortly.

    4. _____

5. Tonight's *government-related* meeting is to get citizen feedback about the proposed discount store.

    5. _____

6. A lot of *thoughtfulness and careful consideration* went into this decision.

    6. _____

7. The ink used to mark these prices is *unable to be removed*.

    7. _____

8. No one wanted the children to be *exposed and opened* to the ridiculous headlines about their father.

    8. _____

9. *Assigned to a remote place in* Iceland, Wilson lost his influence in Washington.

    9. _____

10. We like to be *showing good manners and taste*, so we always send thank-you notes for any gifts we receive.

    10. _____

Exercise 2.3   Synonyms and Antonyms

Fill in the blanks in column A with the required synonyms or antonyms, selecting them from column B. (Remember: A *synonym* is a word *similar* in meaning to another word. *Autumn* and *fall* are synonyms. An *antonym* is a word *opposite* in meaning to another word. *Beginning* and *ending* are antonyms.)

	A	B
_____	1. synonym for *manager*	civic
_____	2. synonym for *aspect*	indelible
_____	3. synonym for *examine*	refined
_____	4. antonym for *unkind*	deliberation
_____	5. synonym for *forethought*	subject
_____	6. antonym for *private*	administrator
_____	7. synonym for *demoted*	perspective
_____	8. antonym for *removable*	benign
_____	9. synonym for *cultured*	peruse
_____	10. synonym for *undergo*	relegated

C. Journal Freewrite

Before you begin the reading on the next page, take out a journal or sheet of paper and spend some time responding to the following prompt.

TIP: Don't worry about grammar and spelling; just write what comes to mind. The purpose of freewriting is to explore ideas, not to produce a polished work.

> Does having money assure you a perfect, happy future? Why or why not? Think of specific examples from your own experience or from books you've read or movies or shows you've seen.

from Happy All the Time

by Laurie Colwin

About the Author
**Laurie Colwin
(1944–1992)** was born
in Manhattan and
worked as an editor for
several publishers,
simultaneously working
on her own writing
career and publishing
short stories in maga-
zines like *The New
Yorker, Redbook,
Cosmopolitan,* and
Harper's. Her novels and
stories humorously
explore troubled char-
acters and relationships.
Her two memoir/cook-
books combine recipes
with funny essays, such
as "Alone in the Kitchen
With an Eggplant."
Happy All the Time, her
second novel, is a witty
depiction of the love
lives of middle- and
upper-class people.

Guido Morris and Vincent Cardworthy were third cousins.
No one remembered which Morris had married which Cardworthy, and no one cared except at large family gatherings
when this topic was introduced and <u>subjected</u> to the <u>benign</u>
opinions of all. Vincent and Guido had been friends since
babyhood. They had been strolled together in the same
pram[1] and as boys were often brought together, either at the
Cardworthy house in Petrie, Connecticut, or at the Morrises'
in Boston to play marbles, climb trees, and set off cherry
bombs in trash cans and mailboxes. As teenagers, they drank
beer in hiding and practiced smoking Guido's father's cigars,
which did not make them sick, but happy. As adults, they
both loved a good cigar.

At college they fooled around, spent money, and wondered what would become of them when they grew up.
Guido intended to write poetry in heroic couplets[2] and
Vincent thought he might eventually win the Nobel Prize for
physics.

In their late twenties they found themselves together again
in Cambridge. Guido had gone to law school, had put in several years at a Wall Street law firm, and had discovered that
his heart was not in his work, and so he had come to graduate school to study Romance languages and literature. He
was old for a graduate student, but he had decided to give
himself a few years of useless pleasure before the true responsibilities of adulthood set upon him. Eventually, Guido was
to go to New York and take over the stewardship of the
Morris family trust[3]—the Magna Charta Foundation, which
gave money to <u>civic</u> art projects, artists of all sorts, and
groups who wished to preserve landmarks and beautify their
cities. The trust put out a bimonthly magazine devoted to the
arts called *Runnymeade.* The money for all this came from a
small fortune in textiles made in the early nineteenth century
by a former sea captain by the name of Robert Morris. On

---

[1]perambulator—a baby carriage
[2]two rhymed lines, each having four stressed syllables
[3]a large amount of money, often left by a deceased person to an
heir or to charity

Unit One The Power of Love   **31**

one of his journeys, Robert Morris had married an Italian wife. Thereafter, all Morrises had Italianate names. Guido's grandfather was Almanso. His father was Sandro. His uncle Giancarlo was the present <u>administrator</u> of the trust but he was getting on and Guido had been chosen to be eventual heir.

Vincent had gone off to the University of London and had come back to the Massachusetts Institute of Technology. He had begun as a city planner, but his true field of interest was sanitation engineering, as it was called, although Vincent called it garbage. He was fascinated by its production, removal, and possible uses. His monographs[4] on recycling, published in a magazine called *City Limits*, were beginning to make him famous in his field. He had also patented[5] a small machine for home use that turned vegetable peelings, newspapers, and other kitchen leavings into valuable mulch,[6] but nothing much had happened to it. Eventually he would go off to New York and give over his talent and energy to the Board of City Planning.

With their futures somewhat assured, they lolled around Cambridge and wondered whom they would marry.

One Sunday afternoon in January, Vincent and Guido found themselves <u>perusing</u> an exhibition of Greek vases at the Fogg Museum. The air outside was heavy and wet. Inside, it was overheated. It was the sort of day that forced you out of the house and gave you nothing back in return. They had been restless indoors, edgy out of doors, and had settled on the Fogg feeling that the sight of Greek vases might cool them out. They took several turns around. Guido delivered himself of a lecture on shape and form. Vincent gave his two minutes on the planning of the Greek city-state. None of this quieted them. They were looking for action, unsure of what kind and unwilling to seek it out. Vincent believed that the childish desire to kick tires and smash bottles against walls was never lost but <u>relegated</u>, in adulthood, to the subconscious where it jumped around creating just the sort tension he was feeling. A sweaty round of handball or a couple of well-set cherry bombs would have done them both a lot of good, but it was too cold for the one and they were too <u>refined</u> for the other. Thus they were left with their own nerves.

On the way out, Guido saw a girl sitting on a bench. She was slender, fine-boned, and her hair was the blackest, sleekest hair Guido had ever seen. It was worn the way Japanese children wear theirs, only longer. Her face seemed to print itself on his heart <u>indelibly</u>.

He stopped to stare at her and when she finally looked back, she glared through him. Guido nudged Vincent and they moved toward the bench on which she sat.

"The <u>perspective</u> is perfect," said Guido. "Notice the subtlety of line and the intensity of color."

"Very painterly," said Vincent. "What is it?"

---

[4]articles, pamphlets, or other pieces of writing devoted to one subject
[5]guaranteed exclusive manufacturing rights for a certain time period
[6]material used in gardens and around trees and plants to prevent weeds and provide nourishment

"I'll have to look it up," said Guido. "It appears to be an inspired mix of schools. Notice that the nose tilts—a very slight distortion giving the illusion of perfect clarity." He pointed to her collar. "Note the exquisite folds around the neck and the drapery of the rest of the figure."

During this recitation, the girl sat perfectly still. Then, with <u>deliberation</u>, she lit a cigarette.

"Notice the arc of the arm," Guido continued. The girl opened her perfect mouth.

"Notice the feeblemindedness[7] that passes for wit among aging graduate students," she said. Then she got up and left.

———
[7]foolishness

Understanding the Reading

Complete the next three exercises and see how well you understood the excerpt from *Happy All the Time.*

Exercise 2.4   Multiple-Choice Questions

Answer the following questions about the reading. Circle the letter of your answer.

TIP: Don't try to answer the questions from memory; go back to the text as often as necessary.

1. As children, Guido and Vincent
   A. were spoiled and behaved very badly.
   B. behaved a little worse than most boys.
   C. were not allowed to play together.
   D. lived in the same house.

2. Guido's and Vincent's early years at college were primarily devoted to
   A. working part-time and attending classes.
   B. studying the principles of physics.
   C. writing heroic couplets.
   D. partying and big dreams.

3. Guido and Vincent entered graduate school in Cambridge mainly to
   A. get more education so they could get better jobs.
   B. study ancient Greek art.
   C. pass the time and possibly find wives.
   D. have the kind of fun they had as teenagers.

4. Neither Vincent nor Guido
   A. was successful in attaining his dreams.
   B. had any extra time to waste fooling around.
   C. was well educated.
   D. had enough money to do what he wanted to.

5. According to Vincent, once you reach adulthood, you
   A. can still play and have fun.
   B. are thankful to finally be responsible and settle down.
   C. become completely serious and boring.
   D. still have childish tendencies but have to quiet them.

Exercise 2.5 Short-Answer Questions

Respond to the following questions in one to two complete sentences. Go back to the text, as you did on the multiple choice.

6. Why is Guido able to give up a career for which he has spent so much time and money preparing?

   _____

   _____

   _____

7. Do you think Vincent will be happy in his job on the Board of City Planning? Why or why not?

   _____

   _____

   _____

8. Do you think the title *Happy All the Time* applies to Guido, to Vincent, to both, or to neither? List some words that you think describe them.

   _____

   _____

   _____

9. Guido and Vincent "lolled around Cambridge and wondered whom they would marry." Predict what you think their romantic futures might hold. For instance, will they get married? What kind of women would be attracted to them?

   _____

   _____

   _____

Exercise 2.6 Extending Your Thinking

Respond to the following question in three to four complete sentences. Use details from the texts in your answer.

10. Compare the frailties, or natural weaknesses, of the male protagonists in "Loretta and Alexander" and *Happy All the Time*. What do we learn about their personalities that has had or might have an effect on their romantic relationships?

(Hint: Think about their levels of confidence, responsibility, and self-assurance.)

_____

_____

_____

_____

_____

_____

Reading Strategy Lesson
Thinking Aloud for Better Comprehension

In the previous lesson, you learned about audience, purpose, and task. Think about the novel excerpt you have just read. What do you think Laurie Colwin's audience, purpose, and task were?

In the author sidebar, you learned that Colwin's novels and stories "humorously explore troubled characters and relationships." The audience for this story is limited only by the language, which is fairly complicated. A wide "young adult and up" readership might enjoy this story. Colwin's purpose was to entertain and possibly to imply a moral lesson. Since _Happy All the Time_ is a novel, Colwin chose a novel as her task.

Determining the writer's audience, purpose, and task can help you to accomplish _your_ reading purpose: to find more meaning in a story, essay, or article, and to connect what the author is saying to your own life.

Thinking aloud is another helpful tool. This means that you verbalize what you're thinking as you read the selection. You can even carry on a conversation with the author.

Example:

Laurie Colwin Writes:	You Think Aloud:
At college, they fooled around, spent money, and wondered what would become of them when they grew up. Guido intended to write poetry in heroic couplets and Vincent thought he might eventually win the Nobel Prize for physics.	_OK, so you're saying these two guys were rich and didn't ever have to worry much about anything. Are they thinking it's going to be quite a while before they "grow up"? Aren't their goals kind of unrealistic?_

Now you can picture Guido and Vincent. You may have decided that you think they're pretty cool, or that you don't like them very much. Either way, you probably are wondering—just as they are—what will happen to them when they do finally grow up. Or, in the back of your mind, you might be thinking, "People like them never have to grow up."

Carrying on a conversation with the author or with a classmate or teacher as you read helps you determine the meaning of various details and zero in on the overall message. Here is another passage from the novel, along with some thoughts and questions you might have as you read:

Laurie Colwin Writes:

In their late twenties they found themselves together again in Cambridge. Guido had gone to law school, had put in several years at a Wall Street law firm, and had discovered that his heart was not in his work, and so he had come back to graduate school to study Romance languages and literature.

You Think Aloud:

Cambridge—that's a city. I think it's where Harvard is. And Wall Street, that's in New York. Does it have something to do with stocks? His family is really wealthy if he could just drop a career like that and go study Romance languages. Does this mean learning French and Italian? He's not going to make much money with that.

Exercise 2.7   Practice the Reading Strategy

I. Following is another passage from *Happy All the Time*. With a partner, take turns reading it out loud and talking through what you think it might mean. In the space to the right, jot down your questions and comments, using the examples as a model.

The air outside was heavy and wet. Inside, it was overheated. It was the sort of day that forced you out of the house and gave you nothing back in return. They had been restless indoors, edgy out of doors, and had settled on the Fogg [Museum] feeling that the sight of Greek vases might cool them out. They took several turns around. Guido delivered himself of a lecture on shape and form. Vincent gave his two minutes on the planning of the Greek city-state.

II. You and your partner should now join with another pair and discuss your questions and comments. Did you have the same questions or come to the same conclusions? Can you get closer to the excerpt's meaning by thinking about what someone else has written?

Exercise 2.8 Apply the Reading Strategy

I. Go over the remainder of the story with a partner and jot down your think-alouds on a separate sheet of paper. When you are done, join with another pair and compare your questions and thoughts, as you did for the previous exercise.

II. In a group discussion or on your own, formulate answers for the following questions:

1. Why are Guido and Vincent so dissatisfied?

2. What might be missing in their lives?

3. Why do they talk about the girl in the museum as if she is an art object?

4. Why do you think she reacted like she did?

Writing Workshop
The Planning Stage

In the previous chapter, you learned the importance of identifying your audience, purpose, and task before you begin to plan your writing. In this lesson, you'll learn some techniques for gathering ideas as part of your prewriting planning process.

Suppose you've been assigned the following essay topic:

> There are many different kinds of love, and love, it is said, makes the world go 'round. Write an essay explaining how at least three different kinds of love can play a part in making people's lives better.

If your first thought is, "How am I ever going to write this?" you're not alone. Many people, adults as well as students, view writing as a monumental task. They sit and look at a blank sheet of paper and worry about how to begin. However, there are certain strategies you can use to make it easier to get started.

Planning Is Key

For a moment, imagine that on Wednesday during lunch you and two friends decide to go to a movie on Friday. Before you actually find yourself in your seat in the theater, you have to do some planning:

- find out what's playing

- decide which movie you will see

- find out what time it starts

- figure out how to get there and back home

So on Thursday at lunch you bring up the subject of the movie again. Your friends can't agree on which movie they want to see. Anyway, they aren't sure that either of the ones they're interested in has opened yet. One wants to go to Regal Cinemas, the other to AMC. You're pretty sure your older sister will give you a ride, but that depends on when the movie you want to see starts, and no one knows how you'll get home. It's quite possible that you'll wind up not going to any movie because there is no **plan**.

Writing an essay also requires a plan, and the first part of the plan is to gather some ideas. Before you even do that, however, you want to identify three things: audience, purpose, and task. Let's look back at the prompt:

> There are many different kinds of love, and love, it is said, makes the world go 'round. Write an essay explaining how at least three different kinds of love can play a part in making people's lives better.

There is no specific audience mentioned. If this is a classroom assignment, the audience is likely to be your teacher. If you found this essay prompt on a standardized test, the audience would probably be a group of scorers you've never met. The audience to keep in mind for an assignment like this is a general audience that includes people your own age and up.

Your purpose and task are stated right in the assignment: *Write an essay explaining how at least three different types of love play a part in making people's lives better.*

Purpose: to explain how at least three different types of love play a part in making people's lives better

Task: essay

Now that you have your audience, purpose, and task firmly in mind, you can proceed to the first step of your plan: gathering ideas.

There are many different ways to gather ideas. The first thing to do is let your mind open up and wander about. During this phase, it can be helpful to use a spider map.

TIP: Don't get discouraged and say, "Everyone already knows about this topic. I don't have anything new to add." Even if your readers already know about your subject, you can still show them what you think of it.

Brainstorming with Spider Maps

This is often a good way to brainstorm by yourself. Don't worry about spelling or punctuation. Try to let your thoughts flow freely and write down whatever comes to mind, no matter how silly it seems. Start by writing your topic in the middle of your paper. Circle it and then draw some legs extending outward. Leave plenty of room between them so you'll have space to write. Here is an example:

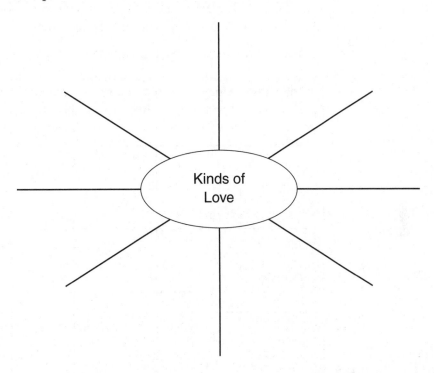

Exercise 2.9   Practice Using a Spider Map

Now create your own spider map in response to the prompt on love (reread it on page 38). First, take out a sheet of paper and draw a spider map outline like the one in the example. Then let your mind wander freely around the topic and write down whatever comes to mind. Some or all of the words you write around the spider's "body" will eventually give your essay some legs to stand on. Once you've jotted down some of the various kinds of love, think about each kind and once again let your thoughts flow. You can make another spider map for each kind if it helps.

Exercise 2.10 Organizing Your Ideas

Look at the ideas you gathered on your spider map and choose three kinds of love you're going to write about. These will be your body paragraphs. Fill them in under the second, third, and fourth headings on the grid. Then go around the map clockwise and choose ideas that go along with each kind of love you identified. Write those ideas briefly in the squares below each kind of love. (You don't have to fill in the introduction and conclusion squares yet. They will be easier to do once you have your body paragraph ideas filled in. You'll work on them later in the unit.)

You're on your way to a great essay!

Introduction	Kind of love:	Kind of love:	Kind of love:	Conclusion

Grammar Mini-Lesson
Compound Sentences

In the previous chapter, you learned that a simple sentence has one subject and one predicate. You learned how to add adjectives and adverbs to short sentences to make them more interesting. In this lesson, you will learn another way to spruce up your writing—sentence combining. Joining two or more simple sentences into compound sentences can help you make transitions between ideas and give your writing a smoother flow.

Compound Sentences

A **compound sentence** consists of two or more simple sentences joined together with a comma plus a coordinating conjunction (*and, or, but*).

> I fell down the stairs. I was not injured. (two simple sentences)
> I fell down the stairs, **but** I was not injured. (compound sentence)

> I'll bring my soccer ball. We can use yours. (two simple sentences)
> I'll bring my soccer ball, **or** we can use yours. (compound sentence)

You can often combine simple sentences by using a semicolon instead of a comma/conjunction pair.

> Mom washed the dishes. I dried them. (two simple sentences)

> Mom washed the dishes, and I dried them. (compound sentence with a comma and a conjunction)

> OR

> Mom washed the dishes; I dried them. (compound sentence with a semicolon)

Note that a semicolon is stronger than a comma, so it does not take a coordinating conjunction. A comma is weaker and does require a conjunction when joining sentences. An easy way to remember this is by thinking of a semicolon's size: it's larger, so it even *looks* stronger. Always use either *just* a semicolon *or* a comma *with* a conjunction.

As a writer, it will be up to you to decide which punctuation option to use. Sometimes you'll want the comma/conjunction, since a conjunction can help you emphasize the transition between ideas (It was raining, *but* we played outside). On the other hand, sometimes you'll want to stick with a semicolon, because of the concise rhythm it creates (I washed the car; he mowed the lawn). Always think about what you are trying to communicate and how you want your writing to flow.

Exercise 2.11 Practice Building Compound Sentences

Make each set of simple sentences into a compound one by using the conjunction shown.

1. Is a cheeseburger all right with you? Do you want something else? (or)

   _____

2. It rained a little. We were able to finish the game. (but)

   _____

3. I think I'd like to see this movie. Maybe I'd like to see that one. (or)

_____

4. Many people thought my decision was unwise. They called me foolish. (and)

_____

5. The delivery truck arrived. There was nothing for me. (but)

_____

6. I'm leaving. I'll be back. (but)

_____

7. Spencer hit the ball hard. It went over the fence. (and)

_____

8. Jessica said she was sorry. Now we're best friends again. (and)

_____

9. They warned us this would happen. We didn't listen. (but)

_____

10. You might have a bad battery. It could be the alternator. (or)

_____

Exercise 2.12 Additional Practice Building Compound Sentences

Make each set of simple sentences into a compound sentence by joining them with a comma and a conjunction *or* with a semicolon.

1. Tyler said he would meet us at 6 A.M. He wasn't there.

_____

2. We had to wait a long time for him. We got angrier and angrier.

_____

3. Fish bite best early in the morning. They also bite just at dusk.

_____

4. We straightened up our tackle boxes. We retied our hooks.

_____

5. We were ready to leave without him. Then we saw him coming.

_____

6. He wore his usual big grin. We forgave him instantly.

_____

7. We've all been friends forever. It seems that way.

_____

8. The boathouse was locked. We hadn't counted on that.

   _____

9. We sighed and turned around to head home. Tyler reached in his pocket.

   _____

10. He said he would have been on time. He had remembered to go back and get the key.

    _____

Polish Your Spelling
Base Words and Derivatives

Being able to spot the base of a word is an important skill because it can help you determine what that word means. Recall how you looked for word-within-word clues in Chapter One's context clues lesson.

Learning to switch between base words and derivatives (words formed from base words) can also help your writing, because you'll be able to play with different ways of saying things. Let's say you were writing about a time you asked a friend a question, and he gave you an unclear answer. You could write, "His response lacked coherency," or you could say, "His answer was incoherent," *or* you could say, "His answer was not coherent at all." When you know how to spell and use different forms of a word, you can vary the ways you express yourself.

In this lesson, we'll focus on how to find and spell the base of a derivative. Later in this volume, we'll look at how to form derivatives *from* base words.

Look at the following diagram. It shows some of the words that you can make from one base word, *cover.*

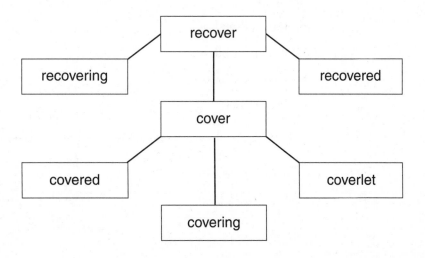

1. It is often possible to change a derivative back into the base word by simply dropping prefixes and suffixes.

> discontent – dis = content
> developed – ed = develop
> unbuttoned – un...ed = button

2. Sometimes you need to restore a letter to the base, such as an *e* that was dropped when the suffix was added:

> blazing – ing = blaz + e = blaze
> unimaginable – un...able = imagin + e = imagine

3. If a final consonant was doubled when the prefix was added, you need to undouble it, that is, drop one of the consonants:

> committed – ed = committ – t = commit
> baggy – y = bagg – g = bag

4. If a final *y* was changed to *i* when the suffix was added, change it back to *y*:

> hurried – ed = hurri – i + y = hurry
> happiness – ness = happi – i + y = happy

Exercise 2.13 Practice Finding Base Words

Find the base words and write them on the lines provided. Refer to the rules and examples if necessary.

1. courageous = _____
2. unconnected = _____
3. scurried = _____
4. tastiness = _____
5. saggy = _____
6. redeveloped = _____
7. unbelievable = _____
8. neighborliness = _____
9. dissatisfied = _____
10. submitted = _____

Chapter Three

Prereading Guide
Words to know and ideas to consider before you jump into the reading.

A. Essential Vocabulary

Word	Meaning	Typical Use
bemused (*adj*) be-MEWSED	confused, bewildered	She had a *bemused* expression on her face as she watched the strange stunts on TV.
entity (*n*) EN-ti-tee	a separate, distinct being or existence	Although those organizations have similar names, they are separate *entities*, with very different beliefs and goals.
exhilarate (*v*) eks-ILL-ur-ate	to energize or thrill; elate	I'm always *exhilarated* by the first snow of the year.
forge (*v*) FORJ	1. to make or form into being with effort 2. to imitate with the intent to defraud; to counterfeit	This sounds like a good plan—let's *forge* ahead and make it happen! They are in detention because they got caught trying to *forge* their parents' signatures.
impulsive (*adj*) im-PUHL-siv	acting without planning ahead; spontaneous	*Impulsive* purchases lead to surprisingly high credit card bills.
inequitable (*adj*) in-EK-wit-uh-bul	unfair or biased; unequal	Many of the world's women receive *inequitable* treatment.
insight (*n*) IN-site	a deeper look into something; perception	Going to the Civil War museum gave us more *insight* into this period in history.
pronounced (*adj*) pro-NOWNST	emphasized, marked, decided	The twins look alike, but there are many *pronounced* differences in their personalities.
provoke (*v*) pro-VOKE	to stir up or call forth a feeling or action; evoke	Her fiery speech *provoked* anger from her listeners and inspired them to get involved in the cause.
vigilance (*n*) VIJ-uh-lunce	watchfulness and attentiveness; alertness	Ian's *vigilance* in checking on his great-grandmother every day after school is admirable.

B. Vocabulary Practice

Exercise 3.1   Sentence Completion

Using your new vocabulary knowledge, choose the best way to complete the following sentences. Circle the letter of your answer.

1. Rafael and Amber are paid _____ for the same job; it's inequitable.
   A. the same
   B. differently

2. I was bemused by the leader's _____ speech.
   A. hilarious
   B. nonsensical

3. This _____ should give you some insights.
   A. situation comedy
   B. special documentary

4. I _____ impulsively.
   A. can't explain why I acted
   B. planned ahead to act

5. The two groups forged a union so they could _____.
   A. fight for what they wanted
   B. focus on their individual goals

6. _____ is very exhilarating to some people.
   A. Taking a stroll
   B. Climbing a rock wall

7. The fact that her hair is long and brown and her sister's is short and blonde is just one of the _____ differences between them.
   A. pronounced
   B. inequitable

8. Vigilance at _____ is essential.
   A. shoe stores
   B. airport security checkpoints

9. Those are two _____; you have to pay for them separately.
   A. entities
   B. insights

10. In an effort to provoke an argument with his little sister, he _____.
    A. helped her with her math homework
    B. blasted the same song over and over

Exercise 3.2   Using Fewer Words

Replace the italicized words with a single word from the following list. The first one has been done for you.

bemused   exhilarating   impulsively   inequitably   insights

entities   forge   pronounced   provoke   vigilant

1. Andrew was *confused and bewildered* by her long e-mail.

    1. _bemused_

2. *Without planning ahead,* Olivia gave her mother a warm and loving hug, and their argument was forgotten.

    2. _____

3. That is a great question and will certainly *stir up* a meaningful discussion.

    3. _____

4. Are the hat and scarf two *distinct things,* or are they being sold as a set?

    4. _____

5. New parents are often so *attentive and watchful* over their new child that they exhaust themselves.

    5. _____

6. If we *put together* a plan, it will be easier to reach our goals.

    6. _____

7. Cartoon characters often have *very emphasized* features.

    7. _____

8. Even at 50, my dad still finds roller coasters *energizing and thrilling.*

    8. _____

9. We must be sure we don't appear to be treating anyone *in an unfair or biased way.*

    9. _____

10. I'd like to get some *deeper looks* into both sides of this issue before I decide what I think about it.

    10. _____

Exercise 3.3   Synonyms and Antonyms

Fill in the blanks in column A with the required synonyms or antonyms, selecting them from column B. (Remember: A *synonym* is a word *similar* in meaning to another word. *Autumn* and *fall* are synonyms. An *antonym* is a word *opposite* in meaning to another word. *Beginning* and *ending* are antonyms.)

	A	B
_____	1. synonym for *perception*	inequitable
_____	2. antonym for *destroy*	insight
_____	3. synonym for *evoke*	entity
_____	4. synonym for *spontaneous*	forge
_____	5. synonym for *alertness*	exhilarate
_____	6. antonym for *unnoticeable*	impulsive
_____	7. synonym for *being*	bemused
_____	8. antonym for *equal*	pronounced
_____	9. synonym for *confused*	provoke
_____	10. synonym for *elate*	vigilance

C. Journal Freewrite

Before you begin the reading on the next page, take out a journal or sheet of paper and spend some time responding to the following prompt.

TIP: Don't worry about grammar and spelling; just write what comes to mind. The purpose of freewriting is to explore ideas, not to produce a polished work.

Describe a time something or someone comforted you when you were feeling sad.

Sonnet 29

by William Shakespeare

About the Author
William Shakespeare (1564–1616) was born in Stratford-on-Avon, England, the son of a prosperous merchant. He went to school in Stratford and married a woman named Anne Hathaway, with whom he had three children. He spent most of his time in London, where he joined the acting company of The Theatre. In 1599, he and several other actors built the famous Globe Theatre. Shakespeare's plays are divided into the tragedies, the comedies, and the histories. He also wrote 154 sonnets, many of which are supposedly written to a "mystery woman" with whom he was in love.

When in disgrace with fortune and men's eyes
I all alone beweep[1] my outcast state,
And trouble deaf heaven with my bootless[2] cries,
And look upon myself, and curse my fate,
Wishing me like to one more rich in hope,
Featured like him, like him with friends possessed,
Desiring this man's art, and that man's scope,[3]
With what I most enjoy contented least;
Yet in these thoughts myself almost despising,
Haply[4] I think on thee, and then my state,
Like to the lark at break of day arising
From sullen earth, sings hymns at heaven's gate;
For thy sweet love remembered such wealth brings
That then I scorn to change my state with kings.

---

[1]cry over
[2]useless
[3]knowledge and intelligence
[4]by luck or chance

Understanding the Reading

Complete the next three exercises and see how well you understood "Sonnet 29."

Exercise 3.4 Multiple-Choice Questions

Answer the following questions about the reading. Circle the letter of your answer.

TIP: Don't try to answer the questions from memory; go back to the text as often as necessary.

1. To feel "in disgrace with fortune and men's eyes" means to feel
   A. sorrowful and ashamed.
   B. humiliated by defeat.
   C. unlucky and unpopular.
   D. deprived and poor.

2. The narrator says, "I all alone beweep my outcast state" to show that he felt
   A. all alone, as if he did not "belong" anywhere.
   B. homesick for his wife and children.
   C. depressed and hopeless about the future.
   D. confused and angry at what life had handed him.

3. In lines 5–7, he says that he envies other men's
   A. optimism and friends.
   B. creative talents.
   C. knowledge and intelligence.
   D. all of these.

4. What makes the narrator "scorn to change [his] state with kings"?
   A. thinking he is just being tested
   B. thinking of his beloved
   C. thinking about the opening of his play
   D. thinking about his wealth

Exercise 3.5 Short-Answer Questions

Respond to the following questions in one to two complete sentences. Go back to the text, as you did on the multiple choice.

5. One of the requirements of a Shakespearean sonnet is to present and describe a problem and then give its solution. What problem and solution are presented in this sonnet?

   _____

   _____

   _____

6. The rhyme scheme of this sonnet is ABABCDCDEBEBFF. Study the last words of each line. Which lines rhyme? See if you can figure out and explain what is meant by "rhyme scheme" and what is meant by those letters.

_____

_____

_____

7. The narrator says he prefers being in love to being a king. What would your choice be? Why?

_____

_____

_____

Exercise 3.6   Extending Your Thinking

Respond to the following question in three to four complete sentences. Use details from the text in your answer.

8. The theme of this unit is "The Power of Love." What power does love have for the narrator as expressed in this sonnet?

_____

_____

_____

_____

_____

_____

Journal Freewrite

Before you begin the second reading, take out a journal or sheet of paper and spend some time responding to a different prompt.

Parents often tell their teenagers that they are too young to be in love. What do you think? How has your view of relationships changed as you've been going through school?

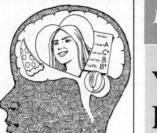

Young Love: The Good, the Bad and the Educational

by Winifred Gallagher

About the Author
Winifred Gallagher
(1947–) has written widely about human behavior and spirituality. She is the author of *Just the Way You Are*, *The Power of Place*, and *Working on God*. She is also a journalist and has written for *The Atlantic Monthly*, *Rolling Stone*, *Discover*, and *The New York Times*, where this article appeared. She divides her time between Manhattan and Long Eddy, New York.

When they fell in love, she was barely into her teens, and he wasn't much older. Some saw a star-crossed couple who found understanding, joy and maturity in each other's arms. Others saw impulsive kids whose reckless passion cut them off from family, friends and more appropriate interests, provoked mood swings, delinquent behavior and experimentation with drugs, and ended in tragedy.

Romeo and Juliet's story is centuries old, but these two very different views of adolescent romance live on, often simultaneously, in the minds of bemused parents.

Lately, teenage romance has caught the attention of a number of researchers, who are increasingly interested in its potentially positive as well as negative effects—not just on adolescence, but on adult relationships and well-being.

According to Dr. Wyndol Furman, an editor of the book *The Development of Romantic Relationships in Adolescence*, understanding teenage dating means under-standing that adolescence is "a roiling emotional caldron[1] whose major fuel—more than parents, peers or school and almost as much as those things combined—is the opposite sex."

Dr. Furman, a professor of psychology at the University of Denver, said adolescents' lack of social skills and emotional control can make relationships difficult. Yet, he said, romantic relationships can also be significant sources of support that offer teenagers fun and companionship, help them forge mature identities and offer them practice in managing emotions.

"Growing up involves risks," he said. "Parents are naturally concerned about their teens' relationships, but they shouldn't want them to just stay home."

Setting guidelines requires an appreciation of the profound differences between 13- and 19-year-olds. Among the so-called "tweens" of middle school, Dr. Furman said, the point of a crush "is mostly to be able to say you have a boy- or girlfriend,"

[1]boiling pot

and to start to know the opposite sex. Next, he said, boys and girls date in groups—"you kiss, then go to the movies"—and become more interested in the close companionship sought by older teenagers.

Teenagers' growing capacity for positive romantic relationships has been traced by Dr. Reed Larson, a professor of human and community development at the University of Illinois. After paging his teenage subjects at random times during the day and inquiring about their activities and emotions, Dr. Larson confirmed what parents since Adam and Eve have observed: adolescents are either very happy or very unhappy much more often than adults, especially concerning romance.

But Dr. Larson correlated their more numerous negative responses to what he called "a certain randomness" and superficiality in their attachments, which make their relationships less rewarding. Indeed, he said, this dissatisfaction is most pronounced among the younger, less experienced teenagers, who "haven't yet learned how to have fun and get along."

He observed, "It takes time for a teenager to realize that a relationship isn't just an infatuation based on haphazard attraction, but an entity on which two people with compatible personalities work together."

. . . For Dr. Furman, red flags are raised by "precocious daters" who pair off before their peers, and by "uneven, inequitable relationships," in which one partner is controlling and the other dependent.

Dr. [Miriam] Ehrensaft [an assistant professor of clinical psychology at the New York State Psychiatric Institute] said she would be concerned about the relationships of teenagers who were already depressed or troubled and about partners who were more than two years apart in age. Notwithstanding the need for vigilance, she said that parents must come to terms with the fact that teenagers will have relationships. She urged, "Rather than saying that's good or bad, try to help them form positive ones."

Preparation for good dating experiences begins well before adolescence. "Parents should give children enough time and attention so that they're not driven outside to find support," Dr. Furman said. "Adults also need to teach kids how to scaffold[2] healthy relationships that are supportive, as opposed to controlling or dependent. Kids need to know that it's the quality of the relationship, not simply having a boy- or girlfriend, that matters."

Once parents have laid the groundwork, Dr. [Miriam] Kaufman [a pediatrician and an associate professor at the University of Toronto Medical School and author of the book *Overcoming Teen Depression*] said, they should try to, well, mind their own business.

"Assume that your teenager's relationship won't be perfect," she said. "Hope that he or she is learning more from it than from your lectures on the subject. Then, be there to listen. If you keep your cool, they'll talk to you more." Dr. Kaufman said she suspected that some parents' anxiety reflected their "discomfort with the idea of teens enjoying themselves, instead of trying to get into Harvard."

"Relationships are an even more important part of life than where you go to college," she said. "And that first flush of love can be really exhilarating. Teens deserve happiness, too."

Dr. Larson agreed that wise parents balanced being available to their teenage children with the understanding that the young needed to learn on their own. To parents seeking additional insight, he said, "Go back and look at your own love letters."

---

[2]build

Understanding the Reading

Complete the next three exercises and see how well you understood "Young Love: The Good, the Bad and the Educational."

Exercise 3.7 Multiple-Choice Questions

Answer the following questions about the reading. Circle the letter of your answer.

TIP: Don't try to answer the questions from memory; go back to the text as often as necessary.

1. The main idea of this article is that
   A. teenagers are too young to know what real love is.
   B. teenage romances can be important learning experiences.
   C. teenagers are reckless and use poor judgment.
   D. the effects of teenage romances are mostly negative.

2. According to Dr. Wyndol Furman, parents should give children plenty of time and attention so the
   A. children will be too busy to think about finding a boyfriend or girlfriend.
   B. children won't get involved with someone much older to replace the parents.
   C. parents can keep close tabs on their children's activities.
   D. children won't feel they must look for emotional support in a romantic relationship.

3. Dr. Ehrensaft and Dr. Kaufman would agree that
   A. depressed teens should not be allowed to date.
   B. teens will and should have romantic relationships.
   C. having a romantic relationship is more important than going to college.
   D. parents should go back and look at their own old love letters.

4. Which of the relationships described below is *not* mentioned as potentially unhealthy by the experts quoted in this article?
   A. One person is controlling, the other dependent.
   B. The partners are more than two years apart in age.
   C. One partner is already distressed or troubled.
   D. One partner physically abuses the other.

Exercise 3.8 Short-Answer Questions

Respond to the following questions in one to two complete sentences. Go back to the text, as you did on the multiple choice.

5. How do you think the two views of Romeo and Juliet's love story live on today?

_____

_____

_____

6. The researchers mention that teenage relationships can have both negative and positive effects. What would be an example of each?

_____

_____

_____

7. What is your reaction to Dr. Larson's statement that younger, less experienced teenagers "haven't yet learned how to have fun and get along"?

_____

_____

_____

Exercise 3.9 Extending Your Thinking

Respond to the following question in three to four complete sentences.

8. The theme of this unit is "The Power of Love." Among most of the people you know, how important is it to have a boyfriend or girlfriend? Explain.

_____

_____

_____

_____

_____

_____

Reading Strategy Lesson
Using Comprehension Tools

The article "The Good, the Bad and the Educational" is typical of one you might be asked to analyze on a standardized test. Four different experts are quoted, and they each present different ideas about a topic (in this case, teenage romance). When you read these kinds of articles, how can you keep all the information straight?

1. Begin with literal comprehension

Literal comprehension basically means that you understand most of the words in the article. You studied some of them in the vocabulary lesson at the beginning of the chapter. Some are footnoted. If there are any other words you don't know, you can use context clues to figure them out. While you don't need to know every single word to grasp the meaning of the selection, certain key words are important. The italicized words in this sentence are crucial to understanding it:

> For Dr. Furman, red flags are raised by "*precocious* daters" who pair off before their peers, and by "uneven, *inequitable* relationships," in which one partner is *controlling* and the other *dependent*.

The word *precocious* is defined in the sentence's context. *Precocious* daters pair off before their peers. So *precocious* must mean people who do things before other people their age. Even if you hadn't studied the word *inequitable* in the vocabulary lesson, you can infer that it means "uneven"—particularly if you know the key words *controlling* and *dependent*. If you aren't sure of those, you can break them down to their base words—*control* and *depend*, and you can probably define them. One person tries to *control* the other, whose actions *depend* on what the other wants.

2. Read ahead

You may find a sentence or paragraph that seems to make little sense even though you know the literal meaning of the words. When that happens, it may be helpful just to keep reading. You may very well find more information that clarifies the earlier confusing passage.

A good example of this is the first paragraph of the article. You may think that the journalist is describing a couple that was recently in the news. Only when you read on to the second paragraph do you learn that she is talking about Romeo and Juliet.

3. Break down long sentences

Some sentences seem to go on forever. Breaking them into smaller parts can help you to understand them better. Here are some tools you can use to make long sentences more manageable:

- **Focus on the most important words in the sentence**, especially nouns and verbs.

- **Find the simplest subject and predicate**, to help you keep track of the person and the action the sentence is primarily about.

- **Look for answers to the 5 W's:** *Who, What, When, Where, Why* (and *How*). Are any of these involved in the sentence?

- **Use chunking,** a technique that breaks the sentence into smaller parts that are easier to understand. Try chunking according to punctuation. Commas often separate answers to questions that fall into the 5 W's.

Let's practice breaking down this example from the article.

> After *paging* his *teenage subjects* at *random times* during the day and *inquiring* about their *activities* and *emotions, Dr. Larson confirmed* what parents since Adam and Eve have observed: adolescents are either *very happy or very unhappy* much *more often* than adults, *especially* concerning *romance.*

- **Focus:** The most important words in the sentence are italicized.
- **Subject and predicate:** *Dr. Larson* (subject), *confirmed* (predicate).
- **5 W's:** The *who* includes Dr. Larson, teenage subjects, adolescents, and adults. *What* did Dr. Larson confirm? That adolescents are either very happy or very unhappy much more often than adults. *When* are they happy or unhappy? When romance is the issue. *How* did he confirm this? He did so by paging his teenage subjects. *When?* At random times during the day. *Why?* To inquire about their activities and emotions.
- **Chunking:** Divide the sentence into chunks. Use the think-aloud technique to make sure you understand each one.

After paging his teenage subjects at random times during the day and inquiring about their activities and emotions,	*So he called kids up and asked them what they'd been doing and how they felt.*
Dr. Larson confirmed what parents since Adam and Eve have observed:	*What he found out was something parents have known for a long time.*
adolescents are either very happy or very unhappy much more often than adults,	*Teenagers have more ups and downs than adults.*
especially concerning romance.	*These ups and downs can be set off by either good or bad things that happen in their love lives.*

Exercise 3.10 Practice the Reading Strategy

Read the following sentences, from Thoreau's essay "Walking." On a separate sheet of paper, follow the steps outlined on pages 56–57 for breaking down long sentences: **focus, subject and predicate, 5 W's,** and **chunking.**

1. Living much out of doors, in the sun and wind, will no doubt produce a certain roughness of character—will cause a thicker

cuticle to grow over some of the finer qualities of our nature, as on the face and hands, or as severe manual labor robs the hands of some of their delicacy of touch.

2. So staying in the house, on the other hand, may produce a softness and smoothness, not to say thinness of skin, accompanied by an increased sensibility to certain impressions.

Exercise 3.11 Apply the Reading Strategy

The following sentences are taken from "The Art of Living: Education" by Robert Grant, published in *Scribner's Magazine* in April of 1895. Read each one and use the comprehension tools you have learned in this lesson. You do not need to write down each step as you did for Exercise 3.10. Instead, circle the key words and underline the main subject and predicate. Then summarize the sentence in your own words. You may need to use a dictionary to look up some of the words.

1. On occasions of oratory in this country, nothing will arouse an audience more quickly than an allusion to our public school system, and any speaker who sees fit to address it is certain to be fervidly applauded.

Summary: _____

_____

_____

2. Moreover, in private conversation, whether with our countrymen or with foreigners, every citizen is prone to indulge in the statement, commonly uttered with some degree of emotion, that our public schools are the great bulwarks of progressive democracy.

Summary: _____

_____

_____

3. If the public schools, in those sections of our cities where our most intelligent and influential citizens have their homes, are unsatisfactory, they could speedily be made as good as any private school, were the same interest manifested by the tax-payers as is shown when an undesirable pavement is laid, or a company threatens to provide rapid transit before their doors.

Summary: _____

_____

_____

Writing Workshop

Producing a First Draft

Putting Your Thoughts Into Writing

In the previous chapter, you created a spider map and a grid with ideas for an essay about different kinds of love. Once again, here is the essay prompt:

> There are many different kinds of love, and love, it is said, makes the world go 'round. Write an essay explaining how at least three different kinds of love can play a part in making people's lives better.

Here is a sample student grid with notes and ideas for the essay:

Introduction	Kind of love: parent-child	Kind of love: friend-friend	Kind of love: romantic	Conclusion
	first love we know	can happen as early as day care	makes you feel special	
	provides us with basic needs	person who is there for you—trust	feel like you can fly	
	teaches us how to love, share, act right	person to laugh and have fun with	can't eat, can't sleep	
	makes us feel secure and OK	person to do hard things with	can end in a broken heart	

How to Begin: Restating the Prompt

It seems like you've got plenty of ideas, right? The hardest thing for many students is to get started and write the first sentence. Whenever you have trouble answering a specific prompt like the one given here, there is an easy way to get your first sentence down: Restate the prompt. This does not mean that you should rewrite it word for word. Instead, phrase it in a slightly different way. For example:

Love plays an important part in making people's lives better.

You've got your first sentence. Now let's go back to the grid and think about what else you want to say in your introduction.

Introduction	Kind of love: parent-child	Kind of love: friend-friend	Kind of love: romantic	Conclusion
Love plays an important part in making people's lives better.	first love we know	can happen as early as day care	makes you feel special	
parent, friend, romantic	provides us with basic needs	person who is there for you—trust	feel like you can fly	
daring to love—positive and negative feelings	teaches us how to love, share, act right	person to laugh and have fun with	can't eat, can't sleep	
makes world go around	makes us feel secure and OK	person to do hard things with	can end in a broken heart	

To get ideas for your introduction, look at the ideas in the columns you've filled in and back at the prompt. The purpose of the introduction is to say to your reader, "Here's what I'm going to talk about in this essay." Here is a sample introduction:

Love plays an important part in making people's lives better. Without the love of a parent or guardian, the love of friends, or the love of a romantic partner, people's lives would be empty. Sometimes it takes courage to open your heart to love, because it can bring negatives as well as positives. Nonetheless, love always has and always will make the world go around.

This introduction indicates that the writer is going to discuss parental love, friendship, and romantic love. The writer will tell us what these relationships provide to keep one's life from seeming empty. We'll also learn about some of the negative things that can happen when you love someone. We'll learn why this writer thinks love is important.

Writing the Body of the Essay

The body of the essay will be developed from the ideas in the second, third, and fourth columns, with one paragraph for each column. As you write your paragraphs, stay "in your lane." In other words, when you write about parent-child love, don't jump over to the ideas in the column about friendship or romantic love.

Here are three sample body paragraphs based on this student's grid of ideas:

> The love of a parent or guardian is the first love we know. Parents are the ones who come running when we cry in the middle of the night. They take care of us when we are sick. They provide us with food, clothing, and shelter, and they teach us how to love other people and share with them. From parents, we learn right from wrong. The love of parents or other adults gives us a sense of security.

> Friendship comes naturally to most people. Parents have friends with children, and these may be the first friends for toddlers. You can see budding friendships among even little children at day-care centers. All through school, friends are very important. A friend is there when you have a problem you can't talk about with your parents. You can trust a true friend not to tell your secrets. You can laugh and enjoy yourself alone, but it's a lot more fun if you have your friends with you. Friends can disappoint you by talking behind your back or deciding not to be friends with you anymore. Even so, who else could you talk to about a romantic relationship if not your best friend?

> Romantic relationships that turn out "happily ever after" are depicted in the movies and on TV every day of the week. The perfect romance is something everybody dreams of having. The first time you fall in love, you might feel so special that you think you can fly. You don't need to eat or sleep. All you can think of is that wonderful person in your life. Unfortunately, you might be in for a broken heart. After that, it takes courage to start anew, but you can indeed find love again.

Writing the Conclusion

Too often, conclusions sound a lot like introductions. It's true that you'll want to summarize what you've said, but that doesn't mean you should repeat it word for word. Instead, restate your ideas and finish with a concluding statement that really winds things up and leaves your readers with something to think about.

To write your conclusion, look at the prompt again. Look over what you have written so far. Then restate your ideas once more in a slightly different way, and wind up with a decisive final sentence called the "clincher." The far right column of the grid shows some ideas for the conclusion:

Introduction	Kind of love: parent-child	Kind of love: friend-friend	Kind of love: romantic	Conclusion
Love plays an important part in making people's lives better.	first love we know	can happen as early as day care	makes you feel special	begin as babies with love but do not appreciate it yet
parent, friend, romantic	provides us with basic needs	person who is there for you—trust	feel like you can fly	give and take starts with first friendships
daring to love—positive and negative feelings	teaches us how to love, share, act right	person to laugh and have fun with	can't eat, can't sleep	romantic love may disappoint; human condition to keep on loving
makes world go around	makes us feel secure and OK	person to do hard things with	can end in a broken heart	we start it all over again as parents

Based on the ideas in the far right column, here is what a conclusion to the essay could look like:

Love begins when we are infants, too young and small to appreciate how much our caregivers are doing for us. We take it for granted. As we get older and start to give back, we learn what it is like not only to receive love but to give it as well. We find out that friends are a great source of pleasure even though they can hurt us. Finally, as teenagers, we begin to look for romantic relationships. We find out how great it feels to be flying high in love, and how hard we hit when the love ends and we fall from the sky. We'll keep trying, though. It is part of the human condition to love. One day we'll find the right person and settle down. Then we may learn what it's like to be on the parent side of the parent-child relationship.

Exercise 3.12 Practice the Writing Lesson

Transfer your ideas from the first grid you did (on p. 40) to this one. You may want to change your mind about where to put some of your ideas, or add more as you copy. Then fill in ideas for your introduction and conclusion.

Introduction	Kind of love:	Kind of love:	Kind of love:	Conclusion

Exercise 3.13 Apply the Lesson and Write Your First Draft

Using your grid as a guide, write your first draft on a separate sheet of paper. Remember to introduce the ideas you will write about in your first paragraph. Then "stay in your lane" as you write three paragraphs using the ideas in columns 2, 3, and 4. Finally, restate what you have said, and tie up your essay with a conclusion that has a punch.

Grammar Mini-Lesson

Writing Complex Sentences

In the last grammar lesson, you learned about compound sentences. Another kind of sentence that can help your writing flow smoothly is the **complex sentence**.

> A **complex sentence** consists of one **independent** clause and one or more **dependent** clauses.

- An **independent clause** has a subject and a predicate, and can stand alone as a sentence.

  Example: She was barely into her teens.
  This is a complete sentence by itself.

- A **dependent clause** has a subject and a predicate but cannot stand alone as a sentence; it is dependent on something else.

  Example: When they fell in love
  This does not make sense by itself; it needs to be linked to something else.

- A **complex sentence** joins together **one independent clause** and **one or more dependent clauses.** (Keep in mind that this is different from a compound sentence, which joins together two independent, simple sentences.)

  Example: <u>When they fell in love,</u> <u>she was barely into her teens,</u>
             DEP. CLAUSE   INDEP. CLAUSE

  <u>and he wasn't much older.</u>
      DEP. CLAUSE

Here is another example of a complex sentence from the chapter's second reading, broken down into clauses.

Complex Sentence	Independent Clause	Dependent Clause(s)
If you keep your cool, they'll talk to you more.	they'll talk to you more	If you keep your cool

Notice that dependent clauses usually begin with a word such as *if*, *although*, *when*, or *as*. (These words are often referred to as subordinating conjunctions, because they make that clause subordinate, or dependent.)

Exercise 3.14 Practice Identifying the Parts of a Complex Sentence

Break down the sentences below into their dependent and independent clauses. Write your answers in the table.

Complex Sentence	Independent Clause	Dependent Clause(s)
1. Before the twelfth century, there were few songs written about love.		
2. Stories were about heroic war exploits, but few women were mentioned.		
3. Love songs began in France, with the troubadours.		
4. Regardless of which century you look at after that, you can find two themes in almost all love songs.		
5. The singer is over-joyed because of love, or in agony over a broken heart.		

Why Write Complex Sentences?

Like strong adjective and adverb choices, complex sentences help you express your ideas with more precision. This sentence shows the connection between parents' wishes to understand their children's relationships and their *own* relationships as teens:

> To parents seeking additional insight, he said, "Go back and look at your own love letters."

Complex sentences help you vary your style and make your essays, stories, letters, articles—whatever you write—more interesting to read.

Punctuating Complex Sentences

- A comma usually follows a dependent clause that introduces a sentence.

  Although Luis was far behind, he did not drop out of the race.
  DEP. CLAUSE   INDEP. CLAUSE

- No comma is usually necessary when an independent clause introduces a sentence.

  Larissa did not order the jacket *because it was too expensive.*
  INDEP. CLAUSE   DEP. CLAUSE

Exercise 3.15 Practice Forming Complex Sentences

Combine each pair of sentences into a complex sentence. Do this by changing the italicized sentence into a dependent clause beginning with an appropriate conjunction from the following list. The first one has been done for you.

after	as if	before	so that	while
although	since	as	when	until

1. Turn on the light. *You can see what you are reading.*
   Turn on the light, so that you can see what you are reading.

2. *Eli was not well.* He came to school.

   _____

   _____

3. *You do not have the right book.* You will not be able to read the assignment in class.

   _____

   _____

4. It is silly to buy a warm coat now. *Spring is on its way.*

   _____

   _____

5. *Winter arrives.* We begin to spend more time indoors.

   _____

   _____

6. She asked me to hold the groceries. *She tried to find her keys.*

   _____

   _____

7. Cashiers are on duty daily from 10 A.M. *The shop closes at 7 P.M.*

_____

_____

8. I have to go now. *My class is about to start.*

_____

_____

9. *We go to school.* We should eat a good breakfast.

_____

_____

10. You flew down the soccer field. *You were a bird.*

_____

_____

Polish Your Spelling
Changing Nouns into Adjectives

In Chapter One, you added suffixes to base words to form new words. In Chapter Two, you removed prefixes and suffixes to find base words. In this chapter, we will continue to work with suffixes. This time, we will be using them to change nouns (people, places, or things) into adjectives (words that describe nouns).

Here are some ways to change nouns into adjectives.

1. Drop -*ness*

NOUN		SUFFIX		ADJECTIVE
ripeness	–	ness	=	ripe
happiness	–	ness	=	happy

2. Drop -*ity*

NOUN		SUFFIX		ADJECTIVE
joviality	–	ity	=	jovial
insanity	–	ity	=	insane*

Note that when you drop a suffix, you may have to restore a vowel, like the e in insane.

3. Add a suffix

NOUN		SUFFIX		ADJECTIVE
beauty	+	ful	=	beautiful
care	+	less	=	careless
victory	+	ous	=	victorious
health	+	y	=	healthy

4. Change a suffix

NOUN		SUFFIX		ADJECTIVE
abundance	→	ance → ant	=	abundant
urgency	→	cy → t	=	urgent

Exercise 3.16 Practice Turning Nouns into Adjectives

Change each noun into an adjective. Write the adjective on the line. Refer to the previous examples if necessary.

NOUN	ADJECTIVE
1. immediacy	_____
2. untidiness	_____
3. profession	_____
4. insistence	_____
5. harm	_____
6. affluence	_____
7. extravagance	_____
8. ice	_____
9. joy	_____
10. availability	_____

Unit One Review

Vocabulary Review

A. Match each word with its definition.

DEFINITION | WORD

_____ 1. lacking in skill or competence | a. subject

_____ 2. assign to a lesser category | b. neurotic

_____ 3. a distinct being | c. exhilarate

_____ 4. showing good taste and manners | d. deliberation

_____ 5. to energize or thrill | e. inept

_____ 6. a view showing a relationship | f. insight

_____ 7. suffering from unstable behavior | g. relegate

_____ 8. a deeper look | h. perspective

_____ 9. to expose | i. entity

_____ 10. thoughtfulness and consideration | j. refined

B. Match each word with its synonym.

SYNONYM | WORD

_____ 11. examine | a. dexterity

_____ 12. centered | b. provoke

_____ 13. unequal | c. unassuming

_____ 14. manager | d. vigilance

_____ 15. evoke | e. variance

_____ 16. modest | f. focused

_____ 17. confused | g. inequitable

_____ 18. agility | h. peruse

_____ 19. alertness | i. bemused

_____ 20. discrepancy | j. administrator

C. Match each word with its antonym.

	ANTONYM	WORD
_____	21. definite	a. civic
_____	22. unkind	b. intact
_____	23. destroy	c. indelible
_____	24. careful	d. benign
_____	25. damaged	e. exquisite
_____	26. unnoticeable	f. impulsive
_____	27. removable	g. conceivable
_____	28. plain	h. forge
_____	29. private	i. pronounced
_____	30. inconceivable	j. indeterminate

Grammar Review

Each question offers three ways to improve the corresponding underlined portion of the essay. If the underlined portion is *not* improved by one of the three suggested changes, choose A., No change. Circle the letter of your answer.

Popular Music

Popular <u>music, a term</u> used to describe
     (1)
music that appeals to a wide audience.
<u>Includes jazz,</u> country and western,
    (2)
<u>movie, soundtracks,</u> soul, and rock. The
    (3)
favorite of most American teens has been
<u>rock, ever</u> since it began in the 1950s.
 (4)
<u>In 1955 Bill</u> Haley's "Rock Around the
    (5)
Clock" was the first wildly popular
rock <u>song but most</u> people think of Elvis
     (6)
Presley as the "King of Rock."

   African-American musicians had been considered "separate" from others but the

1. A. No change
   B. music. It's a term
   C. music, or a term
   D. music is a term

2. A. No change
   B. It includes jazz
   C. Including jazz
   D. Inclusive of jazz

3. A. No change
   B. movies, soundtracks
   C. movie soundtracks
   D. movies and soundtracks

4. A. No change
   B. rock and ever
   C. rock since
   D. rock ever

5. A. No change
   B. Around 1955 Bill
   C. In 1955, Bill
   D. Bill

6. A. No change
   B. song. Most
   C. song. But most
   D. song, but most

rock-and-roll <u>artists became famous</u>

(7)

<u>among them</u> Chuck Berry, Little Richard,

(7)

and Fats Domino. <u>When Motown Records</u>

(8)

<u>was founded in Detroit. The</u> soulful

(8)

"Motown sound" captured teen listeners
with its themes of love, identity, and personal freedom. Folk-rock musicians, especially popular in the 1960s and 1970s,
sang about the same issues.

In 1964, the "British Invasion" began
with the arrival of the Beatles in New
York City. Parents were distressed to see
that the Beatles' hair covered the tops of
<u>their ears. Alarmed</u> when their own sons

(9)

refused to get haircuts. Folk-rock singer
and songwriter Bob Dylan, whose songs
are classics today, advised parents that
"The Times They Are A-Changing."

It's certainly true that the times have
<u>changed and that</u> music styles have

(10)

changed with them. Even in the newest
styles, at least one aspect of rock music
remains. It still addresses the issues that
are important to America's—and the
world's—adolescents.

7. A. No change
   B. artists became famous, among
      them were
   C. artists became famous. Among
      them were
   D. artists became famous among
      them.

8. A. No change
   B. When Motown Records was
      founded in Detroit and the
   C. When Motown Records was
      founded in Detroit the
   D. When Motown Records was
      founded in Detroit, the

9. A. No change
   B. their ears and were even more
      alarmed
   C. their ears, but alarmed
   D. their ears, alarmed.

10. A. No change
    B. changed. That
    C. changed, that
    D. changed or that

Spelling Review

A. Add the suffixes given and write out the new word.

1. courage + ous   _____

2. calculate + or   _____

3. day + ly   _____

4. easy + er   _____

B. Write the base of each word.

5. dissatisfaction   _____

6. righteousness   _____

7. hurried   _____

C. Change the nouns into adjectives.

8. negligence   _____

9. ignorance   _____

10. spiciness   _____

Writing Review

Choose one of the following topics. Plan your essay. Write your first draft. Then revise and edit your draft, and write your final essay. Be sure to identify your audience, purpose, and task before you begin planning.

> Most of the literature in this unit was written in modern times. The exception is Shakespeare's sonnet. Do you think the power of love is as strong today as it was in Shakespeare's day? Explain your answer using specific details and examples. Refer to any or all of the selections in the unit.
>
> OR
>
> This unit contains a novel excerpt, a short story, a newspaper article, and a poem. Each one treats the subject of love in a different way. Choose two of the selections and compare what the two authors have to say about love. Show how they are alike and how they are different by using specific details and examples from the selections.

SPEAK/LISTEN

Lyric Analysis

Using the Internet or CD sheet as a source, find the lyrics to a favorite love song. Write a short analysis of the song. You should answer these questions: To whom is the song addressed? Is this a sad or a happy love song? How do you feel when you listen to it? Play part or all of the song for your class and then share your analysis.

EXPLORE

Getting to Know the Authors

Choose either Budge Wilson, Laurie Colwin, or Winifred Gallagher, and find more biographical information about her on the Internet or in the library. Then read something else that the author has written. For Budge Wilson, you might read another story. For Laurie Colwin, you could read the remainder of the chapter of *Happy All the Time*. Winifred Gallagher has written a number of other articles as well as several books. Summarize your biographical research in one paragraph. In a second one, write a review of the additional material you read.

WRITE

Create Your Own Sonnet

Read more of Shakespeare's sonnets online or at the library. Print out or copy several that you particularly like. Find out the differences among a Shakespearean, a Spenserian, and an Edwardian sonnet. Then choose one form and try writing your own.

CONNECT

Love and the Written Word

How have changing forms of communication over the ages (from love poems and handwritten letters, to phone calls, to e-mails, to text messaging) changed relationships? With a partner, choose a position—technology has improved relationships *or* technology has hindered them. Formulate an argument with specific examples and debate a pair on the opposite side.

UNIT TWO

Alienation and Identity

Chapter Four

Prereading Guide
Words to know and ideas to consider before you jump into the reading.

A. Essential Vocabulary

Word	Meaning	Typical Use
aberration (*n*) ab-ur-AY-shun	a deviation from what is normally considered to be proper; abnormality	A mirage—an imaginary vision—is a psychological *aberration*.
brandish (*v*) BRAN-dish	to wave something around in a showy way; wield	The knights rode forth from the castle, *brandishing* their lances.
confront (*v*) cun-FRUNT	to meet head-on or deal with; face	I'm afraid my parents are going to *confront* me about coming in so late last night.
decree (*n*) de-CREE	an official declaration by an authority; ruling	In many countries, government *decrees* protect rare species.
exterminate (*v*) eks-TUR-mih-nate	to destroy completely; annihilate	The aliens plotted to invade planet Creon, *exterminate* its inhabitants, and steal its natural resources.
negation (*n*) nih-GAY-shun	denial or opposite of something; nullification	Dad's lack of enthusiasm seemed like a *negation* of all we had done for his surprise birthday party.
oppressive (*adj*) uh-PRESS-iv	emotionally, mentally, or physically harsh; cruel	The heat was so *oppressive* that Matt could not finish his usual five-mile run.
propaganda (*n*) prop-uh-GAN-duh	ideas, information, or allegations spread to attack or promote a particular cause, doctrine, or nation	It is not always easy to find the truth; you have to make sure you aren't being taken in by *propaganda*.
regime (*n*) ruh-ZHEEM	a system of government; administration	Close control of the people is a feature of totalitarian *regimes*.
resistance (*n*) re-ZISS-tunce	a force struggling against another; opposition	If we lived under a dictator, I would be part of the *resistance*.

B. Vocabulary Practice

Exercise 4.1   Sentence Completion

Using your new vocabulary knowledge, choose the best way to complete the following sentences. Circle the letter of your answer.

1. My brother _____ the propaganda about the home gym, and now he's sorry.
   A. laughed at
   B. believed

2. A decree went out from the _____ that smoking was no longer allowed in restaurants.
   A. townspeople
   B. local government

3. When France was occupied by Germany during World War II, the resistance focused on _____.
   A. aiding Hitler
   B. beating Germany

4. I decided to confront my fear of water and _____.
   A. avoid the pool
   B. take swimming lessons

5. At Fourth of July parades, the _____ is brandished proudly all over the country.
   A. American flag
   B. fireworks

6. The complete extermination of _____ is not possible.
   A. human curiosity
   B. a species

7. She was _____; her behavior was an aberration.
   A. acting abnormally
   B. acting normally

8. _____ is the negation of blame.
   A. Forgiveness
   B. Anger

9. A number of different regimes _____ Rome over ten centuries.
   A. ignored
   B. governed

10. The United Nations polices the actions of oppressive _____.
    A. governments
    B. weather

Exercise 4.2   Using Fewer Words

Replace the italicized words with a single word from the following list. The first one has been done for you.

aberration   brandished   confront   decree   exterminated

negation   oppressive   propaganda   regimes   resistance

1. The *struggling opposition force* is having a secret meeting tonight.

   1. <u>resistance</u>

2. The senator claimed the news article was *a false, attacking publication.*

   2. _____

3. When Michael got straight A's on his report card, he *waved around in a showy way* it all over school.

   3. _____

4. Absolute rule is the *opposite or denial* of freedom.

   4. _____

5. Many people in the world live under *systems of government* that restrict human rights.

   5. _____

6. Madison doesn't usually act that way, it was just a small *deviation from what is normally considered proper* on her part.

   6. _____

7. Mom was delighted when the bugs eating her roses were finally *completely destroyed.*

   7. _____

8. The game's rules will not change unless there is a(an) *official declaration by an authority* from the national conference.

   8. _____

9. If someone has done something to upset you, the best thing may be to *meet head-on or deal with* the person directly.

   9. _____

10. It isn't very cold today, but the wind makes it *physically harsh.*

    10. _____

Exercise 4.3 Synonyms and Antonyms

Fill in the blanks in column A with the required synonyms or antonyms, selecting them from column B. (Remember: A *synonym* is a word *similar* in meaning to another word. *Autumn* and *fall* are synonyms. An *antonym* is a word *opposite* in meaning to another word. *Beginning* and *ending* are antonyms.)

	A	B
_____	1. synonym for *cruel*	aberration
_____	2. synonym for *opposition*	brandish
_____	3. synonym for *wield*	confront
_____	4. antonym for *avoid*	decree
_____	5. synonym for *ruling*	exterminate
_____	6. antonym for *preserve*	negation
_____	7. synonym for *nullification*	oppressive
_____	8. synonym for *administration*	propaganda
_____	9. synonym for *rumors*	regime
_____	10. antonym for *normality*	resistance

C. Journal Freewrite

Before you begin the reading on the next page, take out a journal or sheet of paper and spend some time responding to the following prompt.

TIP: Don't worry about grammar and spelling; just write what comes to mind. The purpose of freewriting is to explore ideas, not to produce a polished work.

> Imagine that you live in a country where you feel as if all of your activities are being watched. You have few rights and are afraid to leave your home. Would you stay inside and hope things might change—or do something else? Explain.

from My Forbidden Face
by Latifa

About the Author
Latifa (1980–) is the pen name of an Afghan girl who began keeping a diary at age 16 to record what happened to her and her family in Afghanistan after the Taliban came to power. Her diary covers the five-year period from 1996 to 2001, when her family escaped to France. It was published as *My Forbidden Face: Growing Up Under the Taliban: A Young Woman's Story,* and it relates the brutal treatment of women, who were not allowed to work, go to school, or leave their homes without being completely covered and accompanied by a male relative. Latifa's true name may never be known, because she still has family and friends in Afghanistan and fears they would be targeted for violence.

The programs on Radio Sharia are always the same: from 8 to 9 a.m., prayers and readings from the Koran; from 9 to 10:30, religious songs, <u>propaganda</u>, and the announcement of new <u>decrees</u>, some of which are chanted in Arabic, as if to make us believe they're really from the Koran. Then they suspend broadcasting until 6 p.m., when they read the "death notices" for Taliban "heroes." Then comes the "news," which is always the same, hailing Taliban advances without mentioning (of course) any conflicts with the <u>resistance</u> or any villages that are fighting off Taliban attacks. Finally, at 9:30 p.m., after the reading of a few sacred texts, Radio Sharia shuts up.

Around noon, one of us suggests halfheartedly that we fix something to eat. Our home is like a hospital or a penitentiary. The silence is <u>oppressive</u>. No one is doing anything anymore, so we have nothing to talk about. Since we can't talk to one another, we're left alone with our fear and dismay. And when everyone is in the same black hole, it's useless to keep saying we can't see any daylight.

I drag around, don't change my clothes anymore, sometimes wearing the same outfit for three or four days, day and night. The neighbor's telephone never rings anymore; it's still out of order. And when it finally does work again, my father hesitates to use it: We're well aware that the Taliban listen to everything, spy on everything.

Some of Daoud's friends come by the apartment now and then to watch videos in secret.

Farida and Saber occasionally drop in to visit me. They go out, they're more adventurous than I am, but I just don't dare risk setting foot outside. I feel as though the only way I can still resist is to shut myself in, refusing to see *them.*

It isn't until the very beginning of 1997, four months after the Taliban takeover, that Farida persuades me to venture into the streets of Kabul with her, under the pretext of retrieving the latest issues of our review[1] from our friend

---

[1]a periodical review of movies, music, and other things of interest

Maryam, who recently borrowed it from me. I don't see why I have to go along on this errand.

"You must come outside!" insists Farida. "You look awful, and there's no better way to <u>confront</u> reality. If you stay shut in any longer, you'll go crazy."

I vanish under my *chadri*.[2] Then Saber, Farida, and I begin our strange "walk." I haven't been outdoors for months. Everything seems strange to me, and I feel lost, as if I were a convalescent still too weak to be up and about. The street looks too big. I feel as though I were constantly being watched. We whisper under our *chadris* to avoid attracting attention, and Saber sticks close to our sides.

On the way to Maryam's we pass our former high school, there are Taliban guards at the entrance. On the adjacent sports field, ominous garlands of cassette tape have been draped on the volleyball net, the basketball hoop, and the branches of trees. My father had already mentioned them, but I'd thought these displays were temporary. Apparently, they are systematically renewed, streamers of forbidden pleasures: no images, no music.

A bit farther on, we pass four women. Suddenly a black 4 x 4 brakes to a halt next to them with a hellish screech: *Talibs* leap from the vehicle <u>brandishing</u> their cable whips and without a word of explanation begin flogging these women even though they're hidden by their *chadris*. They scream, but no one comes to their rescue. Then they try to run away, pursued by their tormentors, who keep whipping them savagely. I see blood dripping onto the women's shoes.

I'm frozen, I can't move, I've been turned to stone—and they're going to come after me next. Farida grabs my arms roughly.

"Run! We have to get away! Run!"

So with one hand I clamp the peephole of the chadri over my face, and we race off like lunatics until we're completely out of breath. Saber stays behind us, our helpless bodyguard—he knows there's nothing he could do to protect us. I have no idea if the *talibs* are following us; I seem to feel them breathing down my neck and keep expecting every second to feel their whips, to stagger beneath their blows.

Fortunately we're not far from home, so within five minutes we're scrambling up the stairs of our building. On the landing I sob uncontrollably, gasping for air, unable to speak. Farida painfully catches her breath, muttering who knows what, probably cursing the Taliban. She's much more of a rebel than I am.

Saber has caught up with us. Horrified, he explains what happened.

"Farida, they beat those women for wearing white shoes."

"What? That's some new decree?"

"White is the color of the Taliban flag, so women are not allowed to wear white. White shoes mean they're trampling on the flag!"

---

[2] a veil of dark, opaque material, with a peephole for the eyes

Even though they seem to follow one another without rhyme or reason, these decrees have a certain logic: the <u>extermination</u> of the Afghan woman.

A woman went out one day covered only with a chador,[3] holding the Koran clasped to her breast. The Taliban attacked her immediately with their whips.

"You have no right!" she protested. "Look at what is written in the Koran!"

During the struggle, though, the Koran fell from her arms, and none of her assailants made a move to pick it up. Now, the Koran must *never* be placed directly on the ground. If they really respected the Koran, the Taliban would know this. But they completely ignore the customary principles of our religion. Their decrees are just so many <u>aberrations</u> with regard to the sacred texts. The Koran specifically states that a woman may show her nakedness to a man if he is either her husband or her physician. To forbid women to consult a male doctor when women are at the same time forbidden to practice a profession—including that of medicine—is to attempt to destroy them. The paralyzing depression slowly overtaking our mother is an example of this torture, this <u>negation</u> of women.

My mother was a spirited, strong-willed woman who always felt free in her family, free in her studies, and free to choose a husband who had not been selected by her family. When she was in college, she wore skirts or pants. In the sixties, she used to go to the Zainab Cinema, and even took along her sisters. Women in Kabul were demanding their rights at that time, and during the Afghan Women's Year in 1975, the <u>regime</u> of President Daoud showed some democratic good sense when it decreed that "the Afghan woman has the same right as the Afghan man to exercise personal freedom, choose a career, and find a partner in marriage."

---

[3]a scarf covering the head and shoulders, worn by Muslim women

Understanding the Reading

Complete the next three exercises and see how well you understood the excerpt from *My Forbidden Face.*

Exercise 4.4 Multiple-Choice Questions

Answer the questions on the following page about the reading. Circle the letter of your answer.

TIP: Don't try to answer the questions from memory; go back to the text as often as necessary.

1. The first paragraph of this selection is a good description of
   A. heroic acts of the Taliban.
   B. a religious program.
   C. Taliban propaganda.
   D. fair, balanced news.

2. Throughout this selection, the narrator expresses her
   A. hope that things will change.
   B. anger and wishes for vengeance.
   C. determination to defy the Taliban.
   D. depression and fearfulness.

3. The "ominous garlands of cassette tape" are a symbol of
   A. the happier life Afghan people lived before the Taliban.
   B. the Taliban's banning of rap music.
   C. someone being arrested for disobeying a decree.
   D. the Taliban decree against sports.

4. During the regime of President Daoud,
   A. Afghan women began to be oppressed.
   B. Afghan women began to gain rights.
   C. Afghan women were forbidden to attend school.
   D. all of the cinemas were closed.

5. The main idea of this selection is that
   A. the narrator and her family are cowardly.
   B. people should follow the decrees of their government.
   C. women should not expect to have the same rights as men.
   D. life under the Taliban was a nightmare, especially for women.

Exercise 4.5   Short-Answer Questions

Respond to the following questions in one to two complete sentences. Go back to the text, as you did on the multiple choice.

6. The title of the chapter from which the excerpt is taken is "A Canary in a Cage." Is this an appropriate title? Why or why not?

   _____

   _____

   _____

7. Why don't Latifa, Farida, and Saber try to help the women who are being beaten?

   _____

   _____

   _____

8. Farida urges the narrator to go outside and "confront reality."
   In the same situation, would you be more like Farida or Latifa?
   Why?

   _____

   _____

   _____

9. The Taliban claim to be ruling according to the Muslim holy
   book, the Koran. How does the narrator present her belief that
   this is not really the case?

   _____

   _____

   _____

Exercise 4.6   Extending Your Thinking

Respond to the following question in three to four complete sentences. Use details from the text in your answer.

10. The theme of this unit is "Alienation and Identity." How has
    the Taliban takeover changed the narrator's identity, or sense of
    who she is? Why does she feel that the world outside her home
    is an alien (unknown) one?

    _____

    _____

    _____

    _____

    _____

    _____

Reading Strategy Lesson
Considering Author's Purpose and Point of View

In Chapter One, you learned that identifying your audience, purpose, and task will help you as a writer. Similarly, identifying an *author's* purpose for writing, along with his or her point of view, can help you as a reader.

Author's Purpose

Author's purpose questions are frequently found on standardized tests. Regardless of how it is worded, this type of question is simply asking you, "Why did the author write this? For what reason was this piece written?" Look at the example on the next page.

The *primary* purpose Latifa wrote this book was to
A. keep busy while confined in her apartment.
B. practice her writing skills.
C. leave a record of her feelings for her family in case something happened to her.
D. expose the reality of life under the Taliban.

We know that Latifa was bored, so there is probably some truth to choice A. Choice B also has some validity. Since she was not attending school, Latifa may have wanted to keep writing so she would not forget what she had learned. It is quite possible something might happen to her, but she does not mention wanting to leave a record, so C is less likely to be the correct choice.

There is one more answer to consider: "to expose the reality of life under the Taliban." From the notes about the author, you know that this book was published under a fictitious name after Latifa and her family escaped to France. We can assume she submitted her journals to a publisher there because she hoped to inform as many people as possible of what life in Afghanistan under the Taliban was like.

If you draw on your knowledge of history, you may know that the Taliban took over Afghanistan in 1996 and were ousted by the U.S. in 2001. People in many countries were aware of the harsh conditions in which Afghan people lived—particularly women. Books and articles like Latifa's helped to get more information to people who could make a difference.

Did 16-year-old Latifa have this in mind when she first wrote in her journals? Maybe not. But in the end she gathered her pages and her courage and told the world what was happening in her native land. Her **purpose** in doing so was *to expose the reality of life under the Taliban*, choice D.

Point of View

When you read fiction and some other types of writing, it is important to identify the author's point of view, or the vantage point from which he or she "sees" the story. Authors usually choose one point of view and stick to it. Three points of view are most often used.

- **First person:** The narrator is a character in the story and refers to herself or himself using words like *I*, *me*, *we*, and *our*. In the current selection, Latifa tells her story in the first person. She is the narrator of her own story:

  I vanish under my *chadri*. Then Saber, Farida, and I begin our strange "walk." I haven't been outdoors for months.
  Everything seems strange to me, and I feel lost, as if I were a convalescent still too weak to be up and about.

- **Omniscient third person:** The narrator knows what everyone in the story is thinking and feeling at all times. The characters are referred to by name, as "he" or "she," or by another identifier such as "the little boy" or "the teacher." If *My Forbidden Face* had been written in this style, it could have been titled *Her Forbidden Face*. Here is an example of how one part of the selection might have been written in omniscient third person. Notice how, in this version, you are told how everyone is feeling: Latifa, Farida, and even the *talibs*.

> Latifa felt frozen, unable to move, as if she'd been turned to stone. She was sure they would come after her next. Farida could not believe it. How could she get Latifa to realize they had to run? She grabbed her friend's arms roughly and shook her. "Come on! We have to run!" she shouted.
>
> The *talibs* watched them running away. We'll get them next time, they thought.

• **Limited third person:** The narrator knows how one character feels and thinks, and tells the story from that person's limited point of view. Once again we'll use part of the selection, this time changing the point of view to limited third person. Here we see the story from the viewpoint of only Latifa's mother:

> She was a spirited, strong-willed woman who always felt free in her family, free in her studies, and free to choose a husband who had not been selected by her family. She had gone to college, and now Afghan women were told they could not even learn to read or write. She had already decided that would not keep her from schooling her daughter, Latifa, even if they were stuck inside this apartment forever. If only she could give her daughter some of her own strength. She had a feeling she was going to need it.

Why Does Point of View Matter?

Why should you know point of view? The story still gets told, right? Point of view matters because it affects how much you learn about the various characters and events in a story. If you are reading a story told in a first-person or limited third-person point of view, there are things you won't know about the other characters. In an omniscient point-of-view story, however, you'll learn things that the other characters don't even know.

Nonfiction Viewpoints

When you read certain kinds of nonfiction, point of view means something a little different. A nonfiction point of view is how the author sees an issue or idea, where he or she is coming from. To distinguish nonfiction points of view, we'll call them **viewpoints**.

To better understand this concept, think of any issue with two sides, for instance the building of a new shopping mall in a local community. From the viewpoint of some residents, a mall would help create jobs and draw people to the town. From the viewpoint of other residents, however, a mall might create too much traffic and congestion. Some residents might also be concerned that having a mall where a field once stood is bad for the environment.

Latifa's viewpoint is that of a 16-year-old Afghan girl who feels imprisoned in her own home and country. If the Taliban rulers told the story of what was happening in Afghanistan at the same time, their viewpoint would be very different.

Exercise 4.7   Practice the Reading Strategy

I. Author's Purpose. Each item describes a nonfiction selection. On the line beneath the description, state the author's main purpose.

1. A book sorts out the differences between the Taliban decrees and what the Koran says about the same subjects.

Purpose of the book: _____

_____

2. An article in a magazine about pets explains how to teach your dog basic commands like "sit" and "stay."

Purpose of the article: _____

_____

3. A father writes a letter to his son in Marine boot camp. He ends the letter with, "It's not easy, I know. I've been there, done that. I know you can make it through. I'll be so proud when I come to your graduation."

Purpose of the letter: _____

_____

II. Point of View. Read each item carefully. Then identify the point of view from which it is written. Use the following abbreviations:

FP = first person   TPL = third person   TPO = third person
                              limited   omniscient

_____ 4. My father was a lawyer before the lawyer jokes. He honestly believed that people deserved a fair trial and that justice should not play favorites or be the victim of some technicality that let a criminal go free. I sometimes wish I had followed his path, but in those days there were not many women going into the law.

_____ 5. George watched Miss Amelia trudging up the long drive from the dusty road to his house. She would have a casserole with her, still warm from the oven, or maybe an apple pie. At first he had resented these intrusions on his privacy, but lately he had found himself looking forward to her visits, and he didn't even mind that he never got a word of his own into the one-way conversation. He had finally admitted that he was lonely, and that Miss Amelia had known that long before he did.

_____ 6. Downtown, Lake Street smelled like it did when people looked at one another and said, "The fish are up." Dan Elliott thought he would leave work early and toss in a line down at the pier. At Kennedy's Bakery, the fishy smell gave way to that of freshly cooked donuts and strong coffee. She knew she shouldn't do it, but Margie Grey ordered a custard-filled with chocolate frosting. "I've got five days before I have to weigh in on Friday," she told herself. Over in the corner, Audrey Bryant sipped her plain tea and shook her head. "Margie has no willpower," she thought. "She's going to be sorry come Friday."

Exercise 4.8   Apply the Reading Strategy

Use the Internet or printed sources to select a short piece of writing. Then use the following graphic to record the author's purpose and point of view. If you select a nonfiction piece, also explain the viewpoint of the author.

Title of Selection:	Author:

Circle one:	fiction	nonfiction	autobiography

Point of View: (Circle one)

first person   third person omniscient   third person limited

Evidence:

Author's Purpose:

If nonfiction, state the author's viewpoint:

Writing Workshop

What Is a Personal Narrative?

Like the author of *My Forbidden Face*, you are the expert on your own life and how your experiences have affected you. When you write a personal narrative, you don't have to do any research. Your experiences, the events in your life, your thoughts and opinions, and the people you know provide you with the information you need.

This doesn't mean that you don't have to think or plan when you write a personal narrative, however. You are usually given a topic, and you must think about how your personal experience relates to that topic. Read the following five sample topics:

1. Write about a time when you succeeded at something that you found difficult. It could be an athletic or academic accomplishment, a change in your behavior, or a change in the way you think about something.

2. Write about an experience that taught you something important. Be sure to include enough details about your experience that your reader will understand what happened and what important lesson you learned.

3. Write about someone you know personally who has either a positive or negative effect on your life. Describe what the person does and/or says and how this affects you.

4. Write about your favorite place to be. It can be indoors or outdoors, as long as you are happy and comfortable while you are there. Provide details that show your reader why you like this special place.

5. Write about a memorable event from your childhood. It can be something funny or serious. Give enough details so your reader will feel as if he or she is there with you.

Notice that even though you are your own source of details, you still have to plan. To write a personal narrative, follow these steps:

- Choose a topic.

- Narrow your topic by deciding who and what you will write about.

- Use a spider map to gather ideas and details for your narrative. (See page 39.)

- Group details from your map that belong together.

- Write in the first person.

- Write an introductory sentence related to the topic.

- Write your narrative.
- Revise and edit your narrative. If possible, also do peer editing with a classmate or group of classmates.

Exercise 4.9   Practice the Writing Lesson

1. Choose one of the topics on page 90. Write the prompt here:

   _____

   _____

   _____

   _____

2. Narrow your topic. Briefly note who and what you will write about. (Example: my favorite place—in front of my computer.)

   _____

   _____

   _____

3. Use a spider map to gather ideas and details:

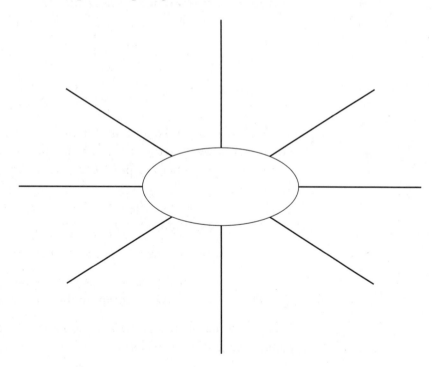

4. Group ideas from your map that belong together. For example, label all the ideas that belong in one paragraph with the letter A, the next group with B, and so forth.

Exercise 4.10 Write Your Personal Narrative

On a separate sheet of paper, write an introductory sentence that relates to the prompt and prepares your reader for what you are going to write about. Then continue with your narrative. Look back at the prompt to make sure you are staying on topic. Use your spider map to help you keep your ideas grouped logically. Then revise and edit your narrative, and produce your final draft. If possible, share it with the class.

Grammar Mini-Lesson
Compound-Complex Sentences

What Is a Compound-Complex Sentence?

A **compound-complex** sentence consists of at least *two* independent clauses and at least one dependent clause. Let's break down a compound-complex sentence from *My Forbidden Face*.

> Everything seems strange to me, and
>   INDEP. CLAUSE   CONJ.

> I feel lost,
> INDEP. CLAUSE

> as if I were a convalescent still too weak to be up and about.
>   DEP. CLAUSE

Independent clauses could stand on their own as sentences. Dependent clauses tie together the independent clauses to form one long sentence, with the help of punctuation and connecting words like *as*, *that*, and *who*.

In Unit One, you learned that two independent clauses joined together form a **compound** sentence. For example:

> Everything seems strange to me, and I feel lost.

Adding some dependent clauses for description makes the sentence more *complex*, so it becomes a **compound-complex** sentence.

> Everything seems strange to me, and I feel lost, as if I were a convalescent still too weak to be up and about.

Exercise 4.11 Practice Forming Compound-Complex Sentences

Each item contains a compound sentence and a simple sentence. Combine them into a compound-complex sentence.

HINT: Change the simple sentence to a dependent clause beginning with one of the following: although, as, because, now that, since, that, though, when, which, who.

Example: Our family finally escaped to France, and we can all breathe more freely. The worst part of our lives seems to be over. Our family finally escaped to France, and we can all breathe more freely now that the worst part of our lives seems to be over.

1. The bell rang. The students quickly left the room, and the teachers went out to stand in the corridors.

   _____

   _____

   _____

2. My mother is out, but I can let you talk to my dad. He might be able to help you.

   _____

   _____

   _____

3. Bandwidth continues to improve. One instrument that functions as a telephone, computer, and television may soon be commonplace.

   _____

   _____

   _____

4. The downpour made visibility almost zero. We finally had to pull over, thinking we would wait until the rain stopped.

   _____

   _____

   _____

5. The days are growing longer, and you can feel the warmth in the air. Spring is approaching.

   _____

   _____

   _____

Exercise 4.12 Additional Practice Forming Compound-Complex Sentences

Now you are given three simple sentences. Combine all three sentences to make one compound-complex sentence.

1. The illiteracy rate is high. Storytelling is alive and well in Afghanistan. Folktales link the past and the present.

   _____

   _____

   _____

2. Folktales teach values and beliefs. They teach behaviors. They are also a form of entertainment.

_____

_____

_____

3. Afghans have always enjoyed music. Much of it is traditional. There are certain dances that go with certain songs.

_____

_____

_____

4. There was no music allowed under the Taliban. No forms of dance were permitted. The people sang and danced quietly in private.

_____

_____

_____

5. The United States drove out the Taliban in 2001. The Afghan people celebrated. They rejoiced by singing and dancing openly in the streets.

_____

_____

_____

Polish Your Spelling
Changing Adjectives to Adverbs

The suffix -*ly* is used to turn adjectives (words that describe nouns) into adverbs (words that describe verbs). Adding -*ly* to the end of a word can seem simple, but you should be aware of certain spelling changes.

To change an adjective to an adverb, we usually just add -*ly*.

ADJECTIVE		SUFFIX		ADVERB
extreme	+	ly	=	extremely
loud	+	ly	=	loudly
harsh	+	ly	=	harshly

Exceptions:

1. If the adjective ends in a consonant plus -le, change the -le to -ly.

ADJECTIVE	ADVERB
reasonable	reasonably
able	ably
ample	amply

2. If the adjective ends in y preceded by a consonant, change y to i before adding -ly.

ADJECTIVE		SUFFIX		ADVERB
ready	+	ly	=	readily
flimsy	+	ly	=	flimsily

3. If the adjective ends in -ic, add al before attaching -ly.

ADJECTIVE		SUFFIXES		ADVERB
drastic	+	al + ly	=	drastically
scientific	+	al + ly	=	scientifically

4. Note that the e is dropped in these three special exceptions:

ADJECTIVE	ADVERB
due	duly
true	truly
whole	wholly

Exercise 4.13 Practice Changing Adjectives to Adverbs

Change each adjective to an adverb and write the new word on the line.

ADJECTIVE   ADVERB

1. comfortable   _____

2. heavy   _____

3. gentle   _____

4. magic   _____

5. happy   _____

6. whole   _____

7. busy   _____

8. tragic   _____

9. true   _____

10. hasty   _____

Chapter Five

Prereading Guide
Words to know and ideas to consider before you jump into the reading.

A. Essential Vocabulary

Word	Meaning	Typical Use
abdicate (*v*) AB-dih-kate	to relinquish a power, right, position, or responsibility; to resign	The king *abdicated* the throne, and his daughter became queen.
anonymous (*adj*) uh-NON-ih-muss	of unknown authorship or origin; unidentified	The person who made the $10,000 donation prefers to remain *anonymous*.
cultivation (*n*) cul-tih-VAY-shun	the act of growing and nurturing; development	The *cultivation* of good study habits should begin when children are young.
deplorable (*adj*) de-PLOR-uh-bull	wretched and miserable; shameful	After the tsunami destroyed their homes, the survivors lived in *deplorable* conditions.
enterprise (*n*) ENT-ur-prize	a business intended to make a profit; company	Olivia has her own small *enterprise*, making and selling beaded jewelry.
fortuitous (*adj*) for-TOO-ih-tuss	occurring by chance; fortunate	It was *fortuitous* that I stopped by today since you need my help.
mystical (*adj*) MISS-tik-ul	spiritual or otherworldly; supernatural	Many cultures have their own *mystical* beliefs.
ostensibly (*adv*) oss-TEN-sih-blee	outwardly or seemingly; supposedly	Although she is *ostensibly* my friend, she sometimes talks behind my back.
stultify (*v*) STUL-tih-fy	to make useless; to impair	Some people believe that watching too much TV *stultifies* your mind.
testimonial (*n*) tes-tih-MOAN-ee-ul	1. a formal tribute to a person's accomplishments	Mom was very pleased that her business associates wanted to give her a *testimonial* at the Plaza Hotel.
	2. praise of a product or system; accolade	I bought the Twist-and-Twirl curling iron because of all the *testimonials* on TV.

B. Vocabulary Practice

Exercise 5.1   Sentence Completion

Using your new vocabulary knowledge, choose the best way to complete the following sentences. Circle the letter of your answer.

1. It's _____ mystical; there is strong scientific proof.
   A. very
   B. not

2. Marisol _____ as president of the club by saying, "I wish to abdicate."
   A. was installed
   B. resigned

3. David is ostensibly going to go to Harvard, but his SAT scores might be _____.
   A. too low
   B. off the chart

4. There's a _____. This place is deplorable!
   A. gardener and cook
   B. hole in the roof

5. Good _____ cultivates healthy bodies.
   A. literature
   B. food

6. My parents met by _____ at the supermarket; they call it their fortuitous moment.
   A. prearrangement
   B. chance

7. People _____ stay in a relationship they find stultifying.
   A. should not
   B. should

8. _____ sent me flowers anonymously.
   A. Ethan
   B. Someone

9. I _____ this shampoo. I'd like to give it a testimonial.
   A. don't like
   B. love

10. I'm going to major in _____ and start my own enterprise.
    A. business management
    B. philosophy

Exercise 5.2 Using Fewer Words

Replace the italicized words with a single word from the following list. The first one has been done for you.

abdicated	anonymous	cultivation	deplorable	enterprises
fortuitous	mystical	ostensibly	stultified	testimonial

1. I was *made useless* by staying up all night on the Internet.

   1. <u>stultified</u>

2. There was something *spiritual and otherworldly* about the way the sun gleamed through the pink clouds.

   2. _____

3. His table manners are *wretched and miserable*.

   3. _____

4. How many *businesses intended to make a profit* do you think there are on First Street?

   4. _____

5. He has *relinquished his responsibilities*, and now it's up to us.

   5. _____

6. *Outwardly or seemingly*, they are going to the movies.

   6. _____

7. The *act of nurturing* of the intellect is something that should never end.

   7. _____

8. Many early poems' authors are *of unknown origin*.

   8. _____

9. We're surprising Scott tonight with a(an) *formal tribute to his accomplishments*.

   9. _____

10. It was *because of a lucky chance* that the bus arrived just as it began to rain.

    10. _____

Exercise 5.3 Synonyms and Antonyms

Fill in the blanks in column A with the required synonyms or antonyms, selecting them from column B. (Remember: A *synonym* is a word *similar* in meaning to another word. *Autumn* and *fall* are synonyms. An *antonym* is a word *opposite* in meaning to another word. *Beginning* and *ending* are antonyms.)

A		B
_____	1. antonym for *pleasant*	abdicate
_____	2. synonym for *accolade*	anonymous
_____	3. antonym for *unlucky*	cultivation
_____	4. synonym for *company*	deplorable
_____	5. synonym for *development*	enterprise
_____	6. synonym for *supernatural*	fortuitous
_____	7. antonym for *identified*	mystical
_____	8. synonym for *supposedly*	ostensibly
_____	9. antonym for *take on*	stultify
_____	10. synonym for *impair*	testimonial

C. Journal Freewrite

Before you begin the reading on the next page, take out a journal or sheet of paper and spend some time responding to the following prompt.

TIP: Don't worry about grammar and spelling; just write what comes to mind. The purpose of freewriting is to explore ideas, not to produce a polished work.

> How do people in your neighborhood communicate? Do they walk by one another without speaking, or do they stop and talk? Describe how they relate to one another.

from The Death and Life of Great American Cities

by Jane Jacobs

About the Author

Jane Jacobs (1916–2006) was born in Scranton, Pennsylvania, and moved to New York City after high school. It was the middle of the Great Depression, and she was able to find only temporary work. During her unemployed periods, she observed life in the city and began writing articles about urban development and planning. Before long she had earned the title "urbanist"—one who studies cities. She felt that small neighborhoods are vital to a city, and when she learned of proposals to replace some of them with giant housing projects and office buildings, she wrote *The Death and Life of Great American Cities.* The book inspired neighborhood protests and demonstrations. Jacobs became well-known for her writings about cities, social values, and the dangers of unrestrained development.

Reformers have long observed city people loitering on busy corners, hanging around in candy stores and bars and drinking soda pop on stoops, and have passed a judgment, the gist of which is: "This is <u>deplorable</u>! If these people had decent homes and a more private or bosky[1] outdoor place, they wouldn't be on the street!"

This judgment represents a profound misunderstanding of cities. It makes no more sense than to drop in at a <u>testimonial</u> banquet in a hotel and conclude that if these people had wives who could cook, they would give their parties at home.

The point of both the testimonial banquet and the social life of city sidewalks is precisely that they are public. They bring together people who do not know each other in an intimate, private social fashion and in most cases do not care to know each other in that fashion.

Nobody can keep open house in a great city. Nobody wants to. And yet if interesting, useful and significant contacts among the people of cities are confined to acquaintanceships suitable for private life, the city becomes <u>stultified</u>. Cities are full of people with whom, from your viewpoint, or mine, or any other individual's, a certain degree of contact is useful or enjoyable; but you do not want them in your hair. And they do not want you in theirs either.

In speaking about city sidewalk safety, I mentioned how necessary it is that there should be, in the brains behind the eyes on the street, an almost unconscious assumption of general street support when the chips are down—when a citizen has to choose, for instance, whether he will take responsibility, or <u>abdicate</u> it, in combating barbarism[2] or protecting strangers. There is a short word for this assumption of support: trust. The trust of a city street is formed over time from many, many little public sidewalk contacts. It grows out of people stopping by at the bar for a beer, getting advice from the grocer and giving advice to the newsstand man, comparing opinions with other customers at the bakery and nodding hello to the two boys drinking pop on the stoop, eying the

---

[1]having trees and shrubs
[2]cruel or rude behavior

girls while waiting to be called for dinner, admonishing the children, hearing about a job from the hardware man and borrowing a dollar from the druggist, admiring the new babies and sympathizing over the way a coat faded. Customs vary: in some neighborhoods people compare notes on their dogs; in others they compare notes on their landlords.

Most of it is <u>ostensibly</u> utterly trivial but the sum is not trivial at all. The sum of such casual, public contact at a local level—most of it <u>fortuitous</u>, most of it associated with errands, all of it metered by the person concerned and not thrust upon him by anyone—is a feeling for the public identity of people, a web of public respect and trust, and a resource in time of personal or neighborhood need. The absence of this trust is a disaster to a city street. Its <u>cultivation</u> cannot be institutionalized.[3] And above all, *it implies no private commitments.*

I have seen a striking difference between presence and absence of casual public trust on two sides of the same wide street in East Harlem, composed of residents of roughly the same incomes and same races. On the old-city side, which was full of public places and the sidewalk loitering so deplored by Utopian[4] minders of other people's leisure, the children were being kept well in hand. On the project side of the street across the way, the children, who had a fire hydrant open beside their play area, were behaving destructively, drenching the open windows of houses with water, squirting it on adults who ignorantly walked on the project side of the street, throwing it into the windows of cars as they went by. Nobody dared to stop them. These were <u>anonymous</u> children, and the identities behind them were an unknown. What if you scolded or stopped them? Who would back you up over there in the blind-eyed Turf?[5] Would you get, instead, revenge? Better to keep out of it. Impersonal city streets make anonymous people, and this is not a matter of esthetic quality nor of a <u>mystical</u> emotional effect in architectural scale. It is a matter of what kinds of tangible <u>enterprises</u> sidewalks have, and therefore of how people use the sidewalks in practical, everyday life.

---

[3]put into practice by an authority
[4]from Thomas More's *Utopia*, a perfect world without conflict where everyone is happy
[5]an area taken over by a gang

Understanding the Reading

Complete the next three exercises and see how well you understood the excerpt from *The Death and Life of Great American Cities.*

Exercise 5.4 Multiple-Choice Questions

Answer the following questions about the reading. Circle the letter of your answer.

TIP: Don't try to answer the questions from memory; go back to the text as often as necessary.

1. The narrator compares city sidewalks and testimonial banquets in order to show
   A. the value of meeting in public spaces.
   B. their differences.
   C. that people should give their parties at home.
   D. that people shouldn't loiter on busy corners.

2. The narrator doesn't recommend opening a house up to strangers, but she
   A. would like to help people who have no place to live.
   B. thinks a certain amount of contact with "sidewalk acquaintances" is useful.
   C. says casual public contact is dangerous.
   D. enjoys going to the homes of casual acquaintances.

3. The narrator emphasizes how important it is to
   A. admire new babies on the street.
   B. get advice from the neighborhood grocer.
   C. develop a neighborhood web of trust and respect.
   D. follow the customs of your neighborhood.

4. The narrator gives the example of the "anonymous children" to show
   A. what happens when children are not supervised.
   B. why people are sometimes afraid to get involved in a situation.
   C. what happens to people who get too close to misbehaving children.
   D. the difference between one side of the street and the other.

5. The main idea of this selection is that
   A. city streets are dangerous.
   B. loiterers usually have children who don't behave.
   C. city streets do not have to be impersonal.
   D. you cannot be friends with someone you meet on the street.

Exercise 5.5 Short-Answer Questions

Respond to the following questions in one to two complete sentences. Go back to the text, as you did on the multiple choice.

6. Jane Jacobs is an observer of city life. What do you think was her purpose for writing this selection?

   _____

   _____

   _____

7. Think about the title, *The Death and Life of Great American Cities*. Describe the difference, from your viewpoint, between a community that has died and one that is alive.

_____

_____

_____

8. What does the narrator mean when she says that by themselves the friendly activities in a neighborhood are "utterly trivial but the sum is not trivial at all"?

_____

_____

_____

9. With what parts of this selection can you identify? If there is nothing in it that seems familiar, why do you think that is so?

_____

_____

_____

Exercise 5.6 Extending Your Thinking

Respond to the following question in three to four complete sentences.

10. The theme of this unit is "Alienation and Identity." How would adults in your neighborhood whom you know only casually identify you (for example, "the girl who . . ." or "the boy who . . .")? Explain. Then choose one of the adults and describe him or her using a similar identifier ("the man who . . .," "the lady who . . .").

_____

_____

_____

_____

_____

_____

Reading Strategy Lesson
Making Inferences and Drawing Conclusions

Independent readers are skilled at making inferences based on what the text implies and drawing conclusions about the material.
What is an **inference**? Look at the example on the next page.

Lindsay:	So what do you think? Does this gold sequin top go with these jeans?
Shara:	Well, um, it's an *interesting* outfit.
Lindsay:	That's good. I want to look interesting, right?
Shara:	You will. You *definitely* will not go unnoticed. Maybe you should ask your sister what she thinks before we leave. She has really good taste in clothes, you know?

Shara doesn't want to hurt Lindsay's feelings by telling her she does not like the top. She implies that it may bring Lindsay a different kind of attention from the kind she wants. Her suggestion that Lindsay ask her sister what she thinks is an **implication** that a second opinion is needed.

Implications can be made by a person you are listening to or by the author of the written material you are reading. Implications are also common in advertising, in films, and on TV shows.

By listening and viewing, you are the receiver of the implications. You decide what is meant by them when you "read between the lines" and look for certain key phrases and clues. Once you discover the deeper meaning in a conversation or reading, you have made an **inference**. You can then use your inferences to **draw conclusions** about what the speaker or text is *really* saying.

When you make inferences and draw conclusions, you go beyond the literal meaning of the text.

Strategies for Inferences and Conclusions

- Ask yourself questions about the important details in a selection. Ask yourself why those details are included. To what main idea do they lead?

- When a sentence seems to summarize the main idea of a paragraph or the entire selection, reread the sentence and ask yourself, "How does this information help me to look 'behind' what is written?"

- Draw on your prior knowledge. Do you know something that helps you make a conclusion or makes you question what the author seems to be implying?

- Read ahead with your conclusions in mind and see if there is additional information that either supports or refutes (disproves) the conclusions you have drawn so far.

- Remember that ideas are not always stated outright. You have to "read between the lines" to find the author's meaning.

On the next page is an example, from *Anne's House of Dreams* by Lucy Maud Montgomery. Keep in mind the strategies you just learned as you draw conclusions from the text.

"Thanks be, I'm done with geometry, learning or teaching it," said Anne Shirley, a trifle vindictively, as she thumped a somewhat battered volume of Euclid into a big chest of books, banged the lid in triumph, and sat down upon it, looking at Diana Wright across the Green Gables garret, with gray eyes that were like a morning sky.

You can easily conclude that Anne Shirley does not like geometry, but what else does this paragraph tell you?

• She has been both a student and a teacher of geometry.

• She has a lot of books.

• Diana Wright is probably her friend.

• Anne's geometry book is "Euclidean." (From prior knowledge, you may know that Euclid is known as the "Father of Geometry.")

After drawing these conclusions, you still have an unanswered question: Why is Anne "done with geometry"? Is it only for the summer? Has she been teaching but quit her job? Reading ahead may answer these questions and help you to draw further conclusions:

"Oh, I've always liked teaching, apart from geometry. These past three years in Summerside have been very pleasant ones. Mrs. Harmon Andrews told me when I came home that I wouldn't likely find married life as much better than teaching as I expected. Evidently Mrs. Harmon is of Hamlet's opinion that it may be better to bear the ills that we have than fly to others that we know not of."

Anne refers to whether she will like "married life," so we can infer that she is to be married and will not continue to teach, as she has for the past three years in a place called Summerside.

Making inferences and drawing conclusions can be a bit more difficult when you are reading a nonfiction selection. Here is an example from *How the Other Half Lives* by Jacob Riis, who wrote about the rapid growth of New York City.

Their [the former wealthy residents of Manhattan] comfortable dwellings in the once fashionable streets along the East River front fell into the hands of real-estate agents and boarding-house keepers; and here, says the report to the Legislature of 1857, when the evils engendered had excited just alarm, "in its beginning, the tenant-house became a real blessing to that class of industrious poor whose small earnings limited their expenses, and whose employment in workshops, stores, or about the warehouses and thoroughfares, render a near residence of much importance." Not for long, however. As business increased, and the city grew with rapid strides, the necessities of the poor became the opportunity of their wealthier neighbors, and the stamp was set upon the old houses, suddenly become valuable, which the best thought and effort of a later age have vainly struggled to efface.

See if you can answer the following questions.

1. Why was "a near residence of much importance" for those who lived in the tenements?
2. What does Jacob Riis mean by "the necessities of the poor became the opportunity of their wealthier neighbors"?
3. What "stamp" have those of a later age fought to efface (erase)?

Answers

1. Poor people had to live close to their workplaces because they had no transportation.
2. Since the poor had no choice but to live close to work, those who could afford to buy the old houses and turn them into tenements took advantage of them.
3. The tenement houses became valuable, and even today apartments in New York City rent for a great deal more than in most other places in the nation.

Exercise 5.7   Practice the Reading Strategy

The following passages are from the Jane Jacobs reading selection. Look back at the selection to find them in context. Consider the details and clues, and then write your inferences and conclusions.

1. Reformers have long observed city people loitering on busy corners, hanging around in candy stores and bars and drinking soda pop on stoops, and have passed a judgment, the gist of which is: "This is deplorable! If these people had decent homes and a more private or bosky outdoor place, they wouldn't be on the street!" (page 101)

a. What is the author's implied opinion of reformers? _____

_____

_____

b. What conclusions can you draw about the author's opinion of the people on the street as compared to the opinions of the reformers? _____

_____

_____

2. Cities are full of people with whom, from your viewpoint or mine, or any other individual's, a certain degree of contact is useful or enjoyable; but you do not want them in your hair. And they do not want you in theirs either. (page 101)

a. What inferences can you make about the kind of people the author is discussing here? _____

_____

_____

b. What information led you to these inferences? (Keep in mind that it may be found elsewhere in the selection.) _____

_____

_____

3. I have seen a striking difference between presence and absence of casual public trust on two sides of the same wide street in East Harlem, composed of residents of roughly the same incomes and same races. (page 102)

Draw a conclusion: Why does the author mention that the people in this neighborhood are of the same incomes and races? _____

_____

_____

Exercise 5.8 Apply the Reading Strategy

Here is another passage by Jacob Riis. This is an excerpt from *The Battle of the Slum*, written in 1902. Read the passage. Consider the details and clues, and then answer the questions.

Jacob Beresheim was fifteen when he was charged with murder. It is now more than six years ago, but the touch of his hand is cold upon mine, with mortal fear, as I write. Every few minutes, during our long talk on the night of his arrest and confession, he would spring to his feet, and, clutching my arm as a drowning man catches at a rope, demand with shaking voice, "Will they give me the chair?" The assurance that boys were not executed quieted him only for the moment. Then the dread and the horror were upon him again.

Of his crime the less said the better. It was the climax of a career of depravity [corruption] that differed from other such chiefly in the opportunities afforded by an environment which led up to and helped shape it. . . .

He was born in a tenement in that section where the Gilder Tenement House Commission found 324,000 persons living out of sight and reach of a green spot of any kind, and where sometimes the buildings—front, middle, and rear—took up ninety-three per cent of all the space in the block. Such a home as he had was there, and of the things that belonged to it he was the heir. The sunlight was not among them. It "never entered" there. Darkness and discouragement did, and dirt. Later on, when he took to the dirt as his natural weapon in his battles with society, it was said of him that it was the only friend that stuck to him, and it was true. Very early the tenement gave him up to the street. The thing he took with him as the one legacy of home was the instinct for the crowd, which meant that the tenement had wrought its worst mischief upon him; it had smothered that in him around which character is built. The more readily did he fall in with the street and its ways. Character implies depth, a soil, and growth. The street is all surface. Nothing grows there; it hides only a sewer.

Jacob Beresheim had not even the benefit of such schooling as there was to be had. He did not go to school, and nobody cared. There was indeed a law directing that every child should go, and a corps of truant officers to catch him if he did not; but the law had been a dead letter for a quarter of a century. There was no census to tell which children ought to be in school, and no place but a jail to put those in who shirked. Jacob was allowed to drift. From the time he was twelve till he was fifteen, he told me, he might have gone to school three weeks—no more.

1. Who or what does Riis seem to blame most for Jacob's crime?

_____

_____

_____

2. What details and clues led you to this conclusion?

_____

_____

_____

3. What does Riis imply might have saved Jacob from leading the life he has led?

_____

_____

_____

4. What details and clues led you to this conclusion?

_____

_____

_____

5. After reading this passage and the main reading selection, would you conclude that Jane Jacobs and Jacob Riis would agree or disagree about the streets of New York? Explain your answer.

_____

_____

Writing Workshop
The Thesis Statement

What Is a Thesis Statement?

A **thesis statement** is a sentence at or near the beginning of an essay that notifies the reader of the main purpose or main idea of the essay. A clear thesis statement spells out for your readers exactly what your essay will be proving or showing.

Thesis statements are not just for readers, however. They can also be an enormous help to you, the writer. Properly done, they give you a kind of map of where you are going with your essay. Thesis statements are also called **controlling ideas**, because they hold you back from wandering off to some unrelated topic when you are engaged in the writing process—if you keep them in mind.

The thesis statement gives you the answers to some questions that you ask yourself when you begin to write an essay: "What am I going to write about?" "What is my opinion?" "What am I going to prove?" Once you have figured out the answers to some or all of these questions (depending on the topic) and written your thesis statement, you have a plan for the remainder of your paper.

How to Formulate a Good Thesis Statement

1. A good thesis has two parts: topic and point of the essay. It is not just a topic sentence. What's your *point* about that topic?

TOPIC	POINT OF THE ESSAY
Diversity of opinion	is what makes America great.
The Internet	spreads ridiculous hoaxes.
The voting age	should be changed to 21.

2. A good thesis statement has a very clear, specific opinion or idea. This is especially important if you are writing a persuasive paper. You must state your position clearly. Be firm and take a definite stance. Notice the difference between these two thesis statements:

    A. Some people think vending machines should be removed from the school cafeteria, but I'm not so sure about that.

    B. Vending machines should definitely remain in the school cafeteria, despite what some school administrators, health officials, and parents claim.

Statement A simply refers to "some people," and the writer's opinion is wishy-washy. "I'm not so sure" does not state an opinion. Statement B makes it clear that the writer feels the vending machines should stay ("definitely remain") and that the claims of *specific* people—school administrators, health officials, and parents—are wrong.

Statement A does not give you a good map to follow. There is simply not much potential for writing three paragraphs from such a weak statement. Statement B, however, gives the writer a clear path to follow. The three body paragraphs will be about

1. school administrators' claims
2. health officials' claims
3. parents' claims

The writer will explain why each group thinks the vending machines should go and will give arguments against each group's ideas.

3. A good thesis statement declares one main idea. You will only confuse yourself and your reader if you try to explain or argue more than one point of a large issue. Compare these statements:

A. Better public transportation could help solve our nation's energy problems.
B. Better public transportation could solve our nation's energy problems and make it much easier for people to get to work or school without having to ask someone who has a car to drive them or making them walk for miles to get to school or work.

Statement A is about one main idea, that better public transportation could help solve our nation's energy problems. Statement B brings in too many other ideas.

4. A good thesis is flexible. It is quite possible that as you write your essay, you'll realize you want to approach the topic in a slightly different way. Maybe your first reaction was to keep the vending machines, for example, but you can't really think of any convincing reasons why. Those "school administrators, health officials, and parents" have very good arguments for removing vending machines. You decide your paper will be more effective if you agree with them. Your thesis changes:

School administrators, health officials, and parents pose some excellent arguments for removing vending machines from school cafeterias.

Even if you don't agree with their position, you can write a paper that presents it. If your assignment is specifically to persuade, then you will have to be a little more forceful in presenting those views as correct. In that case, your thesis statement should let your reader know that you are going to tell *why* the vending machines should go. Your thesis statement must "flex" again:

School administrators, health officials, and parents have joined forces to benefit the health of all the students in our school system by choosing to remove vending machines from school cafeterias.

Exercise 5.9 Practice the Writing Lesson

Rate each of these thesis statements. Place a check mark in the corresponding column, and in the space below the statement briefly explain the problem with any of the statements that you mark "poor."

Good	Poor	Thesis Statement
		1. School libraries should automatically ban a book that any parent objects to.
		2. Electronic voting machines make election fraud both possible and probable because it can be done easily by hackers who are willing to take payoffs and may feel they have to because they are out of work due to too many people in the field.
		3. High schools that require students to serve a certain number of hours of community service before graduation recognize the valuable lessons such an experience can teach.
		4. If every state charged a deposit on bottles and cans, we could reduce highway litter and increase recycling.
		5. Getting enough exercise can make you feel better physically, mentally, and emotionally.

Exercise 5.10 Apply the Writing Lesson

Read the essay prompts on the next page. Write a thesis statement for each. You will be working with one of these topics later, so write each thesis statement as if it were a map for an essay. (Remember: You're not trying to answer each prompt in full here. Write only a concise thesis statement you *could* eventually use for an essay.)

1. The academic and social aspects of school are a big part of your life as a teenager. What things do you like most about school? Identify them and explain why they are your favorites.

   _____

   _____

   _____

2. Since you were small, people have probably been asking you, "What do you want to be when you grow up?" What is your answer to that question now? Give at least three reasons why you feel that way.

   _____

   _____

   _____

3. The U.S. Postal Service is always creating new stamps to honor various people. Who do you think should be on the next stamp? Give at least three reasons why.

   _____

   _____

   _____

4. Many adults believe that video games are harmful to their children's physical and mental health. Explain whether you do or do not agree, and give at least three reasons for your opinion.

   _____

   _____

   _____

5. To save money, your school board has proposed removing art, music, and journalism programs from all middle schools and high schools. Sports programs, however, will remain. Explain your position on this proposal, giving at least three reasons for your view.

   _____

   _____

   _____

Grammar Mini-Lesson

Subject-Verb Agreement

One of the most common mistakes people make in writing and conversation is incorrect subject-verb agreement. In this lesson, we'll review how to check that your subjects and verbs agree, to ensure that you're communicating as effectively as possible.

A **singular subject** requires a **singular verb**. A **plural subject** requires a **plural verb**.

> The *customer is* waiting.
> singular subject (*customer*) + singular verb (*is*)
>
> A *speaker believes* in something.
> singular subject (*speaker*) + singular verb (*believes*)

Notice what happens if we change the subjects:

> The *customers are* waiting.
> plural subject (*customers*) + plural verb (*are*)
>
> *Speakers believe* in something.
> plural subject (*speakers*) + plural verb (*believe*)

TIP: *Verbs ending in* s *are usually singular:* is, was, knows, has, does, eats, sleeps, *and so forth. This is easy to remember:* s *at the end is a* s*ingular verb.*

Mistakes often occur because of uncertainty as to which word in the sentence is the subject. Normally, the subject comes before the verb. In the following cases, however, the subject appears after the verb.

- In a question:
  Are the *people* here yet? (The subject is *people*.)

- In a sentence beginning with *There is, There are, Here is, Here are*, etc.:
  Here *are* your *papers*. (The subject is *papers*, not *here*.)
  Are the *girls* home yet? (The subject is *girls*.)

Be careful: An "of" phrase between a subject and its verb has no effect on agreement.
  A *bag of candy bars* is in the pantry. ("*bag . . . is,*" not "*bars is*")

If you aren't sure which verb to use, try reading the sentence without the "of" phrase:
  A *bag is* in the pantry. (The singular subject *bag* requires the singular verb *is*. You would not say "A bag are in the pantry.")

Exercise 5.11 Practice Making Subjects and Verbs Agree

In each sentence there is a subject without a verb. If that subject is singular, select a singular verb for it. If it is plural, choose a plural verb. Write your answer in the space provided.

1. Cities (is, are) _____ full of people.

2. There (was, were) _____ a crowd on the corner.

3. (Where's, Where are) _____ the reformers?

4. Their judgment (represent, represents) _____ a profound misunderstanding of cities.

5. One group of children (behave, behaves) _____ well.

6. (There's, There are) _____ other children who don't.

7. Their identities (is, are) _____ not known.

8. (Doesn't, Don't) _____ anyone have the nerve to speak to them?

9. People (have, has) _____ to think of what might happen.

10. The sidewalk life of cities (ties, tie) _____ into other types of public life.

Exercise 5.12 Additional Agreement Practice

Read each sentence. If the subject and verb do not agree, rewrite the sentence correctly. If they do agree, write OK.

1. The teacher give the students their books on the first day.

   _____

2. A backpack of books are heavy to carry.

   _____

3. We all brings our books to class anyway.

   _____

4. Don't he ever come to class on time?

   _____

5. Many products in our backpacks were made in other countries.

   _____

6. It's not something we thinks about, though.

   _____

7. Hasn't the teachers come back yet?

   _____

8. All of the tickets to the play has been sold.

   _____

9. Has you seen my flash drive anywhere?

   _____

10. Everyone has a laptop except me.

    _____

Polish Your Spelling

Changing Verbs to Adjectives

As we've seen, you can make your writing more colorful and interesting by using specific adjectives, words that describe. You can add to your bank of adjectives by forming some of them from verbs.

1. You can form an adjective by adding *-ing* to a verb.

VERB	ADJECTIVE	EXAMPLE
run	running	The running water was cold.
surprise	surprising	Maria has made a surprising recovery.

Spelling notes:

- Drop silent *e* before adding *-ing*:
  starve + ing = starving   *freeze + ing = freezing*

- Change *ie* to *y* before adding *-ing*:
  die = dying   *tie = tying*

2. You can form an adjective by adding *-ed* to a regular verb.

VERB	ADJECTIVE	EXAMPLE
starve	starved	The child is starved for attention.
surprise	surprised	Maria was surprised at her recovery.

Spelling notes:

- Drop silent *e* before adding *-ed*:
  increase + ed = increased   *encourage + ed = encouraged*

- If the verb ends in *y preceded by a consonant*, change the *y* to *i* before adding *-ed*:
  worry + ed = worried   *satisfy + ed = satisfied*

- Do *not* change the *y if it is preceded by a vowel*:
  annoy + ed = annoyed   *decay + ed = decayed*

3. If the verb is irregular—for example, *break, broke, broken*—you cannot add *-ed*. Instead, use the last principal part—*broken*—as an adjective.

EXAMPLES:

Don't step on the *broken* glass.

We skated on the *frozen* lake. (freeze, froze, frozen)

Can you help the *lost* child? (lose, lost, lost)

Exercise 5.13 Practice Changing Verbs to Adjectives

Complete each sentence by supplying an adjective formed from the verb in parentheses.

1. Kerri was upset by the _____ score on her test. (devastate)

2. With his _____ breath, he cursed his fate. (die)

3. The president has several _____ engagements today. (speak)

4. The warning is not as _____ as we had feared. (alarm)

5. Their _____ figures grew smaller and smaller. (recede)

6. We were _____ by the snowstorm. (blind)

7. We need _____ eggs to make the egg salad. (boil)

8. Evan was _____ by all the attention he received. (embarrass)

9. After winning the game last Friday, the team was _____. (encourage)

10. You need to provide a _____ notice that you are moving out. (write)

Chapter Six

Prereading Guide
Words to know and ideas to consider before you jump into the reading.

A. Essential Vocabulary

Word	Meaning	Typical Use
advantageous (*adj*) ad-van-TAJE-us	offering gain or profit; beneficial	The deal we made was more *advantageous* to the car dealer than it was to us.
anguish (*n*) ANG-wish	extreme mental or physical pain or suffering; agony	Despite a great deal of *anguish*, Letitia was able to regain complete use of her legs after the accident.
disposition (*n*) dis-po-ZI-shun	the usual mood of a person; temperament	Brady was loved by all for his sweet *disposition*.
distort (*v*) dis-TORT	to disfigure or twist out of shape; alter	It is difficult to find a media source that does not *distort* the truth in some way.
epidermis (*n*) ep-ih-DUR-miss	the surface layer covering the body of a human being or other animal or the outer layer of the tissue of a plant; skin	If you get badly sunburned, your *epidermis* may peel.
figment (*n*) FIG-munt	something imagined, made up, or contrived	Was my crush really smiling at me, or was it a *figment* of my imagination?
peculiar (*adj*) pick-KEWL-yar	1. characteristic of one group, person, or thing; distinctive 2. eccentric, particular, odd	Writing in *hieroglyphics* was peculiar to the ancient Egyptians. My little brother has a lot of *peculiar* eating habits, like putting orange juice in his cereal.
phantom (*n*) FAN-tum	something apparent to sense but with no substantial existence; apparition	The windows rattled and the floors creaked eerily, as if there were a *phantom* in the room.
stenographer (*n*) ste-NAH-gra-fer	someone who writes shorthand or takes dictation; transcriber	The *stenographer* worked furiously to capture everything that was said during the trial.

Word	Meaning	Typical Use
substance (*n*) SUB-stunce	1. a tangible material; matter	I accidentally stepped into the sticky *substance* on the floor.
	2. essence; meaning	Oprah is a woman of considerable *substance* who gives a great deal of her wealth to charitable organizations.

B. Vocabulary Practice

Exercise 6.1 Sentence Completion

Using your new vocabulary knowledge, choose the best way to complete the following sentences. Circle the letter of your answer.

1. _____ had distorted the shape of the trees by the coast.
   A. A constant easterly wind
   B. The north-south highway

2. Those plants are peculiar to _____.
   A. that region
   B. the world

3. It will be advantageous to you to _____.
   A. blow off that test
   B. read tomorrow's assignment

4. The epidermis of a(n) _____ is very thick.
   A. elephant
   B. human infant

5. My _____ caused me a great deal of anguish.
   A. basketball game
   B. knee injury

6. I didn't break the vase; a _____ must have done it.
   A. phantom
   B. figment

7. Allergies are the body's _____ to certain substances.
   A. reaction
   B. ability to bond

8. The stenographer typed up _____.
   A. the company's order
   B. everything said during the interview

9. My little brother's _____ was a figment.
   A. imaginary friend Bob
   B. toy dinosaur

10. We call him _____ because of his disposition.
    A. Sam Smith
    B. Sunny Sam

Exercise 6.2   Using Fewer Words

Replace the italicized words with a single word from the following list. The first one has been done for you.

figment   advantageous   anguish   disposition   distorting

epidermis   phantom   stenographer   peculiar   substances

1. Electronic music began with engineers and composers purposely *twisting out of shape* the sounds of everyday life.

1. distorting_____

2. The heavy evening fog created what looked like a(an) *ghost or apparition* crossing the street.

2._____

3. Most of the time Jordan has a cheerful *general mood*.

3._____

4. Did that part of your story actually happen, or is it a(an) *thing that is imagined or contrived*?

4._____

5. I'm in favor of anything that is *offering gain or profit* to the charitable organizations that do so much for the poor.

5._____

6. The witness couldn't take back what he said; it was recorded by a(an) *person who takes shorthand*.

6._____

7. No one can understand the *extreme pain and suffering* I experienced when my best friend moved away.

7._____

8. Sunblock protects the *surface layer of the body*.

8._____

9. That is a very *odd and eccentric* hat; where on earth did you find it?

9._____

10. You need to be careful with hazardous *tangible materials*.

10._____

Exercise 6.3 Synonyms and Antonyms

Fill in the blanks in column A with the required synonyms or antonyms, selecting them from column B. (Remember: A *synonym* is a word *similar* in meaning to another word. *Autumn* and *fall* are synonyms. An *antonym* is a word *opposite* in meaning to another word. *Beginning* and *ending* are antonyms.)

	A	B
_____	1. synonym for *apparition*	substance
_____	2. synonym for *odd*	anguish
_____	3. antonym for *distorted*	figment
_____	4. synonym for *temperament*	peculiar
_____	5. antonym for *harmful*	epidermis
_____	6. synonym for *matter*	phantom
_____	7. synonym for *skin*	unchanged
_____	8. antonym for *joy*	stenographer
_____	9. synonym for *transcriber*	disposition
_____	10. antonym for *something real*	advantageous

C. Journal Freewrite

Before you begin the reading on the next page, take out a journal or sheet of paper and spend some time responding to the following prompt.

TIP: Don't worry about grammar and spelling; just write what comes to mind. The purpose of freewriting is to explore ideas, not to produce a polished work.

> Describe a time you felt invisible in a crowd or other situation. Why were you unnoticed? How did you feel, and what did you do? (If you can't think of something, imagine a situation in which you *would* feel this way.)

Reading 7

from Invisible Man

by Ralph Ellison

About the Author
Ralph Ellison
(1914–1994) was born
in Oklahoma and later
moved to New York City
to study sculpture.
There he met Langston
Hughes and Richard
Wright, who encour-
aged him to write. He
began to publish essays
and short stories in
magazines. During
World War II, while he
was a cook in the
Merchant Marine, he
began *Invisible Man*,
which tells the story of a
young African-
American man who
searches for his identity
in a hostile society. The
book was published in
1952, and became a
huge national success.
It brought a new aware-
ness of the African-
American experience to
many readers.

I am an invisible man. No, I am not a spook like those who haunted Edgar Allan Poe; nor am I one of your Hollywood-movie ectoplasms. I am a man of <u>substance</u>, of flesh and bone, fiber and liquids—and I might even be said to possess a mind. I am invisible, understand, simply because people refuse to see me. Like the bodiless heads you see sometimes in circus sideshows, it is as though I have been surrounded by mirrors of hard, <u>distorting</u> glass. When they approach me they see only my surroundings, themselves, or <u>figments</u> of their imagina-tion—indeed, everything and anything except me.

Nor is my invisibility exactly a matter of a bio-chemical accident to my <u>epidermis</u>. That invisibility to which I refer occurs because of a <u>peculiar</u> <u>disposition</u> of the eyes of those with whom I come in contact. A matter of the construction of their *inner* eyes, those eyes with which they look through their physical eyes upon reality. I am not complaining, nor am I protesting either. It is sometimes <u>advantageous</u> to be unseen, although it is most often rather wearing on the nerves. Then too, you're constantly being bumped against by those of poor vision. Or again, you often doubt if you really exist. You wonder whether you aren't simply a <u>phantom</u> in other people's minds. Say, a figure in a nightmare which the sleeper tries with all his strength to destroy. It's when you feel like this that, out of resentment, you begin to bump people back. And, let me confess, you feel that way most of the time. You ache with the need to convince yourself that you do exist in the real world, that you're a part of all the sound and <u>anguish</u>, and you strike out with your fists, you curse and you swear to make them recognize you. And, alas, it's seldom successful.

Understanding the Reading

Complete the next three exercises and see how well you understood the excerpt from *Invisible Man*.

Exercise 6.4   Multiple-Choice Questions

Answer the following questions about the reading. Circle the letter of your answer.

TIP: Don't try to answer the questions from memory; go back to the text as often as necessary.

1. When the narrator says, "I might even be said to possess a mind," he is
   A. trying to be funny.
   B. expressing low self-esteem.
   C. being sarcastic.
   D. expressing confusion about his intelligence.

2. According to the narrator, people who do see him view him
   A. based on preconceptions because of his skin color.
   B. based on distortions caused by mirrors.
   C. only if they want to.
   D. as they would a circus sideshow.

3. The narrator says the people he comes in contact with "have a peculiar disposition of the eyes." Another way of saying this is that they
   A. are blind.
   B. don't understand him.
   C. are able to look right through him as if he does not exist.
   D. are wearing blindfolds.

4. From context clues, you can determine that the word *ectoplasms* means
   A. bones and flesh.
   B. the physical substance or outline of ghosts.
   C. figments of the imagination.
   D. character actors.

Exercise 6.5   Short-Answer Questions

Respond to the following questions in one to two complete sentences. Go back to the text, as you did on the multiple choice.

5. Why does the narrator feel as if he is invisible?

   _____

   _____

   _____

6. What problems result if you "ache with the need to convince yourself that you do exist in the real world"?

_____

_____

_____

7. Are there ever benefits to being invisible? Explain.

_____

_____

_____

Exercise 6.6   Extending Your Thinking

Respond to the following question in three to four complete sentences.

8. The theme of this unit is "Alienation and Identity." The narrator says his feelings of invisibility are due to more than just his skin color. Are there "invisible people" in your school or community? Explain.

_____

_____

_____

_____

_____

_____

Journal Freewrite

Before you begin the second reading, take out a journal or sheet of paper and spend some time responding to a new prompt.

What challenges do you think a young person might face when first going out into the community as a wage-earner or career person? What particular problems might he or she have to deal with because of gender, race, or national origin?

from A View from the Bridge
by Arthur Miller

About the Author
Arthur Miller
(1915–2005) was born
in New York City, the
son of Jewish immi-
grants. After college, he
began to freelance as a
writer, and when he
was just 32, his first
play appeared on
Broadway. Much of his
work deals with the
problems of American
working families and
societal pressure to con-
form. Miller went on to
write dozens of plays
and film scripts and is
considered one of the
major playwrights of
the twentieth century.
He was also in the spot-
light for his brief mar-
riage to the famous
actress Marilyn Monroe.

*Reader's Tip: In this excerpt from Miller's play, Catherine is
the 17-year-old niece of Eddie and Beatrice, her legal
guardians. As they prepare to sit down to dinner, Beatrice
and Catherine tell Eddie some news, hoping for a favorable
reaction.*

EDDIE: What's goin' on?

Catherine enters with plates, forks.

BEATRICE: She's got a job.

Pause. Eddie looks at Catherine, then back to Beatrice.

EDDIE: What job? She's gonna finish school.

CATHERINE: Eddie, you won't believe it—

EDDIE: No—no, you gonna finish school. What kinda job,
what do you mean? All of a sudden you—

CATHERINE: Listen a minute, it's wonderful.

EDDIE: It's not wonderful. You'll never get nowheres unless
you finish school. You can't take no job. Why didn't you ask
me before you take a job?

BEATRICE: She's askin' you now, she didn't take nothin' yet.

CATHERINE: Listen a minute! I came to school this morning and the principal called me out of the class, see? To go to
his office.

EDDIE: Yeah?

CATHERINE: So I went in and he says to me he's got my
records, y'know? And there's a company wants a girl right
away. It ain't exactly a secretary, it's a <u>stenographer</u> first, but
pretty soon you get to be secretary. And he says to me that
I'm the best student in the whole class—

BEATRICE: You hear that?

EDDIE: Well why not? Sure she's the best.

CATHERINE: I'm the best student, he says, and if I want, I
should take the job and the end of the year he'll let me take

the examination and he'll give me the certificate. So I'll save practically a year!

EDDIE, *strangely nervous*: Where's the job? What company?

CATHERINE: It's a big plumbing company over Nostrand Avenue.

EDDIE: Nostrand Avenue and where?

CATHERINE: It's someplace by the Navy Yard.

BEATRICE: Fifty dollars a week, Eddie.

EDDIE, *to Catherine, surprised*: Fifty?

CATHERINE: I swear.

Pause.

EDDIE: What about all the stuff you wouldn't learn this year, though?

CATHERINE: There's nothin' more to learn, Eddie, I just gotta practice from now on. I know all the symbols[1] and I know the keyboard. I'll just get faster, that's all. And when I'm workin' I'll keep gettin' better and better, you see?

BEATRICE: Work is the best practice anyway.

EDDIE: That ain't what I wanted, though.

CATHERINE: Why! It's a great big company—

EDDIE: I don't like that neighborhood over there.

CATHERINE: It's a block and half from the subway, he says.

EDDIE: Near the Navy Yard plenty can happen in a block and a half. And a plumbin' company! That's one step over the water front. They're practically longshoremen.

BEATRICE: Yeah, but she'll be in the office, Eddie.

EDDIE: Listen, B., she'll be with a lotta plumbers? And sailors up and down the street? So what did she go to school for?

CATHERINE: But it's fifty a week, Eddie.

EDDIE: Look, did I ask you for money? I supported you this long I support you a little more. Please, do me a favor, will ya? I want you to be with different kind of people. I want you to be in a nice office. Maybe a lawyer's office someplace in New York in one of them nice buildings. I mean if you're gonna get outa here then get out; don't go practically in the same kind of neighborhood.

Pause. Catherine lowers her eyes.

BEATRICE: Go, Baby, bring in the supper. *Catherine goes out.* Think about it a little bit, Eddie. Please. She's crazy to start work. It's not a little shop, it's a big company. Some day she could be a secretary. They

----

[1]In shorthand, symbols stand for words.

picked her out of the whole class. *He is silent, staring down at the tablecloth, fingering the pattern.* What are you worried about? She could take care of herself. She'll get out of the subway and be in the office in two minutes.

EDDIE, *somehow sickened*: I know that neighborhood, B., I don't like it.

BEATRICE: Listen, if nothin' happened to her in this neighborhood it ain't gonna happen noplace else. *She turns his face to her.* Look, you gotta get used to it, she's no baby no more. Tell her to take it. *He turns his head away.* You hear me? *She is angering.* I don't understand you; she's seventeen years old, you gonna keep her in the house all her life?

EDDIE, *insulted*: What kinda remark is that?

BEATRICE, *with sympathy but insistent force*: Well, I don't understand when it ends. First it was gonna be when she graduated high school, so she graduated high school. Then it was gonna be when she learned stenographer, so she learned stenographer. So what're we gonna wait for now? I mean it, Eddie, sometimes I don't understand you; they picked her out of the whole class, it's an honor for her.

Catherine enters with food, which she silently sets on the table. After a moment of watching her face, Eddie breaks into a smile, but it almost seems that tears will form in his eyes.

EDDIE: With your hair that way you look like a madonna, you know that? You're the madonna type. *She doesn't look at him, but continues ladling out food onto the plates.* You wanna go to work, heh, Madonna?

CATHERINE, *softly*: Yeah.

EDDIE, *with a sense of her childhood, her babyhood, and the years*: All right, go to work. *She looks at him, then rushes and hugs him.* Hey, hey! Take it easy! *He holds her face away from him to look at her.* What're you cryin' about? *He is affected by her, but smiles his emotion away.*

CATHERINE, *sitting at her place*: I just—*Bursting out*: I'm gonna buy all new dishes with my first pay! *They laugh warmly.* I mean it. I'll fix up the whole house! I'll buy a rug!

EDDIE: And then you'll move away.

CATHERINE: No, Eddie!

EDDIE, *grinning*: Why not? That's life. And you'll come visit on Sundays, then once a month, then Christmas and New Year's, finally.

CATHERINE, *grasping his arm to reassure him and to erase the accusation*: No, please!

EDDIE, *smiling but hurt*: I only ask you one thing—don't trust nobody. You got a good aunt but she's got too big a heart, you learned bad from her. Believe me.

BEATRICE: Be the way you are, Katie, don't listen to him.

EDDIE, to *Beatrice—strangely and quickly resentful*: You lived in a house all your life, what do you know about it? You never worked in your life.

BEATRICE: She likes people. What's wrong with that?

EDDIE: Because most people ain't people. She's goin' to work; plumbers; they'll chew her to pieces if she don't watch out. *To Catherine*: Believe me, Katie, the less you trust, the less you be sorry.

Eddie crosses himself and the women do the same, and they eat.

Understanding the Reading

Complete the next three exercises and see how well you understood the excerpt from *A View from the Bridge.*

Exercise 6.7   Multiple-Choice Questions

Answer the following questions about the reading. Circle the letter of your answer.

TIP: *Don't try to answer the questions from memory; go back to the text as often as necessary.*

1. At first, Eddie reacts to Catherine's news by
   A. pounding his fist on the table.
   B. congratulating her warmly.
   C. suggesting that they discuss the pros and cons of her decision.
   D. insisting that she finish school instead of taking the job.

2. Catherine and Beatrice mention that Catherine should take the job for all of the following reasons *except*
   A. it pays $50 a week.
   B. she can still take the examination and get her certificate.
   C. the family desperately needs the extra money.
   D. on-the-job training is the best practice.

3. Eddie's main objection to Catherine taking the job is that
   A. she didn't ask him first.
   B. he doesn't like plumbers and sailors.
   C. he wants her to be with a "different kind of people."
   D. he doesn't want her to ride the subway to work.

4. When Eddie says "most people ain't people" he is expressing his fear that
   A. Catherine will be hurt because she trusts people too much.
   B. Catherine will fall in love with a plumber.
   C. the sailors in the Navy Yard will threaten her.
   D. Catherine will never work for a lawyer.

Exercise 6.8 Short-Answer Questions

Respond to the following questions in one to two complete sentences. Go back to the text, as you did on the multiple choice.

5. Stage directions tell the actors how to act and reveal to audiences how the characters are feeling or reacting. Choose one set of directions from the play and explain what it tells about the character to whom it's referring.

   _____

   _____

   _____

6. Beatrice asks Eddie, ". . . you gonna keep her in the house all her life?" What does this remark tell you about how Eddie has probably treated Catherine so far? Is he overprotective or realistic? Explain.

   _____

   _____

   _____

7. Catherine's dreams for herself and Eddie's dreams for her differ. Who has the right to decide what a young person should do with his or her life? Why?

   _____

   _____

   _____

Exercise 6.9 Extending Your Thinking

Respond to the following question in three to four complete sentences. Use details from the texts in your answer.

8. Of all the protagonists in this unit (Latifa, Catherine, and the narrator of *Invisible Man*), who seems to feel the most alienated from other people? Who has the fewest rights? Who has the least hope of being taken seriously?

   _____

   _____

   _____

   _____

   _____

Reading Strategy Lesson
Identifying Conflict

Imagine a story where nobody has any problems, everyone gets along fine, the weather is beautiful . . . and then what? Nothing happens. That's why **conflict** is one of the most important literary elements. Without conflict, there can be no story—it's what drives the plot onward. The character has to have a problem, or several problems.

In Ralph Ellison's novel *Invisible Man*, the main character (who remains nameless throughout the book) has a number of problems with society. In this excerpt from the prologue, we are told only that he has the problem of being looked at as though he does not exist. The remaining chapters flash back to various scenes from his life that explain why he now lives an "invisible" life.

In *A View from the Bridge*, there are several conflicts at once. There is a conflict between Beatrice and Eddie, between Eddie and Catherine, and within Eddie himself. He knows he has the power to tell Catherine she cannot take the job, but as Beatrice points out, he knows he cannot "keep her in the house all her life." The time will come when he has to set Catherine free to function as best she can on her own, and Eddie finally decides that the time is now.

There are four basic types of conflict in literature:

1. Character vs. Character
One or more characters disagree or stand in the way of what each wants.

> Example: Picture a NASCAR race. Every driver is in conflict with every other driver.

2. Character vs. Society
Society has a problem with the way one or more characters behave or believe.

> Example: A NASCAR driver is approached by a small group of protesters outside the racetrack, holding up signs saying it's a waste of gasoline to run those cars around and around the track just for amusement. The driver yells at them to go home—he says that they don't understand his sport—but they continue to show up at his races holding signs.

3. Character vs. Self
A character has a decision to make or is filled with overwhelming feelings of guilt, fear, shame, or some other disturbing emotion.

> Example: This is the first race for one of the drivers on the track. He's practiced a lot, but still, this time he's out on the track in front of a huge audience, and he's driving against big-name drivers. He's not sure how he will do, and he's starting to worry that he'll be bumped off the track and wreck his car.

4. Character vs. Nature

The natural world provides the conflict by forcing the character or characters to deal with extreme heat, cold, isolation on an island, a blinding snowstorm, a hurricane, or any number of other conditions nature can provide.

> Example: Going back to our racetrack, imagine that it begins to rain halfway through the race. The track becomes slick. All of the drivers and their pit crews now have another conflict to deal with.

You can identify the conflict in a story by asking yourself one question: What are the problems?

Exercise 6.10 Practice the Reading Strategy

Read each story part given. On the line that follows, write the main type of conflict represented: **character vs. society, character vs. self, character vs. character,** or **character vs. nature.**

1. Mia and Tiffany have been best friends since first grade. They go everywhere together. They are even in the same classes. One day a new student joins their math class. Mia and Tiffany both think he is just about the hottest guy they've ever seen. Besides that, he talks to them on the way to their next class, and he's funny and not at all conceited. Wow, he's in their English class too. They both rush to sit next to him, but Mia wins. She gives Tiffany a dirty look. She thinks, *Jared is going to be mine, not hers. Whatever it takes.*

   _____

2. Tiffany knows the fight is on for Jared. The next morning she chooses an outfit that her mother would never let her wear to school and packs it in her backpack so she can change into it before the first bell. When she walks out of the girls' room in her rather shocking outfit, complete with too much makeup, she hears some people laughing. It doesn't matter, though. Wait until Mia sees her. *Wait until Jared sees her.* She tells the others to mind their own business.

   _____

3. Mia and Jared talked on the phone for two hours last night. He is as attracted to her as she is to him. He tells her he likes how she doesn't wear a lot of makeup or dress like she wants everyone to notice her. Now Mia catches sight of Tiffany. What has she done to herself? Should she tell her how silly she looks? They're already on the outs. Would that just make things worse? She doesn't want to lose her best friend, especially over a guy.

   _____

4. The school day is over, and neither Jared nor Mia has spoken to Tiffany. Besides that, she missed the bus. She'll have to walk home in the rain. Oh, no! She forgot to change clothes before she left school! At least maybe some of the makeup will wash off in the rain.

Exercise 6.11 Apply the Reading Strategy

On a separate sheet of paper, invent your own character, or use one of the ones above. Create four scenarios, each with a different type of conflict:

    A. character vs. character
    B. character vs. society
    C. character vs. self
    D. character vs. nature

Writing Workshop
Topic Sentences

In the previous chapter, you learned how to write a thesis statement that serves as a guide for your essay. You know that an essay consists of an introduction (with a thesis statement), body paragraphs (any number of them), and a conclusion. Just as your introduction must contain a thesis statement, each paragraph in your essay should have a **topic sentence.**

Here are some functions that a topic sentence serves:

- **It states one of the main points in your discussion.** A topic sentence is a summary of each paragraph's main idea.

- **It tells the reader what the paragraph is about.** If the topic sentence comes at the beginning of a paragraph, it announces or introduces the topic of the paragraph. Sometimes the topic sentence comes in the middle or at the end of the paragraph, but it is generally easiest to put a topic sentence at the beginning.

- **It helps you write the paragraph by controlling what you put in it.** Everything in the paragraph should relate to the topic you introduced in your topic sentence. If you write your topic sentence first, you can keep "checking in" with it as you write your other sentences. As you do so, ask yourself, "Does the sentence I am writing now relate to my topic sentence?"

Each body paragraph is a kind of mini-essay. You state your topic and then you give details about it. Put three or four mini-essays together with an introduction and a conclusion, and you've got a long essay.

When you write your topic sentences, be sure they relate to the main idea of your essay. Let's say you are writing an essay beginning with a quotation by Mark Twain. Your essay begins with this sentence:

> Mark Twain said, "Few things are harder to put up with than the annoyance of a good example."

Your body paragraphs should explain what Twain meant and how it applies to your life (in a personal narrative) or to society in general (in an expository essay). A good way to approach this assignment might be first to list some things you consider to be good, *but annoying*, examples. The examples that follow are for a personal narrative, which you studied previously.

1. My sister, who is always on the honor roll
2. The goalie on our soccer team, who almost never lets anyone score
3. My dog, who always meets me at the door and loves me no matter what
4. Our neighbor, whose rose garden annoys my mother because it always looks like a page from the magazine *Martha Stewart Living*

Which one of these four examples does not fit the criteria of "good example but annoying"? The answer is that 1, 2, and 4 all fit, but 3 does not. Your sister, the team goalie, and the neighbor are all people who are doing an excellent job of something—and that makes others look not so great in comparison. Your dog is doing a great job of being a dog, so you probably feel no annoyance or envy. You decide to develop your topic sentences for your second, third, and fourth paragraphs around your sister, your neighbor, and the goalie.

Examples:

> My sister is an annoyingly brilliant person who is always on the honor roll, while I struggle to make it.

> It's not that I want our team to lose, but our soccer goalie makes the rest of us look like amateurs because nothing gets by her.

> I can understand my mother's annoyance when Mrs. Ralosky's rose garden begins blooming, because it looks like a page out of *Martha Stewart Living*.

Exercise 6.12 Practice Choosing Relative Topic Sentences

Each item on page 135 contains a thesis statement for an essay and four possible topic sentences for three body paragraphs. You need to eliminate one. Find the topic sentence that does *not* relate to the thesis statement. Circle its letter.

1. Living in an apartment is better than living in a house.
   A. If something goes wrong in an apartment, the landlord has to fix it.
   B. You don't have to mow the lawn if you live in an apartment.
   C. Apartments are really small and the rent may skyrocket suddenly.
   D. Apartments often have swimming pools and exercise rooms.

2. Family stories hold families together.
   A. Parents tell stories about cute things their children did as toddlers.
   B. Relatives keep alive the memories of those who have gone before.
   C. Parents often fix recipes their own parents made.
   D. Parents tell heartbroken teenagers the stories of their own first loves and losses.

3. Community colleges offer training for many careers that pay well and do not require a four-year college degree.
   A. People who enjoy cooking can complete a one-year course in culinary arts.
   B. If you want to go to law school, it will take seven years of college.
   C. Cosmetology offers all sorts of possibilities, from stylist to makeup artist.
   D. Health-care workers are in high demand, and their benefits and pay match the need.

4. When we think of stars, most of us think of those faraway twinkles in the sky, but our sun is also a star, and it is both beautiful and useful.
   A. The pull of the sun's gravity keeps Earth and all of the planets in our solar system in orbit.
   B. Life could not exist without the heat and light that the sun provides.
   C. Getting repeated sunburns can lead to skin cancer.
   D. Everyone has seen breathtaking sunrises and sunsets, but most of us do not give a second thought to what actually causes them.

5. Ice hockey is an extremely fast-paced game that is played in about 30 countries.
   A. The modern game of ice hockey developed in Canada.
   B. Professional and college games run for 60 minutes, with a 15-minute intermission at 20 and 40 minutes.
   C. Ice hockey players must be able to skate extremely well, but there are other skills that are also important in the game.
   D. I have some hockey skates, but I have never played hockey.

Exercise 6.13 Apply the Writing Lesson

Choose one of the essay prompts from Exercise 5.10 in the previous writing lesson (page 113). Copy your thesis statement on the first line. Remember that thesis statements can "flex," so you may want to change yours as you think further about your essay. Then write three topic sentences you could use for three body paragraphs in an essay responding to the prompt.

My thesis statement: _____

_____

Topic sentence 1: _____

_____

Topic sentence 2: _____

_____

Topic sentence 3: _____

_____

Grammar Mini-Lesson
Avoiding Double Negatives

The use of double negatives is a very common mistake. Once you understand what you are really saying (or writing) when you use a double negative, it will be easier to stop.

In *A View from the Bridge*, Eddie and Beatrice use double negatives. Miller has them talk this way to show that they are not well-educated people, which goes along with why it is important to Eddie that Catherine finishes school. Catherine speaks with slightly better grammar than her aunt and uncle.

> Eddie: You'll *never* get *nowheres* unless you finish school. You *can't* take *no* job.

In making a negative statement, you should use only one negative word. In the first example, Eddie incorrectly uses two, saying "you'll *never* get *nowheres*." What he is saying, in effect, is "you will get somewhere" and "you have to take a job," just the opposite of what he really means. This is because two negatives change the meaning. (Also note that *nowheres* is not standard English.)

If Eddie wanted to say what he really means, he could say:

> You'll never get *anywhere* unless you finish school. You can't take *a* job.
>
> OR
>
> You'll get *nowhere* unless you finish school. You can take *no* job.

Those sentences each contain just one negative, so the meaning is clear. Let's now correct Beatrice's error.

> Beatrice: Listen, if nothin' happened to her in this neighborhood it *ain't* gonna happen *noplace* else . . . She's *no* baby *no* more.

How can Beatrice say what she really means? First of all, *ain't* is not standard English. We'll change that to "is not." *Noplace* is also nonstandard English. It is correctly spelled as two words: *no place*. But the sentence still contains two negatives (*is not* and *no place*). "She's no baby no more" also contains two negatives (*no* and *no*). If Beatrice wanted to say what she really means, she could say:

> Listen, if nothing has happened to her in this neighborhood, it isn't going to happen anyplace else. She's not a baby anymore.

Here are some negative words. Be careful to use only one of them in each negative statement.

no	never	no one
scarcely	not	nobody
barely	only	hardly
nothing	neither	none
nowhere	but (when it means *only*)	words ending in *-n't* (meaning *not*)

Exercise 6.14 Practice Completing a Negative Sentence

Complete each sentence by choosing the correct word and writing it on the line. Look back at the list of negative words if you need help.

1. I didn't know _____ about it. (anything, nothing)

2. My friend has hardly _____ clothes. (any, no)

3. We looked all over for crepe paper; we couldn't find _____. (any, none)

4. Where are Emma and Ashley? I haven't seen _____ of them. (either, neither)

5. Our teacher did not fail _____ on that test. (anybody, nobody)

6. He did it himself. He doesn't have _____ else to blame. (no one, anyone)

7. My little sister _____ barely five feet tall. (is, isn't)

8. Some of us haven't _____ gone camping. (never, ever)

9. I _____ but two sheets of paper left. (have, haven't)

10. She told us that she _____ nothing to do with the prank. (didn't have, had)

Exercise 6.15 Different Sentence, Same Meaning

Following is one correct way of making a negative statement. On the line, make the same statement in another equally correct way. The first two have been done for you.

1. You have not answered any of my questions.
   You have answered none of my questions.

2. Don't mention it to anyone.
   Mention it to no one.

3. There are no apples left.

4. I didn't care for either of them.

5. She had never been to the library.

6. They didn't have anybody to take them to the store.

7. He has nothing to boast about.

8. I looked for errors but I found none.

9. This line of questioning isn't getting us anywhere.

10. There aren't any signs of improvement.

Polish Your Spelling
Changing Verbs into Nouns

Three suffixes for turning verbs into nouns are *-ion*, *-ation*, and *-ure*. They all have the same meaning: "act or result of."

VERB		SUFFIX		NOUN
liberate	+	ion	=	liberation
afflict	+	ion	=	affliction
adore	+	ation	=	adoration
consider	+	ation	=	consideration
expose	+	ure	=	exposure
press	+	ure	=	pressure

Exercise 6.16 Practice Changing Verbs into Nouns

Turn the following verbs into nouns by adding -*ion*, -*ation*, or -*ure*.
Look back at the examples if necessary.

VERB	NOUN
1. discuss	_____
2. seize	_____
3. close	_____
4. imagine	_____
5. construct	_____
6. appreciate	_____
7. erase	_____
8. infect	_____
9. perspire	_____
10. pollute	_____

Unit Two Review

Vocabulary Review

A. Match each word with its definition.

	DEFINITION	WORD
_____	1. formal tribute to one's accomplishments	a. enterprise
_____	2. something made up	b. brandish
_____	3. to meet head-on	c. cultivation
_____	4. extreme mental or physical pain	d. resistance
_____	5. someone who takes dictation	e. substance
_____	6. the act of growing and nurturing	f. testimonial
_____	7. opposition of one force against another	g. figment
_____	8. tangible material	h. confront
_____	9. to wave around in a showy way	i. anguish
_____	10. a business intended to make a profit	j. stenographer

B. Match each word with its synonym.

	SYNONYM	WORD
_____	11. cruel	a. aberration
_____	12. supposedly	b. disposition
_____	13. apparition	c. negation
_____	14. ruling	d. epidermis
_____	15. impaired	e. oppressive
_____	16. temperament	f. ostensibly
_____	17. abnormality	g. mystical
_____	18. skin	h. phantom
_____	19. supernatural	i. decree
_____	20. nullification	j. stultified

C. Match each word with its antonym.

ANTONYM	WORD
_____ 21. truth	a. anonymous
_____ 22. take on	b. confront
_____ 23. unlucky	c. abdicate
_____ 24. harmful	d. deplorable
_____ 25. avoid	e. exterminate
_____ 26. indistinctive	f. distorted
_____ 27. pleasant	g. advantageous
_____ 28. identified	h. propaganda
_____ 29. preserve	i. peculiar
_____ 30. unchanged	j. fortuitous

Grammar Review

Each sentence below may contain an error in the word or phrase that is underlined. Circle the letter of the error or, if there is no error, mark D.

1. <u>Two</u> situations that <u>increased</u> homelessness <u>has developed</u> in
     A   B   C
   America in the past few decades. <u>No error</u>
                                    D

2. <u>To begin with</u>, people <u>don't have no place</u> to live because they
         A   B
   <u>can't afford</u> the high rents that are charged, even for
     C
   substandard housing. <u>No error</u>
                 D

3. <u>Even with wages</u> that can pay the monthly <u>rent, people</u> may not
         A   B
   have the money for first and last <u>month's rent</u> and a hefty sum
                               C
   for a security deposit. <u>No error</u>
                   D

4. <u>Media reports of</u> low <u>unemployment</u> and steady economic
         A   B
   <u>growth leaving</u> out part of the story. <u>No error</u>
     C   D

5. They forget to mention the parts that means the difference
      A   B
   between having a home and living on the street, in a car, or in a
                              C
   homeless shelter. No error
                     D

6. Many large companies are outsourcing jobs, which
                  A   B
   mean that they pay less money for people in other countries to
           C
   do the jobs that Americans used to do. No error
                                  D

7. Americans who lose their jobs may soon get another, so they
                       A   B
   are not counted as "unemployed," even though their new jobs
                                   C
   may pay a lot less. No error
                   D

8. Also, the actual buying power of wages has declined steadily,
     A   B
   and making more money means that a low-wage worker
    B
   isn't no better off than a decade ago. No error
      C   D

9. Homeless people often feel as if they are invisible in our society,
                A   B
   as if nobody don't care nothing about them. No error
           C   D

10. In reality, many Americans is just one paycheck, one illness, or
      A   B   C
    one disaster away from losing their homes. No error
                                    D

Spelling Review

A. Change the adjectives into adverbs.

1. whole   _____

2. glorious   _____

3. busy   _____

B. Change the verbs into adjectives.

4. The bright sun was _____. (blind)

5. No one claimed the _____ chair. (break)

6. There was a _____ turnout for the party. (surprise)

C. Change the verbs into nouns.

7. discuss   _____

8. appreciate   _____

9. expose   _____

10. pollute   _____

Writing Review

Choose one of the following topics. Plan your essay. Write your first draft. Then revise and edit your draft, and write your final essay. Be sure to identify your audience, purpose, and task before you begin planning.

Article One of the United Nations' Universal Declaration of Human Rights reads:

"All human beings are born free and equal in dignity and rights. They are endowed with reason and conscience and should act towards one another in a spirit of brotherhood." Choose one character or narrator from the reading selections in this unit. Explain the connection (either negative or positive) between the character or narrator and this article of the declaration.

OR

Compare and contrast Latifa (*My Forbidden Face*) and Catherine (*A View from the Bridge*). Consider their ages, families, hopes, dreams, and the people to whom they must answer. How are the two girls alike? How are they different?

Unit Two Extension Activities

 SPEAK/LISTEN

Presenting Miller

Arthur Miller is considered one of the most important writers of the twentieth century. Find out more about his life and get a list of his works on the Internet or at the library. Read *A View from the Bridge* or another of Miller's plays, or watch one that has been made into a movie—for example, *The Crucible* or *Death of a Salesman*. In a report to your class, briefly summarize the main events of the play/movie you chose and explain what big ideas about life (themes) you think Arthur Miller expressed.

 EXPLORE

Special-Interests or Unified Goals?

Although Ralph Ellison was African-American and well aware of racism, his approach to the problem was what he called a writer's duty: to "tell us about the unity of American experience beyond all considerations of class, of race, of religion." There are many organizations devoted to the interests of one group. Conduct Internet research on special-interest groups. List four organizations. (Their interests may seem to conflict.) Explore how each group does or does not contribute to the idea that America can be diverse, yet unified. Write a few paragraphs about your findings.

 WRITE

Current Events and Your Life

Latifa's family escaped from Afghanistan before her diaries were published. For three days, watch the news, read a newspaper, or read articles online. Each day, write a diary entry in which you summarize what you read or watched and explain how it affects you or might affect you in the future.

CONNECT

Standout Cities

Work in a small group. Choose a large city within a 500-mile radius of you. (Each group should work with a different city.) Gather information about your city from the Internet or at the library. What makes it a place people from other states and countries would like to visit? If it does not have much to offer, are any efforts underway to make it more attractive? Create an advertisement for it that might appear on television. You can write a jingle, act out a short skit, or both. Your advertisement should paint your city in a favorable light that will encourage tourists to visit it.

Writers on Writing

Chapter Seven

Prereading Guide
Words to know and ideas to consider before you jump into the reading.

A. Essential Vocabulary

Word	Meaning	Typical Use
ambiguity (*n*) am-bih-GYEW-ih-tee	uncertainty or vagueness; imprecision	His speech was ineffective because of its *ambiguity*.
articulate (*adj*) ar-TIK-yu-lat	skilled with words; well-spoken	Darnell is very *articulate*, so I know he will give a great presentation.
coherent (*adj*) ko-HERE-unt	logical and rational; understandable	The dream Blake had made no *coherent* sense.
conspiracy (*n*) con-SPEER-uh-see	a secret plan between two or more people to do something wrong; plot	Some people believe that world leaders are involved in a *conspiracy*.
crucial (*adj*) KROO-shul	absolutely necessary; critical	It is *crucial* that you arrive by 6 because the bus leaves at 6:10.
explicit (*adj*) eks-PLISS-it	clearly defined or stated; precise	Mom was pretty *explicit* about me cleaning my room before I could go out.
innumerable (*adj*) ih-NOOM-ur-uh-bul	too many to be counted; countless	A clear night is breathtaking, with *innumerable* stars in the sky.
interloper (*n*) INT-ur-low-pur	one who intrudes where he or she is not expected or wanted; meddler	My younger sister Sam was an *interloper* at my sleepover party.
irony (*n*) EYE-run-ee	the opposite of what one expects; paradox	There is some *irony* in the situation—I thought Dustin was such a bad driver, and I'm the one who had the accident.
pallid (*adj*) PAL-id	lacking in color; pale	Ricardo is back at school, but he still seems weak and looks *pallid* since he had the flu.

B. Vocabulary Practice

Exercise 7.1   Sentence Completion

Using your new vocabulary knowledge, choose the best way to complete the following sentences. Circle the letter of your answer.

1. Due to the ambiguity of the instructions, we _____.
   A. didn't know what to do
   B. knew exactly what to do

2. Heather felt _____ after surgery, as if she wasn't speaking coherently.
   A. fine
   B. foggy

3. _____ is crucial to being admitted to a top college.
   A. A good GPA
   B. Being popular

4. When there is a blizzard, the _____ are innumerable.
   A. temperatures
   B. snowflakes

5. The other girls saw her as an interloper, probably because she was _____.
   A. stunningly gorgeous
   B. from a different city

6. Ironically, our veterinarian is _____.
   A. very tall
   B. allergic to cats

7. Pallid bats get their name from their_____ fur.
   A. dark brown
   B. creamy white

8. Mrs. Li gave explicit directions about how to care for the children, so there _____.
   A. would be no problems
   B. were unanswered questions

9. Early _____ were called "conspiracies for higher wages," and the participants were fined or imprisoned.
   A. worker strikes
   B. efforts to import cheap goods

10. He won the contest because of his very articulate _____.
    A. pitching
    B. essay

Exercise 7.2   Using Fewer Words

Replace the italicized words with a single word from the following list.

| ambiguity | articulate | conspiracy | coherent | crucial |
| explicit | innumerable | interloper | ironic | pallid |

1. He was often a(an) *person who intrudes where he is not wanted* and liked to crash private parties.

   1._____

2. Taylor was so *lacking in color* that the school nurse called her mother to come and get her.

   2._____

3. Due to the *uncertainty and vagueness* of Zack's directions, we were soon lost.

   3._____

4. Why don't you ask Shelby to help you with your speech? She is very *skilled with words*.

   4._____

5. Zimbabwe was one of the first African nations to formulate a(an) *logical and rational* strategy for conservation.

   5._____

6. The Constitution grants us *clearly defined or stated* rights.

   6._____

7. The plants and animals that call wetlands home are *too many to be counted*.

   7._____

8. Sometimes life can play tricks on you that are *the opposite of what you expect*.

   8._____

9. The tragedy of 9/11 was part of a(an) *secret agreement between two or more people to do something wrong*.

   9._____

10. Some people think cell phones are *absolutely necessary* to their existence.

    10._____

Exercise 7.3   Synonyms and Antonyms

Fill in the blanks in column A with the required synonyms or antonyms, selecting them from column B. (Remember: A *synonym* is a word *similar* in meaning to another word. An *antonym* is a word *opposite* in meaning to another word.)

	A	B
_____	1. synonym for *plot*	innumerable
_____	2. synonym for *precise*	irony
_____	3. synonym for *countless*	ambiguity
_____	4. antonym for *irrational*	explicit
_____	5. synonym for *well-spoken*	conspiracy
_____	6. antonym for *unimportant*	pallid
_____	7. synonym for *paradox*	coherent
_____	8. antonym for *clarity*	interloper
_____	9. synonym for *pale*	crucial
_____	10. synonym for *meddler*	articulate

C. Journal Freewrite

Before you begin the reading on the next page, take out a journal or sheet of paper and spend some time responding to the following prompt.

TIP: Don't worry about grammar and spelling; just write what comes to mind. The purpose of freewriting is to explore ideas, not to produce a polished work.

> Even people who enjoy writing find it difficult sometimes. What do you find most challenging about writing? Explain. (Think about personal writing as well as school assignments.)

from Notes of a Native Son

by James Baldwin

About the Author
James Baldwin
(1924–1987) was born in Harlem in New York City, the oldest of nine children. By age 14, Baldwin was spending much of his time at the public library and realized how much he loved both reading and writing. In 1948, he moved to Paris, where he wrote his first novel, *Go Tell It on the Mountain*, about the struggles of an African-American family. He also wrote about black identity and racial struggle in *Notes of a Native Son.* In 1957 he returned to the U.S. to join the civil rights movement, and was one of its most influential and intellectual spokesmen. Like Martin Luther King Jr., he advocated peaceful protest. He wrote many other novels, plays, essays, and short stories while continuing to work for equality.

Any writer, I suppose, feels that the world into which he was born is nothing less than a <u>conspiracy</u> against the cultivation of his talent—which attitude certainly has a great deal to support it. On the other hand, it is only because the world looks on his talent with such a frightening indifference that the artist is compelled to make his talent important. So that any writer, looking back over even so short a span of time as I am here forced to assess, find that the things which hurt him and the things which helped him cannot be divorced from each other; he could be helped in a certain way only because he was hurt in a certain way; and his help is simply to be enabled to move from one conundrum[1] to the next— one is tempted to say that he moves from one disaster to the next. When one begins looking for influences one finds them by the score. I haven't thought much about my own, not enough anyway; I hazard[2] that the King James Bible, the rhetoric[3] of the store-front church, something ironic and violent and perpetually understated in Negro speech—and something in Dickens' love for bravura[4]—have something to do with me today; but I wouldn't stake my life on it. Likewise <u>innumerable</u> people have helped me in many ways; but finally, I suppose, the most difficult (and most rewarding) thing in my life has been the fact that I was born a Negro and was forced, therefore, to effect some kind of truce with this reality. (Truce, by the way, is the best one can hope for.)

One of the difficulties about being a Negro writer (and this is not special pleading, since I don't mean to suggest that he has it worse than anybody else) is that the Negro problem is written about so widely. The bookshelves groan under the weight of information, and everyone therefore considers himself informed. And this information, furthermore, operates usually (generally, popularly) to reinforce traditional attitudes. Of traditional attitudes there are only two—For or Against—and I, personally, find it difficult to say which attitude has caused

[1]puzzle or mystery
[2]guess
[3]convincing language
[4]a show of brilliance

me the most pain. I am speaking as a writer; from a social point of view I am perfectly aware that the change from ill-will to good-will, however motivated, however imperfect, however expressed, is better than no change at all.

But it is part of the business of the writer—as I see it—to examine attitudes, to go beneath the surface, to tap the source. From this point of view the Negro problem is nearly inaccessible. It is not only written about so widely; it is written about so badly. It is quite possible to say that the price a Negro pays for becoming articulate is to find himself, at length, with nothing to be articulate about. ("You taught me language," says Caliban to Prospero, "and my profit on't is I know how to curse.") Consider: the tremendous social activity that this problem generates imposes on whites and Negroes alike the necessity of looking forward, of working to bring about a better day. This is fine, it keeps the waters troubled; it is all, indeed, that has made possible the Negro's progress. Nevertheless, social affairs are not generally speaking the writer's prime concern, whether they ought to be or not; it is absolutely necessary that he establish between himself and these affairs a distance which will allow, at least, for clarity, so that before he can look forward in any meaningful sense, he must first be allowed to take a long look back. In the context of the Negro problem neither whites nor blacks, for excellent reasons of their own, have the faintest desire to look back; but I think that the past is all that makes the present coherent, and further, that the past will remain horrible for exactly as long as we refuse to assess it honestly.

I know, in any case, that the most crucial time in my own development came when I was forced to recognize that I was a kind of bastard of the West; when I followed the line of my past I did not find myself in Europe but in Africa. And this meant that in some subtle way, in a really profound way, I brought to Shakespeare, Bach, Rembrandt, to the stones of Paris, to the cathedral at Chartres, and to the Empire State Building, a special attitude. These were not really my creations, they did not contain my history; I might search in them in vain forever for any reflection of myself. I was an interloper; this was not my heritage. At the same time I had no other heritage which I could possibly hope to use—I had certainly been unfitted for the jungle or the tribe. I would have to appropriate these white centuries, I would have to make them mine—I would have to accept my special attitude, my special place in this scheme—otherwise I would have no place in *any* scheme. What was the most difficult was the fact that I was forced to admit something I had always hidden from myself, which the American Negro has had to hide from himself as the price of his public progress; that I hated and feared white people. This did not mean that I loved black people; on the contrary, I despised them, possibly because they failed to produce Rembrandt. In effect, I hated and feared the world. And this meant, not only that I thus gave the world an altogether murderous power over me, but also that in such a self-destroying limbo I could never hope to write.

One writes out of one thing only—one's own experience. Everything depends on how relentlessly one forces from this experience the last drop, sweet or bitter, it can possibly give. This is the only real concern of the artist, to recreate out of the disorder of life that order which is art. The difficulty then, for me, of being a Negro writer was the fact that I was, in effect, prohibited from examining my own experience too closely by the tremendous demands and the very real dangers of my social situation.

I don't think the dilemma outlined above is uncommon. I do think, since writers work in the disastrously <u>explicit</u> medium of language, that it goes a little way towards explaining why, out of the enormous resources of Negro speech and life, and despite the example of Negro music, prose written by Negroes has been generally speaking so <u>pallid</u> and so harsh. I have not written about being a Negro at such length because I expect that to be my only subject, but only because it was the gate I had to unlock before I could hope to write about anything else. I don't think that the Negro problem in America can be even discussed coherently without bearing in mind its context; its context being the history, traditions, customs, the moral assumptions and preoccupations of the country; in short, the general social fabric. Appearances to the contrary, no one in America escapes its effects and everyone in America bears some responsibility for it. I believe this the more firmly because it is the overwhelming tendency to speak of this problem as though it were a thing apart. But in the work of Faulkner, in the general attitude and certain specific passages in Robert Penn Warren, and, most significantly, in the advent of Ralph Ellison, one sees the beginnings —at least—of a more genuinely penetrating search. Mr. Ellison, by the way, is the first Negro novelist I have ever read to utilize in language, and brilliantly, some of the <u>ambiguity</u> and <u>irony</u> of Negro life.

About my interests: I don't know if I have any, unless the morbid desire to own a sixteen-millimeter camera and make experimental movies can be so classified. Otherwise, I love to eat and drink—it's my melancholy conviction[5] that I've scarcely ever had enough to eat (this is because it's *impossible* to eat enough if you're worried about the next meal)—and I love to argue with people who do not disagree with me too profoundly, and I love to laugh. I do *not* like bohemia, or bohemians, I do not like people whose principal aim is pleasure, and I do not like people who are *earnest* about anything. I don't like people who like me because I'm a Negro; neither do I like people who find in the same accident grounds for contempt. I love America more than any other country in the world, and, exactly for this reason, I insist on the right to criticize her perpetually. I think all theories are suspect, that the finest principles may have to be modified, or may even be pulverized[6] by the demands of life, and that one must find, therefore, one's own moral center and move through the world hoping that this center will guide one aright. I consider that I have many responsibilities, but none greater than this: to last, as Hemingway says, and get my work done.

I want to be an honest man and a good writer.

---

[5]sad belief
[6]crushed

Understanding the Reading

Complete the next three exercises and see how well you understood the excerpt from *Notes of a Native Son.*

Exercise 7.4   Multiple-Choice Questions

Answer the following questions about the reading. Circle the letter of your answer.

TIP: Don't try to answer the questions from memory; go back to the text as often as necessary.

1. A paraphrase for James Baldwin's description of writing is
   A. being born into a world that was against him from the start.
   B. moving from one puzzle or disaster to the next.
   C. getting used to the world being indifferent.
   D. reinforcing traditional attitudes about society.

2. Which of these does Baldwin *not* mention as an influence on his writing?
   A. the King James Bible
   B. Dickens's love for bravura
   C. the rhetoric of the storefront church
   D. his mother's encouragement

3. Baldwin's opinion regarding the past is that
   A. what's done is done and it should be forgotten.
   B. it must be assessed honestly to make sense of the present.
   C. reparations should be made to African-Americans.
   D. it is always nice to reminisce about the good old days.

4. The main idea of this selection is that
   A. Baldwin's responsibilities are not very different from those of most serious writers.
   B. everyone in America bears responsibility for "the Negro problem."
   C. Baldwin thinks he would have been a better photographer than a writer.
   D. Baldwin admires Ernest Hemingway.

5. Using context clues, you can determine that the word *heritage* (bottom of page 152) most likely means
   A. a person's life experiences.
   B. desire to travel back to one's homeland.
   C. cultural traditions and history of a group of people.
   D. a person who is not honest.

Exercise 7.5   Short-Answer Questions

Respond to the following questions in one to two complete sentences. Go back to the text, as you did on the multiple choice.

6. How does Baldwin explain his difficulty in writing from his own experience?

_____

_____

_____

7. Why do you think Baldwin says, "I don't like people who like me because I'm a Negro"?

_____

_____

_____

8. Baldwin says he loves to argue with people who don't disagree with him too much. What do you enjoy arguing about? What would you rather not discuss?

_____

_____

_____

9. Why does Baldwin call himself an interloper? Have you ever felt like one?

_____

_____

_____

Exercise 7.6   Extending Your Thinking

Respond to the following question in three to four complete sentences. Use details from the text in your answer.

10. The theme of this unit is "Writers on Writing." Does James Baldwin think it was more difficult for him as an African-American writer than it would have been if he had been some other race? Why or why not?

_____

_____

_____

_____

_____

Reading Strategy Lesson
Knowing Your Purpose for Reading

There is always a purpose for reading something. You read comics to get a few laughs. You read your e-mail to stay in touch with friends who don't live nearby as well as with those who do. You read blogs to see what people are saying about things that interest you.

Why Identify a Purpose?

Have you ever asked your teacher, "Why do we have to do this?" Most students have. They want to know the **purpose** for reading a story or writing an essay or figuring out a math problem. When you can see a clear purpose for doing something, it's easier to generate enthusiasm for it.

When you read textbooks, your purpose is to learn information and develop skills that will help you later on in school and in life. In language arts classes, you often read short stories, poetry, or nonfiction selections like James Baldwin's *Notes of a Native Son*.

If you hadn't yet read the selection, how could you determine your purpose for reading it? Would you expect to be entertained? Persuaded? Informed?

Keep in mind the title of this unit: "Writers on Writing." Also think about the author information. What did you learn about James Baldwin?

- His writing helped many races and nationalities understand what it meant to be an African-American.

- His writing was important during the civil rights movement.

- He advocated peaceful protest as a way to improve conditions for his fellow African-Americans.

Given the title of the unit and Baldwin's background, you can infer that the selection will be about what it was like for James Baldwin to be an African-American writer. Your purpose, then, is to be informed. This will not be a short story. It probably won't be humorous. It's a serious piece that will require your careful concentration and full attention. You will have to read fairly slowly, and read the footnotes. It can also help to interact with the text, by putting yourself in the author's place, or thinking about what points the author makes that you agree or disagree with. You may have to reread some parts to get the full meaning. It is a piece that will require you to think hard while you read and after you finish.

If this were a humorous short story, you would adjust your purpose and your reading style to the task. You could read faster, and a once-through would be enough. Your purpose would have been to be entertained, to enjoy the story.

Before you begin various reading tasks, always take a few moments to define your purpose. It will help you to set your reading pace and style and get the most out of the time you spend.

Exercise 7.7 Practice the Reading Strategy

Following are descriptions of ten different types of reading we may do in our daily lives. Describe a probable purpose for reading each one. Then assign them personal difficulty ratings, using the scale below.

1	2	3	4
simple and fun to read	simple to read but requires some thought	more difficult and requires a lot of thought	very difficult and requires the most thought

Reading Task	Purpose	Rating
1. an excerpt from a book called *A Beginner's Guide to Credit*	*to find out how to use credit wisely*	*2*
2. the latest novel by your favorite writer		
3. an article titled "Help Yourself to Better Study Habits"		
4. an e-mail from your friend who just took his or her driver's test		
5. five pages of a history textbook about the French and Indian War		
6. a newspaper article with the headline "Local Girls Win Place in Regional Softball Tourney"		
7. the nutrition information panel on your breakfast cereal box		

Reading Task	Purpose	Rating
8. a Web site devoted to a celebrity		
9. a blog about college football		
10. the "Review" section following a chapter in a science textbook		

Exercise 7.8   Apply the Reading Strategy

For the next two days, keep a reading log. Set it up like the table you just completed. Describe at least ten things that you read and your purpose for doing so. Give each a difficulty rating.

Writing Workshop
Using Transitions

So far in this book, you have learned to gather and organize your ideas and write thesis statements and topic sentences.

There is another important kind of sentence that will improve your writing: the **transition sentence**. The transition sentence links ideas between two paragraphs, like a bridge over a river. The transition sentence may come at the end of one paragraph and lead into the next, or it may come at the beginning of the second paragraph.

Here is how Baldwin made the transition between his second and third paragraphs in the selection for this chapter:

Last sentence of paragraph 2:
> I am speaking as a writer; from a social point of view I am perfectly aware that the change from ill-will to good-will, however motivated, however imperfect, however expressed, is better than no change at all.

First sentence of paragraph 3:
> But it is part of the business of the writer—as I see it—to examine attitudes, to go beneath the surface, to tap the source.

The last sentence in the second paragraph reminds us that James Baldwin is speaking as a writer. The first sentence in the third paragraph picks up this idea again with "But it is part of the business of the writer . . . ."

REMEMBER: A **paragraph** is a group of sentences dealing with one topic. When you want to talk about a new topic, write a **transition sentence** and begin a new paragraph. The transition can come at the end of one paragraph or at the beginning of the next.

If you think of something later that belongs in a previous paragraph, go back and put it in the paragraph where it belongs.

Exercise 7.9 Practice the Writing Lesson

This passage would be more effective if it were divided into three paragraphs. Read it and answer the questions that follow.

> Serious protests against segregation began in the 1960s. Activists demonstrated throughout the South and in many Northern cities, holding rallies, boycotting segregated businesses, and working to register black voters. They tried to rally people all over the country to demand an end to Southern segregation. Speaking out for civil rights required courage and determination. Many protesters were beaten by the police, and others were killed. Medgar Evers, Martin Luther King Jr., and three civil rights activists in Mississippi were assassinated by opponents of integration. The activists' voices did not go unheeded. Congress passed new and stronger civil rights laws in 1964, 1965, and 1968. By the 1970s, aggression against civil rights workers had finally begun to lessen in the South. Formal segregation was also gone.

1. What sentence in the paragraph above should begin the second paragraph? Write that sentence here. Explain your choice.

   _____

   _____

2. What sentence in the paragraph above should begin the third paragraph? Write that sentence here. Explain your choice.

   _____

   _____

Writing Transition Sentences

While it is fairly easy to pick out transition sentences that were written by someone else, you will need to practice constructing your own. Here are some tips:

1. Begin a new paragraph with a sentence that refers directly to an idea or a point you made in the previous paragraph.

Look at this example:

> End of paragraph 1:
> They tried to rally people all over the country to demand an end to Southern segregation.
>
> Beginning of paragraph 2:
> Speaking out for civil rights required courage and determination.

At the end of the first paragraph, the writer talks about rallying many people to support the civil rights movement. Logically, the first sentence of the next paragraph says that in order to join the movement, one had to have courage and determination.

2. Use enumeration.

To use enumeration, begin your essay by mentioning a certain number of points, reasons, etc., that you will discuss. Then begin your paragraphs with *First . . ., Second . . ., Third . . .,* and so forth. Enumeration is the easiest way to link paragraphs, but you shouldn't rely on it often or use it when it isn't appropriate.

3. Begin with phrases signaling that you are going to talk about another of your points or ideas.
Examples:

> The most important reason
> Another cause
> A final reason

4. Use transition words and phrases.
Study the following table and refer to it when you write an essay.

To Link Thoughts	To Compare Like Ideas	To Contrast Ideas	To Summarize
again, also, and, and then, besides, further, furthermore, in addition, last, likewise, moreover, next	also, as well as, in the same way, likewise, similarly	although, but, even though, granted, however, in spite of, nevertheless, on the contrary, on the other hand, otherwise, still, yet	consequently, finally, in brief, in conclusion, in short, thus, to sum up
To Emphasize	**To Show Cause and Effect**	**To Show Sequence**	**To Enumerate**
certainly, clearly, indeed, in fact, surely, to be sure, truly, undoubtedly, without a doubt	accordingly, due to, in consequence, hence, consequently, since, therefore, thus	after, afterward, at the same time, before, during, earlier, in the first place, in the second place, last, later, next, while	first, second, etc.

Exercise 7.10 Apply the Lesson to Your Own Writing

James Baldwin wrote about the difficulties and joys he found in writing. Now it's your turn to do the same. On a separate sheet of paper, write three paragraphs about your writing experiences. Use transition phrases or sentences to link your paragraphs. (For ideas, look at the journal entry you wrote for this chapter.)

Grammar Mini-Lesson
Active and Passive Voice

- An **active verb** describes an action done *by* its subject.
  The radio station *broadcast* the news.
  (The verb *broadcast* is active because it describes an action done by the radio station. The *radio station* is the subject of this sentence.)

- A **passive verb** describes an action done *to* its subject.
  News *was broadcast* by the radio station.
  (The verb phrase *was broadcast* is passive because it describes an action done *to the news*. *News* is the subject in this sentence.)

When you use an active verb, you are writing in the **active voice**. When you use a passive verb, you are writing in the **passive voice**. Here are some additional examples of active and passive voice:

Active: Recklessness *causes* accidents.
Passive: Accidents *are caused* by recklessness.

Active: He *will read* the book.
Passive: The book *will be read* by him.

Active: The children *ate* the birthday cake.
Passive: The birthday cake *was eaten* by the children.

Which voice sounds more clear, brief, and natural? In general, it is better to use the active voice. This is particularly true with news writing, when you want an article to sound lively and current.
Compare these sentences:

Passive: A tree was planted by our science class.
Active: Our science class planted a tree.

The second sentence uses fewer words and states the action clearly. The use of the passive verb in the first sentence makes the sentence unnatural sounding. Think about it. If you were asked, "What did you do in school today?" which would you say: "A tree was planted by our science class" or "Our science class planted a tree"?
Active verbs are far more common than passive verbs. You should use the active voice whenever possible, especially when the passive voice sounds awkward.

The passive voice does have some uses, however. One good use of passive verbs is to help you avoid the vague pronoun *they*, as in the following:

Poor: *They* grow cherries in Michigan.
(Who are *they*? The sentence is not clear on this point. *They* could refer to the people who own a particular cherry orchard or to all of the cherrygrowers in Michigan.)

Better: Cherries *are grown* in Michigan.

Making *cherries* the subject of the sentence puts the focus on them—not on who grows them.

You can form the passive voice by adding some form of the verb *to be* to the past participle of a verb. Forms of the verb *to be* are *is*, *was*, *will be*, *has been*, etc.

Examples:

is broken	has been collected	was introduced
will be told	are being sent	were misplaced

When you write, be aware of whether you're using the passive or active voice. Always make sure you're using the one that helps you express yourself as clearly and interestingly as possible.

Exercise 7.11 Practice Using Active and Passive Verbs

Improve each of the following sentences by rewriting it with an active or a passive verb, as needed.

Example: An agreement will be entered into by us.
We will enter into an agreement.

1. Roadside trash was picked up by us.

   _____

2. Not a second glance was given to the gift by Spencer.

   _____

3. Your help could definitely be used by me.

   _____

4. They grow excellent oranges in Florida.

   _____

5. An interesting time will be had by everyone.

   _____

6. Their new uniforms were received by the cheerleaders.

   _____

7. A gold bracelet was worn by Madison.

   _____

8. They arrest people who are in the park after it closes.

_____

9. The moon was jumped over by the cow.

_____

10. The stars were hidden by the clouds.

_____

Polish Your Spelling
Homonyms

Homonyms are words that are pronounced alike but are different in meaning and in spelling. Study the examples below and on page 164.

Homonym	Meaning	Typical Use
already	before; previously	The mail had *already* come.
all ready	everyone prepared	Are we *all ready*?
altar	tablelike structure in a place of worship	The bride was led to the *altar*.
alter	change	Can you *alter* my dress?
altogether	completely	I was *altogether* confused.
all together	everyone at one time	We left *all together*.
bare	without covering	Our feet were *bare*.
bear	endure	He cannot *bear* commercials.
bear	large shaggy animal	There's a *bear* outside the tent!
brake	device for stopping	Quick, step on the *brake*!
break	shatter; fracture	Don't *break* your iPod.
capital	seat of government	The *capital* of Maine is Augusta.
capitol	building where law-makers meet	Can you tell me what street the *capitol* is on?
coarse	rough	Denim is *coarse* cotton cloth.
course	way; path	Let's keep to our *course*.

Homonym	Meaning	Typical Use
complement	something that completes	Dressing is a *complement* to salad.
compliment	praise	I'd like to *compliment* you on your award.
desert	abandon	Please don't *desert* me.
dessert	last course of a meal	Let's have cake for *dessert*.
hear	perceive by ear	Can you *hear* the music?
here	in, or to, this place	Please come *here*.
its	belonging to it	The cat hurt *its* paw.
it's	it is	*It's* starting to snow.
lead	heavy metal	*Lead* in the water is not good.
led	conducted	Who *led* the orchestra?
passed	went by	We *passed* the library.
past	1. gone by	She came to all *past* meetings.
	2. time gone by	The *past* is history.
	3. close to and beyond	We went *past* the library.
peace	opposite of war	Give *peace* a chance.
piece	fragment or part	I ate a *piece* of the pie.
sight	something seen	What a beautiful *sight*!
site	place or location	This is the new building *site*.
their	belonging to them	They paid *their* money.
there	in that place	Were you ever *there*?
they're	they are	*They're* about to leave.
to	in the direction of	We went *to* the pool
two	one plus one	I have *two* brothers.
too	1. also	Jake and I are *too* cold
	2. excessively	*too*.
who's	who is	*Who's* on the phone?
whose	belonging to whom	*Whose* jacket is this?
your	belonging to you	Is this *your* work?
you're	you are	*You're* altogether wrong.

Exercise 7.12 Practice Choosing the Right Homonym

Choose the homonym that fits the sentence's meaning. Write it on the line.

_____   1. We were (lead, led) into a trap.

_____   2. (Its, It's) time to go.

_____   3. I wasn't (to, two, too) hungry.

_____   4. Are they (all ready, already) gone?

_____   5. (Whose, Who's) the guy with the spiky hair?

_____   6. (Your, You're) always the first one in line.

_____   7. Have you ever been to a (desert, dessert)?

_____   8. We (passed, past) your house last night.

_____   9. The river continued on its (course, coarse).

_____ 10. I think I can (here, hear) the bus coming.

Chapter Eight

Prereading Guide
Words to know and ideas to consider before you jump into the reading.

A. Essential Vocabulary

Word	Meaning	Typical Use
amend (*v*) uh-MEND	to change in order to make better; improve	It takes a two-thirds majority vote to *amend* the Constitution.
assent (*n*) uh-SENT	expression of a willingness to go along with; agreement	Hayley made the motion to adjourn the meeting, and received everyone's *assent*.
facile (*adj*) FASS-ul	achieved with little difficulty; easy	There is no *facile* solution to this complex problem.
halting (*adj*) HALT-ing	uncertain and indecisive; hesitant	The *halting* way she replied indicated she didn't really want to go with him.
immersion (*n*) ih-MUR-zhun	complete mental attention; concentration	She is writing a book about Emily Dickinson, and her *immersion* in the research keeps her very busy.
irksome (*adj*) IRK-sum	causing weariness or annoyance; tiresome	The children I take care of after school can be very *irksome* at times.
kinship (*n*) KIN-ship	close connection due to similarities; affinity	He was elected president of the freshman class because of his *kinship* with fellow students.
renounce (*v*) ree-NOWNCE	to give up or reject; relinquish	After he did poorly at the recital, Max was ready to *renounce* his dream of being a famous pianist.
transitory (*adj*) TRANZ-ih-tor-ee	lasting only a short time; temporary	Brooke is all aglow with another of her *transitory* relationships.
visage (*n*) VISS-ij	facial features and expression; countenance	She would recognize his *visage* anywhere, even in the dark theater.

B. Vocabulary Practice

Exercise 8.1   Sentence Completion

Using your new vocabulary knowledge, choose the best way to complete the following sentences. Circle the letter of your answer.

1. The handout on _____ was too facile for me.
   A. advanced calculus
   B. basic addition

2. Total immersion is the only way I'm going to _____.
   A. find out if I like violin
   B. get up in the morning

3. Her _____ were an outstanding feature of her visage.
   A. long legs
   B. large eyes

4. I was _____ in what I said; I need to amend it.
   A. right
   B. wrong

5. Fortunately, the _____ were transitory.
   A. below-zero temperatures
   B. baseball teams

6. Many people find _____ irksome.
   A. eating ice cream sundaes
   B. revising essays

7. The review _____ the new writer for his "halting prose."
   A. praised
   B. criticized

8. The _____ is meant to give the people's assent to one candidate.
   A. presidential election process
   B. voting booth

9. Although we're not related, we feel a close kinship with one another and _____.
   A. get along well
   B. don't get along

10. He opposed his country's policies so he renounced his _____ and moved away.
    A. house
    B. citizenship

Exercise 8.2 Using Fewer Words

Replace the italicized words with a single word from the following list.

amended	assent	facile	haltingly	immersion
irksome	kinship	renounce	transitory	visage

1. He spoke *uncertainly and indecisively*, afraid of angering people in the room.

   1._____

2. Most people do not *give up or reject* a goal without giving it a good try.

   2._____

3. He gave his *expression of a willingness to go along with us*, and we presented our plan to the student government.

   3._____

4. A butterfly's life is *brief in duration*.

   4._____

5. This letter needs to be *changed to make it better*.

   5._____

6. The best way to learn a new language is *giving your completemental attention*.

   6._____

7. Jamal found his little sister's whining *caused weariness and annoyance*.

   7._____

8. Their *close connection due to similarities* made them feel like sisters.

   8._____

9. He could not get her *facial expression and features* out of his mind.

   9._____

10. Global warming does not have a solution that will be *achieved with little difficulty*.

    10._____

Exercise 8.3 Synonyms and Antonyms

Fill in the blanks in column A with the required synonyms or antonyms, selecting them from column B. (Remember: A *synonym* is a word *similar* in meaning to another word. An *antonym* is a word *opposite* in meaning to another word.)

	A	B
_____	1. synonym for *hesitant*	immersion
_____	2. synonym for *relinquish*	amend
_____	3. synonym for *tiresome*	kinship
_____	4. synonym for *concentration*	halting
_____	5. antonym for *permanent*	assent
_____	6. synonym for *affinity*	facile
_____	7. synonym for *improve*	renounce
_____	8. antonym for *disagreement*	visage
_____	9. antonym for *difficult*	irksome
_____	10. synonym for *countenance*	transitory

C. Journal Freewrite

Before you begin the reading on the next page, take out a journal or sheet of paper and spend some time responding to the following prompt.

TIP: Don't worry about grammar and spelling; just write what comes to mind. The purpose of freewriting is to explore ideas, not to produce a polished work.

> Choose an author you like, living or dead, and write a letter to him or her. You might ask questions or simply explain why you admire his or her work.

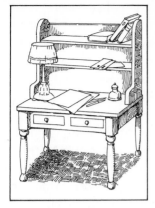

from Letters to a Young Poet

by Rainer Maria Rilke

About the Author

Rainer Maria Rilke (1875–1926) was born in Prague, Czechoslovakia, and endured an unhappy childhood at a military school. Fortunately, an uncle realized that Rilke was literarily gifted and helped him enroll in a German preparatory school. At age 20, he published his first volume of poetry. In the years that followed, he wrote many other poetry collections, and his work was highly admired by other writers. It was not until after his death, however, that he gained widespread recognition as a truly great poet.

Reader's Tip: Many young poets wrote to Rilke asking for advice about their work. This letter is a response to one of those young poets.

Paris
February 17, 1903

Dear Sir,

Your letter arrived just a few days ago. I want to thank you for the great confidence you have placed in me. That is all I can do. I cannot discuss your verses; for any attempt at criticism would be foreign to me. Nothing touches a work of art so little as words of criticism: they always result in more or less fortunate misunderstandings. Things aren't all so tangible and sayable as people would usually have us believe; most experiences are unsayable, they happen in a space that no word has ever entered, and more unsayable than all other things are works of art, those mysterious existences, whose life endures beside our own small, <u>transitory</u> life.

With this note as a preface, may I just tell you that your verses have no style of their own, although they do have silent and hidden beginnings of something personal. I feel this most clearly in the last poem, "My Soul." There, something of your own is trying to become word and melody. And in the lovely poem "To Leopardi" a kind of <u>kinship</u> with that great, solitary figure does perhaps appear. Nevertheless, the poems are not yet anything in themselves, not yet anything independent, even the last one and the one to Leopardi. Your kind letter, which accompanied them, managed to make clear to me various faults that I felt in reading your verses, though I am not able to name them specifically.

You ask whether your verses are any good. You ask me. You have asked others before this. You send them to magazines. You compare them with other poems, and you are upset when certain editors reject your work. Now (since you have said you want my advice) I beg you to stop doing that sort of thing. You are looking outside, and that is what you should most avoid right now. No one can advise or help you—no one. There is only one thing you should do. Go into yourself. Find out the reason that commands you to write; see whether it has spread its roots into the very depths of your heart; confess to yourself whether you would have to die if you were forbidden to write. This most of all: ask yourself in the most silent hour of your night: *must* I write? Dig into yourself for a deeper answer. And if this answer rings out in <u>assent</u>, if you meet this solemn question with a strong, simple "*I must*," then build your life in accordance with this necessity; your whole life, even into its humblest and most indifferent hour, must become a sign and witness to this impulse. Then come close to Nature. Then, as if no one had ever tried before, try to say what you see and feel and love and lose. Don't write love poems; avoid those forms that are too <u>facile</u> and ordinary: they are the hardest to work with, and it takes a great, fully ripened power to create something individual where good, even glorious, traditions exist in abundance. So rescue yourself from these general themes and write about what your everyday life offers you; describe your sorrows and desires, the thoughts that pass through your mind and your belief in some kind of beauty—describe all these with heartfelt, silent, humble sincerity and, when you express yourself, use the Things around you, the images from your dreams, and the objects that you remember. If your everyday life seems poor, don't blame *it*; blame yourself; admit to yourself that you are not enough of a poet to call forth its riches; because for the creator there is no poverty and no poor, indifferent place. And even if you found yourself in some prison, whose walls let in none of the world's sounds— wouldn't you still have your childhood, that jewel beyond all price, that treasure house of memories? Turn your attention to it. Try to raise up the sunken feelings of this enormous past; your personality will grow stronger, your solitude will expand and become a place where you can live in the twilight, where the noise of other people passes by, far in the distance.—And if out of this turning-within, out of this <u>immersion</u> in your own world, *poems* come, then you will not think of asking anyone whether they are good or not. Nor will you try to interest magazines in these works: for you will see them as your dear natural possession, a piece of your life, a voice from it. A work of art is good if it has arisen out of necessity. That is the only way one can judge it. So, dear Sir, I can't give you any advice but this: to go into yourself and see how deep the place is from which your life flows; at its source you will find the answer to the question of whether you *must* create. Accept that answer, just as it is given to you, without trying to interpret it. Perhaps you will discover that you are called to be an artist. Then take that destiny upon yourself, and bear it, its burden and its greatness, without ever asking what reward might come from outside. For the creator must be a world for himself and must find everything in himself and in Nature, to whom his whole life is devoted. But after this descent into yourself and into your solitude, perhaps you will have to <u>renounce</u> becoming a poet (if, as I have said, one feels one could live without writing, then one shouldn't write at all). Nevertheless, even then, this self-searching that I ask of you will not have been for nothing. Your life will still find its own paths from there, and that they may be good, rich, and wide is what I wish for you, more than I can say.

What else can I tell you? It seems to me that everything has its proper emphasis; and finally I want to add just one more bit of advice: to keep growing, silently and earnestly, through your whole development; you couldn't disturb it any more violently than by looking outside and waiting for outside answers to questions that only your innermost feeling, in your quietest hour, can perhaps answer.

It was a pleasure for me to find in your letter the name of Professor Horaček; I have great reverence for that kind, learned man, and a gratitude that has lasted through the years. Will you please tell him how I feel; it is very good of him to still think of me, and I appreciate it. The poems that you entrusted me with I am sending back to you. And I thank you once more for your questions and sincere trust, of which, by answering as honestly as I can, I have tried to make myself a little worthier than I, as a stranger, really am.

Yours very truly,
Rainer Maria Rilke

Understanding the Reading

Complete the next three exercises and see how well you understood the excerpt from *Letters to a Young Poet*.

Exercise 8.4   Multiple-Choice Questions

Answer the following questions about the reading. Circle the letter of your answer.

TIP: Don't try to answer the questions from memory; go back to the text as often as necessary.

1. Rilke refuses to criticize the actual verses the young poet sent him because he
   A. is afraid to tell the young poet he is a failure.
   B. doesn't want to tell the poet he has no talent.
   C. feels most criticism is misunderstood.
   D. thinks the poetry is too hard to understand.

2. Which piece of advice is *not* given to the young poet?
   A. First find out what kind of poetry magazines are buying.
   B. Don't write love poems.
   C. Look deep into your own experiences.
   D. Ask yourself: "Must I write?"

3. According to Rilke, what mistake is the poet making that "above all else" he or she should not make?
   A. looking to Rilke for approval
   B. looking outward for approval
   C. asking publishers for advice
   D. trying to imitate other poets

4. Rilke says there is only one criterion that makes a piece of art good. That is if
   A. someone will pay for it.
   B. someone else appreciates it.
   C. it can be published.
   D. it is written because the poet must write it.

Exercise 8.5   Short-Answer Questions

Respond to the following questions in one to two complete sentences. Go back to the text, as you did on the multiple choice.

5. Rilke tells the young poet that works of art are "those mysterious existences, whose life endures beside our own small, transitory life." What do you think he means? Provide an example.

   _____

   _____

   _____

6. From his letter, what sort of person can you conclude Rilke was?

   _____

   _____

   _____

7. Do you think the young poet who received this letter felt encouraged? Why or why not?

   _____

   _____

   _____

Exercise 8.6   Extending Your Thinking

Respond to the following question in three to four complete sentences.

8. The name of this unit is "Writers on Writing." Rilke tells the young poet, ". . . for the creator there is no poverty and no poor, indifferent place" (page 172). Explain what you think Rilke meant and what this means to you as a writer.

   _____

   _____

   _____

   _____

   _____

Journal Freewrite

Before you begin the second reading, take out a journal or sheet of paper and spend some time responding to a different prompt.

> Think about the last essay, story, or poem you wrote, for school or on your own. Tell your written work how you think and feel about it. Address your written work as if it were a person.

The Author to Her Book

by Anne Bradstreet

About the Author
Anne Bradstreet (ca. 1612–1672) was born in England. She married at age 16 and moved to America two years later, sailing on the ship *Arbella*. Her identity during her life came from first her father and then her husband, who were both governors of the Massachusetts Bay Colony, but we now think of her as America's first female poet. She loved her family, nature, and learning, and she questioned the silent role of women in the new colony. She mostly kept her poetry to herself and her friends, and it wasn't widely read until the twentieth century, when feminist scholars brought it into the spotlight.

Reader's Tip: In this poem, Anne Bradstreet compares her relationship with her book of poetry to the relationship between a mother and child. Notice how the poem parallels the growth of a child. Also keep in mind the sidebar information about Anne Bradstreet's life in a puritanical society that was critical of women who expressed their thoughts and feelings.

Thou ill-formed offspring of my feeble brain,
Who after birth didst by my side remain,
Till snatched from thence by friends, less wise than true,
Who thee abroad, exposed to public view,
Made thee in rags, <u>halting</u> to th' press to trudge,
Where errors were not lessened (all may judge).
At thy return my blushing was not small,
My rambling brat (in print) should mother call,
I cast thee by as one unfit for light,
Thy <u>visage</u> was so <u>irksome</u> in my sight;
Yet being mine own, at length affection would
Thy blemishes <u>amend</u>, if so I could:
I washed thy face, but more defects I saw,
And rubbing off a spot still made a flaw.
I stretched thy joints to make thee even feet,
Yet still thou run'st more hobbling than is meet;[1]
In better dress to trim thee was my mind,
But nought save homespun cloth i' th' house I find.
In this array[2] 'mongst vulgars[3] may'st thou roam.
 In critic's hands beware thou dost not come,
And take thy way where yet thou art not known;
If for thy father asked, say thou hadst none;
And for thy mother, she alas is poor,
Which caused her thus to send thee out of door.

---

[1]proper
[2]clothing
[3]undesirable people

Understanding the Reading

Complete the next three exercises and see how well you understood "The Author to Her Book."

Exercise 8.7 Multiple-Choice Questions

Answer the following questions about the reading. Circle the letter of your answer.

TIP: Don't try to answer the questions from memory; go back to the text as often as necessary.

1. When Bradstreet wrote that her poems "didst by my side remain" (line 2), she probably meant she
   A. kept them in her pocket.
   B. held them by the hand.
   C. did not want anyone else to see them.
   D. kept them in a desk drawer.

2. The "friends, less wise than true" (line 3)
   A. had the poems published to make Bradstreet look foolish.
   B. had good intentions but acted unwisely.
   C. stole the poems and took credit for writing them.
   D. showed the poems to Bradstreet's husband.

3. In Lines 11–16, Bradstreet refers to trying to make her child more presentable. She is actually talking about
   A. the frustration of editing the poems in her book.
   B. painfully rewriting the poems on nicer paper and with better ink.
   C. repairing the torn and spotted covers of her books of poetry.
   D. how embarrassed she was to be the child's mother.

4. Bradstreet negatively criticizes her poetry in all of the lines that follow *except*
   A. "Thou ill-formed offspring of my feeble brain."
   B. "I cast thee by as one unfit for light."
   C. "If for thy father askt, say, thou hadst none."
   D. "And rubbing off a spot, still made a flaw."

Exercise 8.8 Short-Answer Questions

Respond to the following questions in one to two complete sentences. Go back to the text, as you did on the multiple choice.

5. Pride was seen as an unforgivable sin in the puritanical world of the Massachusetts Bay Colony. How does this help explain Bradstreet's criticism of her own work?

   _____

   _____

   _____

6. Do you think Anne Bradstreet really felt that her poems were "unfit for light"? What reasons might she have for saying that?

_____

_____

_____

7. In view of Bradstreet's society's attitudes toward women, how could you interpret the line "If for thy father asked, say thou hadst none" as a note of pride in her accomplishment?

_____

_____

_____

Exercise 8.9   Extending Your Thinking

Respond to the following question in three to four complete sentences. Use details from the texts in your answer.

8. Rainer Maria Rilke advised a young poet to write from the heart and to look inward rather than outward to judge one's poetry. Would Anne Bradstreet agree with Rilke? Explain why or why not, using evidence from "The Author to Her Book."

_____

_____

_____

_____

_____

_____

Reading Strategy Lesson
Finding Meaning in Poetry

Have you ever read a poem through and thought, "I have no idea what this is about"? It is often difficult to understand a poem—especially one written nearly 400 years ago—the first time you read it. One reason poetry can be hard to tackle is that poets rarely waste words. You can't skim a poem. You have to read every word and look at what each one might contribute to that poem's meaning.

However, there are several tips you can use to make the process less intimidating. Let's look at a poem by Robert Louis Stevenson, called "The Land of Counterpane," and use it to go through each of the tips. (Note that a counterpane is a bedspread or comforter.)

The Land of Counterpane

When I was sick and lay a-bed,
I had two pillows at my head,
And all my toys beside me lay,
To keep me happy all the day.

And sometimes for an hour or so
I watched my leaden soldiers go,
With different uniforms and drills,
Among the bed-clothes, through the hills;

And sometimes sent my ships in fleets
All up and down among the sheets;
Or brought my trees and houses out,
And planted cities all about.

I was the giant great and still
That sits upon the pillow-hill,
And sees before him, dale and plain,
The pleasant land of counterpane.

Now let's look at four tips that can help you examine the poem.

1. Read according to the poem's punctuation. If there is a comma at the end of a line, pause briefly. If there is a semicolon, pause a little longer. If there is a period, stop as you would at the end of a sentence. If there is no punctuation at the end of a line, keep going on to the next line. In the first verse of the poem, there is a comma after the first three lines and a period at the end, so you pause briefly after lines 1–3 and stop after line 4. The second verse is punctuated differently:

And sometimes for an hour or so	*(no stop—keep going)*
I watched my leaden soldiers go,	*(brief pause)*
With different uniforms and drills,	*(brief pause)*
Among the bed-clothes, through the hills;	*(longer pause, but then on to the first line of the third verse)*

2. Look for figurative language. Poets use figurative language to make comparisons. It is the opposite of *literal language*, which says just what it means. The most common types of figurative language are similes, metaphors, and personification.

• A **simile** compares two things by using *like* or *as*.

My love is like a red, red rose.

My love is as sweet as candy.

He acted as if he were Hamlet himself.

- A **metaphor** is a more direct comparison that says something *is* something else.

> I was the giant great and still
> That sits upon the pillow-hill,
> And sees before him, dale and plain,
> The pleasant land of counterpane.

Stevenson doesn't say that he was *like* a giant or that the pillow was *like* a hill. He *was* the giant "sitting on the pillow-hill." The counterpane is a land of dales and hills.

The first verse of Stevenson's poem tells us the situation: He's sick in bed. Then we are transported to "the land of counterpane," where he watches his soldiers drill, sends out his ships, and builds cities. The bedclothes become hills and valleys, and the toys seem to come to life.

Anne Bradstreet also uses metaphor. Her whole poem is an *extended metaphor*. In other words, her whole poem is written about a child, but the child is really her book of poetry.

- **Personification** gives human qualities to inanimate or nonhuman things. Stevenson personifies his "leaden soldiers" by writing about them as if they were actually marching. Anne Bradstreet personifies her book by writing to it as if it were her child. Here are some other examples of personification:

> The trees bowed down their weary heads.
>
> The cement mixer opens its gaping mouth.
>
> The golden eyes of houses in the night . . .
>
> The moon's a harsh mistress.

3. Look for imagery. Imagery is language that appeals to the senses—hearing, sight, touch, taste, or smell. Stevenson uses sight imagery. What do you "see" when you read his poem?

Notice the sensory images in another example:

> Popcorn, popcorn, buttery hot,
> Nachos and burgers and everything—why not?
> The crack of the bat on the speeding ball
> And the crowd is up for the umpire's call.
> He's safe at first, guys on all the bases,
> Pitcher is grimacing, making weird faces,
> As I sip my soda, sweet bubbly foam,
> Waiting for the batter up to bring 'em all home.

Put all of your senses in gear when you read poetry, and you'll enjoy it more and understand it better.

4. Use the think-aloud technique. You learned to talk to the author and to yourself when you read a story or an article. It works with poetry, too. When you read a line that doesn't make sense, ask yourself what it could mean. For example, look at Bradstreet's line:

Who thee abroad, exposed to public view

What does "thee abroad" mean? How was "thee" exposed to public view?

Remember that the title is "The Author to Her Book." She is speaking to her book of poems, so "thee" is that book. "Abroad" means in a different country. In this case, since Anne Bradstreet lived in an English colony, her "friends less wise than true" must have taken her poetry to England. The most likely way for poetry to be "exposed to public view" is to be published.

Exercise 8.10 Practice the Reading Strategy

In a small group, use the following poem, "Moonrise in the Rockies," to practice the poetry-reading techniques you learned. First, a group member should read it line by line, stopping at the end of each line. Another member should then read the poem according to the punctuation. Then everyone should read the poem in unison, according to the punctuation. Answer the questions below.

Moonrise in the Rockies
by Ella Higginson

The trembling train clings to the leaning wall
　　Of solid stone; a thousand feet below
Sinks a black gulf; the sky hangs like a pall[1]
　　Upon the peaks of everlasting snow.

Then of a sudden springs a rim of light,
　　Curved like a silver sickle.[2] High and higher—
Till the full moon burns on the breast of night,
　　And a million firs[3] stand tipped with lucent fire.

————
[1]drape　　　[2]cutting tool　　　[3]evergreen trees

1. How did the second reading of the poem affect your understanding and appreciation of it?

　　_____

　　_____

　　_____

2. Identify each type of figurative language as a simile, metaphor, personification, or poetic imagery:

　　a. the trembling train clings　　　　　　_____

　　b. curved like a silver sickle　　　　　　_____

　　c. moon burns on the breast of night　　_____

　　d. a million firs stand tipped with lucent fire　_____

Exercise 8.11 Additional Practice Reading Poetry

Read "The Creek-Road" by Madison Cawein. Answer the questions that follow.

The Creek-Road
by Madison Cawein

Calling, the heron flies athwart[1] the blue
That sleeps above it, reach[2] on rocky reach
Of water sings by sycamore and beech,
In whose warm shade bloom lilies not a few.
It is a page whereon the sun and dew
Scrawl sparkling words in dawn's delicious speech;
A laboratory where the wood winds teach,
Dissect each scent and analyze each hue.
Not otherwise than beautiful, doth it
Record the happenings of each summer day;
Where we may read, as in a catalogue,
When passed a thresher;[3] when a load of hay;
Or when a rabbit; or a bird that lit;
And now a barefoot truant and his dog.

————
[1]across
[2]portion of a river
[3]something that separates plant grain crops into grain or seeds and straw

1. How does Cawein use figurative language in this poem? Give at least three examples.

   _____

   _____

   _____

   _____

2. What sensory images did you see, hear, feel, touch, and/or taste as you read this poem?

   _____

   _____

   _____

   _____

3. What is the main idea expressed in this poem?

   _____

   _____

   _____

   _____

Writing Workshop

Creating Poetry

Why Write Poetry?

You can find enjoyment in poetry for your own sake, even if you don't want to be published. Poetry gives you a way to play with words, and enables you to experiment freely—you are not bound by grammar and punctuation conventions as you are with prose. In addition, it lets you express your feelings. As Rainer Maria Rilke said, you should not look outward for approval of poetry, but inward. If you like what you write, that is what counts.

Have you always thought that poems must have words that rhyme? Not so. In fact, a good way to ruin a poem is to use rhyming words just for the sake of rhyme. This poetry pitfall can leave you trapped in a poem with little or no real meaning, just a list of rhyming words loosely connected by others.

How to Get Started

You learned about poetic imagery, similes, metaphors, and personification in the previous section. Since those are all important elements of poetry, creating some of your own is a good way to free your mind and let your poetic heart speak.

Exercise 8.12 Practice the Writing Lesson

Take out a sheet of paper. Spend ten minutes writing your own similes, metaphors, images, and personifications. Or just string together some words that don't normally go together and see what happens. Write them sideways, upside down, diagonally, or any other way you want to. Here's a sample list to help you get in the right frame of mind:

star headlights fall on the dark road ribbon	whale-large expectations
dandelions like gold medallions	deafening silence
ferocious hamster	sad little diner
galaxies of gum wrappers	soldiered through life

Exercise 8.13 Write Your Own Poem

Share your list from Exercise 8.12 with the class or a small group. Listening to other people's lists may remind you of other things you can add to your own. For example, if someone reads "oceans of lotions" you might think of "tons of toothpaste"—two good images for a poem about a drugstore.

After everyone has finished reading and adding to their lists, it's time to create your own poem. Circle the things on your list that you like best and that relate in some way to each other. Remember that there are no "wrong" poems. Then start writing. Stop when your inner self is satisfied with the result.

Here is an example written from the list given in Exercise 8.12:

Diner
by Mary L. Dennis
Like a ferocious hamster with whale-large expectations
he stored one thought in his plump cheeks:
Some day he would have his own restaurant.
He was thinking *Bon Appetit*,
big crowds discovering his hole-in-the-wall dive,
maybe a show on the Food Network,
breaking eggs with one hand,
flipping frittatas in mid-air.
Now there is only a flapping "For Sale" sign
in front of his sad little diner.
The bright gold medallions of dandelions in the yard
unnoticed by the few who pass on this dark old ribbon of road,
headlights falling like stars,
tail-lights blinking goodbye.

Grammar Mini-Lesson
Sticking to One Tense

Read these excerpts from Rilke's letter:

> *Nothing touches* a work of art so little as words of criticism.
>
> *They* always *result* in more or less fortunate misunderstandings.
>
> *Things aren't* all so tangible and sayable as people would usually have us believe.

Each time you use a verb, you are using one of its **tenses**. In the examples above, Rilke speaks in the present tense.

When you write, it is important to choose one tense as your **governing** tense, that is, the one you will use to express most of your ideas.

The most appropriate choice for an essay is the present, used to express ideas that you have right now. With creative writing, the tense you choose depends on your purpose and when your story takes place. No matter which tense you choose, however, it is important that you use it consistently.

See if you can find the verb tense mistakes in the following sentences:

1. Courage is when you are afraid to do something but you did it anyway.

2. Good examples of courage are people who put others first, people who stood up for a cause, and people who would overcome physical challenges.

The first and second verbs in the first sentence, *is* and *are*, are in the present tense, but the third verb, *did*, is in the past tense. In the second sentence, *put* is in the present tense, but *stood* and *would overcome* do not line up with one another.

Here are revisions that align all of the verb tenses:
1. Courage is when you are afraid to do something but you *do* it anyway.
2. Good examples of courage are people who put others first, people who *stand* up for a cause, and people who *overcome* physical challenges.

Exercise 8.14 Practice Sticking to One Tense

Write the correct tense of the verb in parentheses.

1. The traffic ahead of us had been stopped for half an hour, so I _____ ahead to see what was wrong. (run, ran)

2. The driver stops the van and _____ everybody to get out. (tells, told)

3. I stood up with my job application filled out, and someone _____ up and took it. (come, came)

4. Eric looks around at the other players and suddenly _____ a three-pointer. (shoots, shot)

5. The assistants quieted everyone down. The president _____ his speech. (begins, began)

6. I asked her if she was ready to go, but she _____ she wasn't. (said, says)

7. All of a sudden she cried, "Let's go!" and _____ my arm. (pulled, pulls)

8. As we turned onto Silver Springs Boulevard, the traffic _____. (worsens, worsened)

9. Brandon leads the group around the track at an easy pace. It's like his feet _____ hardly touching the ground. (are, were)

10. As soon as Mom heard there was a hurricane 1,200 miles away, she _____ to worry. (starts, started)

Exercise 8.15 Apply the Grammar Lesson to Revise a Paragraph

The paragraph on the next page has verb tenses that do not agree with one another. Cross out the mistakes and write in your corrections. It has been started for you.

saw

When I ~~seen~~ my first Shakespeare play live on stage, I am

amazed at how much better it would be than reading it. There

is the costumes, of course, and then there is the scenery. The

scenery isn't all that great, but it helped a little envisioning it.

The music adds a lot, too. I cry when Romeo and Juliet die.

Polish Your Spelling
IE or EI?

In some words, the sound of long *e* as in *eve* is spelled *ie* (*achieve*, *believe*). In certain other words, the same sound is spelled *ei* (*ceiling*, *receive*).

You have probably heard the *i* before *e* rhyme. The rhyme is a good way to recall the rule:

Write *i* before *e*	(*brief, chief, fierce, piece, yield*)
Except after *c*	(*conceit, deceit, perceive*)
Or when sounded like *ay*	(*sleigh, vein, freight*)
As in *neighbor* and *weigh*.	

As is often true with the English language, there are some exceptions to the rule. The seven most common exceptions are these:

either	neither	foreign	height
leisure	seize	weird	

Exercise 8.16 Practice the Spelling Rules for IE and EI

Rewrite each word on the blank line, inserting either *ie* or *ei*.

1. outw__ __gh _____

2. bes__ __ged _____

3. fr__ __ght _____

4. w__ __rd _____

5. for__ __gner _____

6. c__ __ling _____

7. y__ __ld _____

8. misch__ __f _____

9. v__ __n _____

10. dec__ __ver _____

Chapter Nine

Prereading Guide
Words to know and ideas to consider before you jump into the reading.

A. Essential Vocabulary

Word	Meaning	Typical Use
compassion (*n*) cum-PASH-un	feelings of sympathy and concern for those with problems; caring	Mother Teresa demonstrated a great deal of *compassion*.
complexity (*n*) com-PLEKS-ih-tee	difficulty and confusion; intricacy	The *complexity* of some algebra equations is more than I can comprehend.
developmental (*adj*) de-vel-up-MENT-ul	relating to physical and mental growth; progress related	There are special schools for children with *developmental* problems.
empathy (*n*) EMP-uh-thee	identification with another's situation and feelings; understanding	I have a lot of *empathy* for you since I know what it feels like to have your heart broken.
ethnicity (*n*) eth-NISS-ih-tee	the language, history, race, religion, and/or customs shared by a large group of people; culture	My parents are of different *ethnicities*, so we have combined the customs and cultures of both in our family celebrations.
inherent (*adj*) in-HARE-unt	existing as a natural part of something or someone; native	In coal extraction, environmental damage is an *inherent* problem.
onerous (*adj*) AHN-ur-us	imposing a burden; troublesome	The task of editing the school yearbook is an *onerous* one.
prolific (*adj*) pro-LIFF-ik	intellectually or physically productive; fruitful	Shakespeare was a *prolific* playwright.
specious (*adj*) SPEE-shus	sounding true but actually false; deceptive	People should try to see through *specious* statements.
tenet (*n*) TEN-ut	a belief held as true by an organization, especially a political or religious group; principle	Free speech is one of the *tenets* of democracy.

B. Vocabulary Practice

Exercise 9.1   Sentence Completion

Using your new vocabulary knowledge, choose the best way to complete the following sentences. Circle the letter of your answer.

1. Tyra's compassion for homeless animals led her to
   _____.
   A. go shopping for cute collars
   B. volunteer to walk dogs at the shelter

2. The complexity of the street layout made it _____.
   A. hard to find our way
   B. easy to get where we were going

3. Developmental disorders can _____ a person's ability to learn.
   A. impair
   B. improve

4. Instead of _____, perhaps we should try to have some empathy.
   A. understanding her
   B. criticizing her

5. I'm a natural-born American, but my ethnicity is
   _____.
   A. Italian
   B. Californian

6. She was just _____ kind; it was inherent.
   A. naturally
   B. taught to be

7. _____ is an onerous burden.
   A. Being expected to get a 4.0
   B. Being sent to the store for milk

8. For some reason, _____ always seem to be more prolific than flowers.
   A. vegetables
   B. weeds

9. Your specious reasoning makes your argument _____.
   A. unconvincing
   B. a good one

10. Early American _____ followed the tenets of Puritanism.
    A. singers and dancers
    B. Pilgrims

Exercise 9.2   Using Fewer Words

Replace the italicized words with a single word from the following list.

compassion   complexity   developmental   empathy   ethnicities

inherent   onerous   prolific   specious   tenet

1. She seems to have a special talent with horses that is *existing as a natural part of her*.

   1._____

2. Joshua's *sympathy and concern for others with problems* is admirable.

   2._____

3. Competition is a basic *belief held as true* of capitalism.

   3._____

4. Movies with sad endings usually evoke *identification with the situations and feelings of/for the characters*.

   4._____

5. California is a state with especially diverse *languages, customs, races, and religions*.

   5._____

6. American colonists found taxes levied by Britain *imposing of a troublesome burden*.

   6._____

7. Mice are very *physically productive*.

   7._____

8. I can't get anywhere talking with her because of her *sounding true but actually false statements*.

   8._____

9. Authors aim children's literature at specific *physical and mental growth-related* groups.

   9._____

10. Due to the *difficulty and confusion* of this pattern, it will take me quite a while to knit this sweater.

   10._____

Exercise 9.3 Synonyms and Antonyms

Fill in the blanks in column A with the required synonyms or antonyms, selecting them from column B. (Remember: A *synonym* is a word *similar* in meaning to another word. An *antonym* is a word *opposite* in meaning to another word.)

	A	B
_____	1. synonym for *principle*	complexity
_____	2. synonym for *culture*	empathy
_____	3. synonym for *deceptive*	inherent
_____	4. antonym for *unproductive*	compassion
_____	5. synonym for *troublesome*	developmental
_____	6. antonym for *simplicity*	ethnicity
_____	7. synonym for *caring*	specious
_____	8. antonym for *acquired*	tenet
_____	9. synonym for *identification*	onerous
_____	10. synonym for *progress related*	prolific

C. Journal Freewrite

Before you begin the reading on the next page, take out a journal or sheet of paper and spend some time responding to the following prompt.

TIP: Don't worry about grammar and spelling; just write what comes to mind. The purpose of freewriting is to explore ideas, not to produce a polished work.

> Think about some stories and novels that you have read. They could even be selections from this book. In your opinion, what is the difference between a good novel or story and a bad one?

Interview with Amy Tan

excerpt from bookreporter.com

About Amy Tan

Amy Tan (1952–) was born in Oakland, California. Her parents were Chinese immigrants who fled China to escape the Chinese Civil War. At San José City College, she earned degrees in English and linguistics. She worked with developmentally disabled children for a time and then started a business-writing company. Although successful, she soon realized she preferred writing creatively. Her first story, "Endgame," was published in a small literary magazine and reprinted in *Seventeen*. Her first novel, *The Joy Luck Club*, spent eight months on *The New York Times* bestseller list, and was made into a movie. Since then, she has written *The Kitchen God's Wife*, *The Hundred Secret Senses*, *The Bonesetter's Daughter*, *Saving Fish From Drowning*, two children's books, and *The Opposite of Fate: A Book of Musings.*

THE BOOK REPORTER: Did winning awards for your first book [*The Joy Luck Club*] make you feel like your second book was "under a microscope" or pressed for a second success of the same magnitude?

AMY TAN: I felt many pressures, the most <u>onerous</u> one coming from myself. I did not know what people saw in my first book. And as I tried to write the second, I could not quiet the anxiety that I would fail for all kinds of reasons. There was first and foremost my need to create something that was different, yet honest, personally meaningful, and which contained the aesthetic merits[1] I valued in good fiction. At the same time, I would often replay in my head the reviews, but only the really bad ones, the mocking ones that said my life wasn't interesting enough to fill a book, that sort of thing, personal jibes. I realized that the public does not simply judge your art but your persona,[2] or their imaginings of what that must be, which, of course, becomes a fiction of sorts. On top of that, I did not want to disappoint my publisher and their hopes for a book that would do well. Yet, I did not think I could "write a bestseller." I could only write a book. And seven false starts later, I finally wrote that second book, *The Kitchen God's Wife*, which, as it turned out, went to number one on the bestseller lists and all that. But the anxiety still continues, gets worse with each book.

TBR: One of your strengths as a storyteller is the insight with which you depict the <u>complexities</u> of mother/daughter relationships. What effects, good and bad, has this storytelling had on your relationship with your own mother?

AT: By writing parts of my stories in a mother's voice, I had to imagine what my mother had gone through, what she had hoped, as well as what she regretted. And in doing so, I learned a very important lesson about imagination. And that is that much of imagination is <u>empathy</u> and <u>compassion</u>.

---

[1]artistically pleasing qualities
[2]who you are; your whole self

And that to have compassion you must have imagination, to imagine fully another person's life. I remember that after my first book came out, my mother was complaining about something that had happened to her. She was about to go on one of her two-hour laments when suddenly she stopped herself and said, "I don't have to tell you. You understand. You're just like me." And I realized that we both understood each other emotionally. My mother now has Alzheimer's disease, but she retains this uncanny intuition[3] about me, particularly about things that bother me. She'll call me and say, "I think you sad today." And she'll be right. She dreams about how I am feeling. She is always concerned over whether I have had enough to eat. And it's those little concerns of hers that are no longer annoying but so precious.

TBR: What were the catalysts that led you down the path to children's literature and how does the creative process differ for you from adult fiction?

AT: When I was a child, I dreamed of becoming an artist, not a writer. I wanted to make picture books. The words in those books were secondary, for the pictures would inspire the words. In a way, I think that is still true for me. I write from imagery in my mind. In the 1970s, I started drawing again. I was working as a language development specialist with young children, birth to five, with developmental disabilities and I would create language materials—pictures when I didn't find the ones I wanted that would motivate the kids to communicate. Again pictures inspiring words. As it turns out, my best friend, Gretchen Schields, is an illustrator, and her sense of imagery closely complements mine—being lush, dense, and at times, gothic. So it was only natural that we use our collective imaginations and collaborate,[4] with her providing the drawings and me the story. One of those children's books we did together, *The Chinese Siamese Cat*, is now going to be a TV production.

TBR: You have expressed strong feelings about a book being judged for art's sake only, without borrowing on one's ethnicity as a writer. What do you see as the inherent dangers in one's work being judged on historical and cultural qualities instead of—or as well as—its aesthetic ones?

AT: From the beginning of time and book reviews, literary critics have always tried to find social, political, and cultural meaning in fiction. Students of literature are forced to do so—to find the hidden symbols and all that. But I'll tell you a secret: The reasons writers write may be different from the reasons readers read. The reasons may be aesthetic or emotional or simply a matter of having fun. And we may not be consciously planting those symbols. I certainly don't.

---

[3]strange ability to know something without seeing it or being told
[4]use what was in both of our imaginations and work together

This is not to say that readers are wrong when they read for cultural meaning or what have you. But cultural messages are not necessarily my intention as a writer. I do become alarmed when I hear certain people saying that works by writers, particularly ethnic writers, should perform a specific role—educating others or providing positive role models, for example—because that assumes you can delimit[5] what the work should be, as well as how it should be written. Art is created out of freedom and not a <u>specious</u> desire to win approval by others or to serve popular policies. And yet that notion that literature has a proscribed[6] role is one that is sometimes put forth in literature classes and among some critics. It is the same rhetoric that conscripted[7] literature to serve the <u>tenets</u> of Marxism and the Cultural Revolution in China. And as a result, a lot of good writers were trounced,[8] and those who followed party line were placed on the pedestals. That's an effective way to kill good literature.

TBR: What do you see as the social role of literature, particularly of American literature in our society today?

AT: I don't think American literature should have any specific social role, except perhaps to provide pleasure and reflection. I think we are pretty good as Americans at discovering what the role of books is for each of us as we go along. I would hope, however, that part of that discovery is that reading good fiction can help enrich what you notice in life, that it is like a meditation on what details you might also observe and bring into your own life. Reading, I think, helps you live well and fully.

TBR: What advice would you give young readers who want to grow up to be writers?

AT: Know why you want to write, why it's necessary. No one can tell you what those reasons are. But if you want to write only to be published then you will likely get discouraged and quit before that happens. An ambition for fame is not enough. The reason you write should be substantial enough that you would continue to write no matter what. I would also advise young writers to continue reading <u>prolifically</u>. Know the difference between good writing and bad. Be willing to revise. Go to readings by other writers and stay inspired. Don't ask them how much money they got as an advance. Ask them what they value in writing.

TBR: What do you find most frustrating, and most rewarding, about the way you are depicted specifically as a Chinese-American writer and role model, and do you see this changing at all?

---

[5]restrict or narrow
[6]specifically assigned
[7]recruited by force; drafted
[8]punished or defeated

AT: It's annoying when reviewers refer to new writers who are Asian-American as "the new Amy Tan." Those writers must feel stymied and pigeonholed.[9] And I feel positively calcified and decrepit.[10] It's frustrating when people who are using my work in multicultural classes take the stories too literally. I saw one question on a study guide that asked, "If you are invited to a Chinese family's house for dinner, should you bring a bottle of wine?" The correct answer was supposedly based on one of my stories! It's amusing when I go on book tour and I am asked everything related to anything having to do with Asian-Americans, China, and even Chinese cooking.

TBR: You've stated that with your writing you want to "create a work of art." Which book comes closest to your conception of what you want your artistic creation to be?

AT: I have yet to write that book. Each book I write succeeds in ways aesthetically that I did not expect. Each book also fails in ways I would have hoped it would not. I think most writers are compelled in part to continue writing because we are trying to come closer to what our work of art should be. For me, language and a seamless and deceptively simple quality to the story are hugely important.

---

[9]hindered by being put into a certain category
[10]hardened and old

Understanding the Reading

Complete the next three exercises and see how well you understood the interview with Amy Tan.

Exercise 9.4 Multiple-Choice Questions

Answer the following questions about the reading. Circle the letter of your answer.

TIP: Don't try to answer the questions from memory; go back to the text as often as necessary.

1. Amy Tan says that each time she writes a book she becomes more
   A. famous.
   B. confident.
   C. overwhelmed with fan mail.
   D. anxious.

2. How does Tan say that empathy and imagination are related?
   A. They are the same thing.
   B. One is true; one is false.
   C. Empathy requires imagination.
   D. Imagination requires empathy.

3. How does Tan's early interest in art affect her writing?
    A. She illustrates all her own books.
    B. Mental pictures supply inspiration for her writing.
    C. She illustrates children's books.
    D. She can always fall back on art as a career.

4. Tan points out that when people read a book she has written, they
    A. make up a sort of fictional story of their own about her.
    B. usually are disappointed if no Chinese recipes are included.
    C. either love it or hate it.
    D. compare her to other Chinese writers.

5. Using context clues, you can determine that the word *jibes* (page 191) most likely means
    A. physical attacks.
    B. unkind remarks.
    C. personal narratives.
    D. book reviewers.

Exercise 9.5   Short-Answer Questions

Respond to the following questions in one to two complete sentences. Go back to the text, as you did on the multiple choice.

6. What do you think Amy Tan means when she says, "The reasons writers write may be different from the reasons readers read"?

    _____

    _____

    _____

7. Tan says that the little concerns her mother expressed used to annoy her but are now "precious." How does this statement relate to your own experience? Have you ever seen someone in a new light? Explain.

    _____

    _____

    _____

8. What part of this selection did you find most helpful for writers? Why?

    _____

    _____

    _____

9. Tan says that reading "helps you live well and fully." Do you agree? Why or why not?

_____

_____

_____

Exercise 9.6   Extending Your Thinking

Respond to the following question in three to four complete sentences. Use details from the text in your answer.

10. Amy Tan says she is alarmed when she hears "certain people" say that writers' works should perform a specific role such as education or providing positive role models. Why do you think this bothers her? Do you agree?

_____

_____

_____

_____

_____

Reading Strategy Lesson
Question-Answer Relationships on Multiple-Choice Tests

What Is the QAR Technique?

When you take a quiz or test in class or for a state assessment, you are often given a short passage to read and then asked to answer multiple-choice and short-answer questions. The QAR technique helps you to answer more quickly and confidently.

QAR means **Question-Answer Relationship**. To use the technique, you determine the relationship between the question and the answer. There are three basic types of answers for multiple-choice questions.

1. Right There
To find "right there" answers, you go back to the text and find words similar to the ones in the answer choices. If it is "right there," you need look no further.

Example:
> In this selection, bookreporter.com interviewed Amy Tan, author of *The Joy Luck Club* and other novels. The selection is mostly about

A. the reasons bookreporter.com chose to interview Amy Tan.
B. what it is like to have a family member with Alzheimer's disease.
C. what conditions in China were like during the Cultural Revolution.
D. how Amy Tan feels about her work as a writer.

When you look back at the selection, you'll notice that Amy Tan's first long answer is mostly about how it feels to be a writer. The interviewer makes no mention of why Tan was chosen for the Web site. It's true that she does mention the Cultural Revolution and her mother's Alzheimer's disease, but these are not the main topics.

2. Think and Search
A "think and search" question asks you to do exactly that: think about the question, think about the answers, and search for the information in the selection. If you've read especially carefully and comprehended well, you may only need to think about the question to choose the correct answer.
Example:
   Which of the following topics is *not* discussed in the interview?
   A. the stress of being a well-known author
   B. the role of literature in society
   C. the differences between novels and movie versions
   D. the author's relationship with her mother

Remember that you are looking for the topic that is *not* discussed. As you think about these answer choices, you may recall that the interview began with Tan's discussion of the pressure of being a writer and being expected to follow one smash hit with another. Pressure and stress are the same thing, so this topic is discussed in the interview. The interviewer does ask Tan about the role of literature in society, so B is not the answer. Tan discusses her relationship with her mother at length, so D is not the answer. By a process of elimination, you can guess that the correct answer is C, but you may want to quickly scan (see page 198) the selection just to make sure this topic was not discussed. (If you have limited time, mark C and come back later if you have time left.)

3. On Your Own
"On your own" questions require you to evaluate what you have read and make a decision about what the author meant. You will probably need to use scanning and skimming (see page 198) to review the selection as a whole and make your decision.
Example:
   When Amy Tan says "An ambition for fame is not enough" in her advice for young writers, she means
   A. you should ask other authors what they value in writing.
   B. being published shouldn't be your only reason for writing.

C. you have to read a lot before you can write well.

D. revision is a necessary process.

The exact answer to the question is not stated in the interview. Tan does mention that young writers should ask authors what they value in writing, they should read prolifically, and they should be willing to revise. But none of these choices relates closely enough to the question. The only choice that does is B. In the interview, Tan says, "The reason you write should be substantial enough that you would continue to write no matter what." This could be stated another way: Being published shouldn't be your only reason for writing.

For short-answer questions, you are almost always on your own to make an evaluation, a judgment, or a connection, or to express your own opinions or feelings.

Example:

Tan says that reading "helps you live well and fully." Do you agree? Why or why not?

You are the only person who can answer this question. Can you relate Tan's statement to your own life or someone else's? Perhaps you don't agree. Either way, you will need to look within yourself to find the reasons for your opinion.

GOING BACK TO THE TEXT FOR ANSWERS

Skimming can help you read quickly and find the general ideas of a text. Skim a selection once through before doing a more careful reading. You can also use skimming to review a piece later.

To skim:

1. Read the title along with any subtitles or subheads and any boldfaced, italicized, or footnoted words.
2. Look at any illustrations that are included. They can be clues about the passage.
3. Read the first and last sentence of each paragraph.
4. Finally, let your eyes skim over the text, taking in key words.

Scanning, on the other hand, is when you look for *specific* information. For example, if you need to pick up some milk at the grocery store, you scan the store for the location of the dairy case. If you need to pick up a fact from a selection, you scan the passage for the location of the fact you want.

Use scanning when you are looking for "right there" answers and evaluating "think and search" answers. Use skimming before you read a selection and to review a selection for "On your own" multiple-choice and short-answer questions.

Exercise 9.7   Practice the Reading Strategy

Evaluate each of the following questions according to QAR and indicate whether it is a "right there," a "think and search," or an "on your own" question. Also write down whether you would need to use skimming or scanning or both to find the answer.

1. Amy Tan says she believes the only specific role books should have is to
   A. provide role models.
   B. provide pleasure and reflection.
   C. educate people.
   D. answer readers' questions about life.

Type of question: _____

Techniques to find the answer: _____

2. When reviewers refer to new Asian-American writers as "the new Amy Tan," Tan feels mostly
   A. stymied and pigeonholed.
   B. annoyed at the reviewers and sorry for the writers.
   C. like giving up writing.
   D. angry at the new writers.

Type of question: _____

Techniques to find the answer: _____

3. Tan apparently considers reading good fiction
   A. something people should do if they feel like it.
   B. something people should continue to do throughout life.
   C. an activity for when you are bored.
   D. something you would only do if you had to.

Type of question: _____

Techniques to find the answer: _____

Exercise 9.8   Apply the Reading Strategy

On a separate sheet of paper, write a "right there," a "think and search," and an "on your own" multiple-choice question based on one of the selections in this chapter. Also, write an "on your own" short-answer question. Trade your questions with a partner. Respond to the questions and note which kind each question is.

Writing Workshop
Conducting an Interview

You conduct informal interviews all the time, without even realizing it. When you talk to, e-mail, or text-message friends, you often ask them questions. Sometimes your questions are simple, like "Do you have the pages for the history assignment?" or "How come you weren't at school today?"

Some of your questions are probably more *prying*, that is, you're looking for information that your friend may not be willing to talk about and that you might have to try to draw out of him or her. For example, "So, do you like this guy or not? Everyone says he likes you," or "Is it true you got grounded for staying out too late?"

Then there are the public, personally probing interviews, which you can see every day on television news and talk shows. The questions usually ask for very private or even potentially scandalous information. They make the interviewee squirm and feel uncomfortable.The person asking the questions is often looking for an audience reaction or is just being nosy!

Striking the Right Balance

Suppose you have to interview someone for a class assignment or school newspaper article. Where do you draw the line between the mundane (the usual) and the shocking? If you ask questions that are too bland, your interview will be boring. If your questions are too personal, the person you are interviewing may cut your session short.

The first step is to formulate your interview questions ahead of time.

1. Decide what makes your interviewee (the person you are going to interview) especially interesting. Is she the teacher voted "Teacher of the Year"? Is he the band director who led your school band all the way to state finals?

2. Formulate your questions around the 5 W's and H: Who? What? When? Where? Why? How? For example: Where did the teacher of the year grow up? What made her decide to go into teaching? How did the band director turn the band around? Why did it matter to him?

3. Decide on an appropriate level of personal-detail questions. For example, you wouldn't ask the band director how many times he's been married or ask the teacher her age.

Exercise 9.9   Practice Writing Interview Questions

Choose from the following list, or make your own decision about whom to interview. Ask the person if he or she is willing to be interviewed. Then write at least ten interview questions on a separate sheet of paper.

- a member of your school's faculty

- the president of a school club

- a local business owner

- an elderly relative or neighbor
- someone who works at a fast-food restaurant or grocery store
- a parent or other caregiver or relative
- a doctor, nurse, or veterinarian
- a police officer or firefighter

Exercise 9.10 Conduct Your Own Interview

Now it's time to use your questions in an actual interview. During the interview, don't forget to take good notes. Also, pay attention to how your interviewee is reacting to your questions. If he or she seems to be showing signs of discomfort or annoyance, switch to another question.

With your interviewee's permission, share the interview with your class. Listeners can ask questions after interviews are read.

Grammar Mini-Lesson
Using Possessives Correctly

Using Possessive Nouns

The **possessive** is the form of a noun that indicates ownership or possession.

The italicized nouns in the following phrases are **possessives**:

Jordan's hair	hair belonging to Jordan
students' money	money belonging to the students
women's rights	rights possessed by women
girls' names	the names of the girls

Notice that by using the possessives, we are able to express ideas in fewer words and avoid choppiness.

Why do some possessives end in *'s* (*Jordan's*, *women's*) while others end in *s'* (*students'*, *girls'*)? Understanding the answer to this question is one of the keys to using possessives correctly.

1. If the possessor is a *singular* noun, add *'s*.
the student's book
the girl's coat
the bird's feathers
James's car   (Names ending in *s* still need *'s* to make them possessive because they are singular nouns.)

2. If the possessor is a plural noun that ends in *s*, add only an apostrophe. For instance, if there are several students who have books, several girls with coats, and more than one bird with feathers, you would write

the students' books
the girls' coats
the birds' feathers

3. If the possessor is a plural noun that does not end in s, add 's.
Women is already the plural of *woman*, so *women's* is the possessive. Other examples:

salesmen's earnings
children's playground

Exercise 9.11 Practice Using Possessives for Conciseness

Rewrite each of the following phrases with a possessive.

1. cell phone owned by the boy   _____

2. uniforms of the band members   _____

3. toys belonging to the children   _____

4. wishes of my parents   _____

5. mother of the child   _____

6. duties of congressmen   _____

7. shoes for women   _____

8. mouth of the horse   _____

9. problems facing the city   _____

10. the letter Nicholas wrote   _____

Exercise 9.12 Additional Practice Using Possessives

Write the correct possessive form of the noun in parentheses.

1. My _____ name is Kristin. (aunt)

2. _____ jobs are not easy. (soldier)

3. In late winter, the stores mark down girls' and _____ coats. (women)

4. The contest will be held in the _____ gym. (boys)

5. Why are these _____ gloves so much more expensive than the men's? (ladies)

6. _____ house is only two blocks from school. (Christopher)

7. The usher took the _____ tickets. (gentlemen)

8. Most candidates for office try to gain the _____ confidence. (voters)

9. The bear _____ mother stayed close to them. (cubs)

10. _____ parents are taking her shopping for her birth-day. (Alexis)

Polish Your Spelling
When to Use -ABLE and -IBLE

QUESTION: Should you use *-able* or *-ible* to complete *irrit__ __ __ __*?

HINT: If you remember that there is a word ending in *-ation* that begins with *irrit-* (*irritation*), that is your clue to use *-able*. Both word endings begin with the letter *a*.

CORRECT SPELLING: *irritation*

Most words follow this rule. If there is an *-ation* word, then there is an *-able* word.

Examples:

-ATION	-ABLE
imagination	imaginable
presentation	presentable
application	applicable
adoration	adorable

Exception: The word *sensible* ends in *-ible*, despite the existence of the word *sensation*.

If there is no *-ation* word, there is no easy way to tell how to spell the adjective form of the word. For example, there is no such word as *dependation*, so you need to memorize that the correct way to spell the adjective form of *depend* is *dependable*.

Frequently Used -ABLE Adjectives

acceptable	conceivable	disposable	miserable
advisable	consumable	excusable	perishable
applicable	dependable	hospitable	predictable
available	desirable	imaginable	presentable
believable	despicable	intolerable	probable

Frequently Used -IBLE Adjectives

convertible	feasible	invisible	plausible
digestible	flexible	irresistible	possible
divisible	horrible	legible	responsible
edible	incredible	negligible	sensible
eligible	inexhaustible	permissible	terrible

The suffix *-able* or *-ible* does not change when a prefix is added or removed:

un	+	predict*able*	=	unpredict*able*
ir	+	respons*ible*	=	irrespons*ible*
im	+	prob*able*	=	improb*able*
in	+	exhaust*ible*	=	inexhaust*ible*

Exercise 9.13 Practice Using -ABLE or -IBLE

Following are some adjectives with either *-able* or *-ible* omitted.
Write the complete adjective on the line.

Example: _____ undependable _____

1. unavail _____

2. indigest _____

3. present _____

4. imposs _____

5. horr _____

6. dur _____

7. permiss _____

8. perish _____

9. imagine _____

10. terr _____

Unit Three Review

Vocabulary Review

A. Match each word with its definition.

DEFINITION		WORD
_____	1. opposite of what one expects	a. developmental
_____	2. causing weariness or annoyance	b. visage
_____	3. relating to growth	c. ethnicity
_____	4. secret plan	d. interloper
_____	5. close bond due to similarities	e. compassion
_____	6. one who intrudes	f. tenet
_____	7. facial features and expression	g. irksome
_____	8. belief held as true	h. conspiracy
_____	9. shared customs, language, etc.	i. irony
_____	10. concern and sympathy for others	j. kinship

B. Match each word with its synonym.

SYNONYM		WORD
_____	11. troublesome	a. renounce
_____	12. improve	b. transitory
_____	13. fruitful	c. immersion
_____	14. understanding	d. innumerable
_____	15. precise	e. prolific
_____	16. relinquish	f. amend
_____	17. countless	g. onerous
_____	18. temporary	h. empathy
_____	19. pale	i. explicit
_____	20. concentration	j. pallid

C. Match each word with its antonym.

ANTONYM	WORD
_____ 21. simplicity	a. coherent
_____ 22. inarticulate	b. inherent
_____ 23. unimportant	c. assent
_____ 24. confident	d. facile
_____ 25. acquired	e. specious
_____ 26. difficult	f. ambiguity
_____ 27. disagreement	g. articulate
_____ 28. irrational	h. crucial
_____ 29. clarity	i. complexity
_____ 30. true	j. halting

Grammar Review

Each question offers three suggestions for improving the corresponding underlined portion of the essay. If the underlined portion is not improved by one of the three suggested changes, choose A., No change. Circle the letter of your answer.

Writer's Block

Writer's block is not a place where all the writers in a neighborhood live. It's a bewildering condition <u>suffered from often by</u>
                                                                (1)
<u>many writers</u>, including students and
    (1)
professionals who <u>make a living from</u>
                        (2)
<u>there writing</u>. <u>It helps to know what's</u>
    (2)   (3)
<u>causing the block</u>. <u>One of the problems</u>
        (3)   (4)
<u>that is common where you had a writer's</u>
                        (4)

1. A. No change
    B. of which many writers often suffer from
    C. often faced by many writers
    D. suffering many writers often

2. A. No change
    B. make a living from their writing
    C. made a living from they're writing
    D. made a living from there writing

3. A. No change
    B. Its a help knowing what's causing the block.
    C. Helpful it is to know what causes the block.
    D. It help's to know whats causing the block.

4. A. No change
    B. One of the situations of writer's block
    C. One of the problems where you have a writer's block
    D. A common writer's block situation

block situation is that the editor of the
$\qquad$ (4) $\qquad\qquad$ (5)
writer's brain keeps interfering at the same
$\qquad$ (5)
time the creative process is going on. Its
$\qquad\qquad$ (6)
best to "turn off" the editor until the
creative genius part of your brain has
finished its work. This may be a problem
$\qquad\qquad$ (7)
that belongs to you if you feel each
$\qquad$ (7)
sentence must be perfect before you move
on to the next. If you spent a long time
$\qquad\qquad$ (8)
looking for just the write word, that
$\qquad$ (8)
interrupted the creative process. Just let
$\qquad$ (8)
your ideas flow onto the paper or into the
computer. Most students first drafts are
$\qquad\qquad$ (9)
not perfect. They supply the editor of your
$\qquad$ (9) $\qquad\qquad$ (10)
brain with an entire piece to critique and
$\qquad$ (10)
change until you have a paper you can
turn in with pride.

5. A. No change
   B. the editing function of the writer's brain
   C. the writers' brains editors
   D. the writers brains is an editor who won't stop

6. A. No change
   B. going on, it's
   C. going on. It's
   D. going on; its

7. A. No change
   B. a problem that belong to you
   C. your problem
   D. a problem that you have

8. A. No change
   B. Spending too much time looking for just the right word interrupts
   C. If you spend a lot of time looking for the right word, it causes an interruption to
   D. If you spent a long time looking for just the right word, that interrupted

9. A. No change
   B. Most students' first drafts are not perfect
   C. Most students' first draft's are not perfect
   D. Most students's first drafts are not perfect

10. A. No change
    B. They provide the editor which belongs to your brain
    C. They provide your brain's editor
    D. They supply the brain belonging to your editor

Spelling Review

A. Write the correct homonym on the line.

1. Of _____ I could be wrong. (coarse, course)

2. _____ difficult to know for sure. (It's, Its)

3. Soon it will be _____ late to matter. (two, too, to)

B. Fill in the blanks with *ei* or *ie* to spell each word correctly.

4. w__ __rd

5. v__ __n

6. dec__ __ve

7. for__ __gn

C. Complete each word with either *-ible* or *-able* to spell the word correctly.

8. plaus_____

9. sens_____

10. miser_____

Writing Review

Choose one of the following topics. Plan your essay. Write your first draft. Then revise and edit your draft, and write your final essay. Be sure to identify your audience, purpose, and task before you begin planning.

> Look back at the selections by Anne Bradstreet and James Baldwin. Also reread the author information about each one. What similarities can you find between the societies in which these two authors wrote? How are their attitudes about society alike or different?
>
> OR
>
> Both Rainer Maria Rilke and Amy Tan give advice to young writers. What three bits of advice—from one or both of them—will be most memorable and helpful to you as you continue through school and the many writing projects ahead of you?

❋ SPEAK/LISTEN

Today's Keynote Speaker . . .

Imagine that one of the authors in this unit is going to speak to your entire school. You have been chosen to introduce him or her. Research the author's life and works using the Internet or library books. You should try to find information not included in the About the Author sidebar, and you should assume your audience knows nothing about the writer. Then write a brief introduction for the speaker. Present it to your classmates.

❋ EXPLORE

Tricks of the Trade

Most writers who become famous are asked for advice or about tricks they use for motivation. For example, in order to avoid writer's block, Ernest Hemingway always stopped writing for the day when he knew what his next sentence would be. Choose a favorite author and find out about his or her "tricks of the trade," using the Internet or other resources. Share your findings with your class so you can all begin using some professional writers' techniques.

❋ WRITE

Author to Author

Imagine that two of the authors represented in this unit have a discussion about writing. Write the script of their conversation. Include stage directions. (Look back at *A View From the Bridge* in Unit Two for a model.) Your script should be between three and five minutes long.

❋ CONNECT

Inspirational Tips

Work with a small group to create your own writers' tips with advice and information gathered from the authors in this section. You should have at least five solid tips that will help anyone who follows them to be a better writer. Design a series of small posters with one tip on each. Illustrate each poster with a related picture to help you and your fellow students remember your ideas.

UNIT FOUR

Imagining a World

Chapter Ten

Prereading Guide
Words to know and ideas to consider before you jump into the reading.

A. Essential Vocabulary

Word	Meaning	Typical Use
antagonism (*n*) an-TAG-uh-nizm	feeling of ill will; hostility	There is so much *antagonism* between them that they will probably never learn to get along.
assurance (*n*) ah-SHUR-unce	a certainty that you are right; self-confidence	Although he is only eight, Deepak can spell almost any word with *assurance.*
candid (*adj*) KAN-did	unrehearsed and down-to-earth; forthright	Celebrities are often featured in *candid* and unflattering pictures in the tabloids.
deter (*v*) de-TUR	to try to prevent an occurrence; dissuade	My dad tried to *deter* me from going out with Spike, and unfortunately I must admit he was right.
diplomatic (*adj*) dip-lo-MAT-ik	having to do with government relations, particularly concerning sensitive matters; civic	His *diplomatic* security clearance took a long time to come through.
diversify (*v*) dih-VER-sih-fie	to add variety and to offer or to have more options; expand	Nutrition experts advise us to *diversify* our diets by eating more fruits and vegetables.
insinuate (*v*) in-SIN-yu-ate	to convey a thought by suggestion; imply	What are you *insinuating* by saying that my new haircut is "unusual"?
investigative (*adj*) in-VESS-tih-gate-iv	a process involving fact-finding; analytical	*Investigative* journalists dig deeply to find the truth behind the headlines.
portal (*n*) PORT-ul	way to enter a building or area; gateway	For many years, Ellis Island was a *portal* to America for those arriving from foreign shores.
unprecedented (*adj*) un-PRESS-uh-dent-ed	not having happened before or unique; unheard-of	This TV will give you *unprecedented* picture and sound quality.

B. Vocabulary Practice

Exercise 10.1 Sentence Completion

Using your new vocabulary knowledge, choose the best way to complete the following sentences. Circle the letter of your answer.

1. It was unprecedented for the track team to have someone
   _____.
   A. who could run that quickly
   B. who loved to run

2. He said, "That was _____," but I think he was insinu-ating that it was foolish.
   A. bright
   B. dumb

3. Automobile makers have diversified by offering _____ models.
   A. more
   B. fewer

4. To move ahead on this video game, you have to keep _____ various portals.
   A. avoiding
   B. going through

5. Diplomatic relations between _____ have broken down.
   A. Rob and Matt
   B. the two countries

6. The investigative reporter _____.
   A. made a groundbreaking discovery
   B. wrote about the latest celebrity fashions

7. You should not let anyone deter you from _____.
   A. pursuing your goals
   B. careless driving

8. For good reason, most _____ are antagonistic toward dogs.
   A. people
   B. cats

9. We had a very candid conversation, and _____.
   A. said how we really felt
   B. hid what we were feeling

10. The valedictorian spoke with assurance. She held her head high _____ contact with audience members.
    A. but couldn't make eye
    B. and made eye

Exercise 10.2 Using Fewer Words

Replace the italicized words with a single word from the following list.

antagonism assurance candid deterring diplomatic

diversified insinuating investigative portals unprecedented

1. This problem could be solved by going through *government-related* channels.

   1._____

2. The report will take a while to complete since it's highly *related to finding facts*.

   2._____

3. This is *something that hasn't happened before*!

   3._____

4. The *ways to enter* [of] some beautiful cathedrals are intricately carved or painted.

   4._____

5. There is a lot of *feeling of ill will* between the two cousins.

   5._____

6. It would be nice to always speak with such *a certainty that you are right*.

   6._____

7. The interview was *unrehearsed and down-to-earth*.

   7._____

8. Stop *conveying a thought by suggestion* that I did something wrong.

   8._____

9. I'm *trying to prevent* him from making a big mistake.

   9._____

10. In the past half century, school curricula have become much more *varied and offer more options*.

    10._____

Exercise 10.3 Synonyms and Antonyms

Fill in the blanks in column A with the required synonyms or antonyms, selecting them from column B. (Remember: A *synonym* is a word *similar* in meaning to another word. An *antonym* is a word *opposite* in meaning to another word.)

	A	B
_____	1. synonym for *confidence*	investigative
_____	2. synonym for *civic*	diversify
_____	3. synonym for *imply*	assurance
_____	4. antonym for *usual*	deter
_____	5. antonym for *rehearsed*	antagonism
_____	6. synonym for *gateway*	diplomatic
_____	7. synonym for *analytical*	portal
_____	8. antonym for *encourage*	candid
_____	9. synonym for *expand*	insinuate
_____	10. antonym for *friendliness*	unprecedented

C. Journal Freewrite

Before you begin the reading on the next page, take out a journal or sheet of paper and spend some time responding to the following prompt.

TIP: Don't worry about grammar and spelling; just write what comes to mind. The purpose of freewriting is to explore ideas, not to produce a polished work.

> What do you think we can be doing now to protect our environment for the future? What can be done on a local level? On a global level?

Reading 13

from Ecotopia

by Ernest Callenbach

About the Author
Ernest Callenbach
(1929–) was born in
Williamsport,
Pennsylvania. After
earning a master's
degree in English from
the University of
Chicago, he moved to
California, where he
worked for the
University of California
Press for 36 years, edit-
ing *Film Quarterly* and
the Natural History
Guides. His interest in
environmental issues
grew, and he wrote
Ecotopia and *Ecotopia
Emerging*, books about a
sustainable ecosystem
(an ecosystem that does
not deplete resources)
that was created
through selective use of
technology. He is cred-
ited with coining the
word *ecotopia* (see the
Reader's Tip) and used it
in his *Ecotopian
Encyclopedia*. He has
written several other
books, all on the subject
of sustainability.

Reader's Tip: The word ecotopia *is a combination of the
word* utopia *(a place where everything is perfect) and the
prefix* eco-, *relating to the natural world, or ecology. In this
science fiction selection, reporter Will Weston visits the "stable-
state ecosystem," a place where people and nature live in perfect balance. The fictional country Ecotopia was formed
when northern California and the states of Oregon and
Washington seceded[1] from the Union. Weston is the first
American visitor to the area in the 19 years since its independence.*

WESTON'S NEXT ASSIGNMENT: ECOTOPIA
The *Times-Post* is at last able to announce that William
Weston, our top international affairs reporter, will spend six
weeks in Ecotopia, beginning next week. This <u>unprecedented</u>
journalistic development has been made possible through
arrangements at the highest <u>diplomatic</u> level. It will mark the
first officially arranged visit by an American to Ecotopia since
the secession cut off normal travel and communications.

The *Times-Post* is sending Weston on this unique and difficult <u>investigative</u> assignment in the conviction that a <u>can-
did</u>, on-the-spot assessment of Ecotopia is essential—20
years after its secession. Old <u>antagonisms</u> have too long
<u>deterred</u> close examination of what has been happening in
Ecotopia—a part of the world once near, dear and familiar to
us, but closed off and increasingly mysterious during its
decades of independence.

The problem now is not so much to oppose Ecotopia as to
understand it—which can only benefit the cause of international good relations. The *Times-Post* stands ready, as
always, to serve that cause.

CROSSING THE ECOTOPIAN BORDER
On board the Sierra Express, Tahoe–San Francisco, May 4. I
have now entered Ecotopia—the first known American to
visit the new country since its Independence, 19 years ago.

---
[1]formally separated

My jet landed at Reno. Though it is not widely known, the Ecotopian government prohibits even international flights from crossing its territory—on grounds of air and noise pollution. Flights between San Francisco and Asia, or over the pole to Europe, must not only use a remote airport 40 miles outside the city, but are forced to follow over-water routes; and American jets for Hawaii must fly via Los Angeles. Thus to reach San Francisco I was compelled to deplane at Reno, and take an expensive taxi ride to the train station at the north end of Lake Tahoe. From Tahoe there is frequent and fast service.

The actual frontier is marked by a picturesquely weathered wooden fence, with a large gate, obviously little used. When my taxi pulled up, there was nobody around. The driver had to get out, go over to a small stone guard-house, and get the Ecotopian military to interrupt their card game. They turned out to be two young men in rather unpressed uniforms. But they knew of my coming, they checked my papers with an air of informed authority, and they passed the taxi through the gate—though only after making a point of the fact that it had required a special dispensation[2] to allow an internal combustion engine to pass their sacred <u>portals</u>. I replied that it only had to take me about 20 miles to the train station. "You're lucky the wind is from the west," one of them said. "If it happened to be from the east we might have had to hold you up for a while."

They checked my luggage with some curiosity, paying special attention to my sleeping pills. But I was allowed to keep everything except my trusty .45 and holster. This might be standard garb in New York, I was told, but no concealable weapons are permitted in Ecotopia. Perhaps noticing my slightly uneasy reaction, one of the guards remarked that Ecotopian streets are quite safe, by day or night. He then handed me a small booklet, *Ecotopia Explains*. This document was nicely printed but with rather quaint drawings. Evidently it had been prepared chiefly for tourists from Europe and Asia. "It might make things easier to get used to," said the other guard, in a soft, almost <u>insinuatingly</u> friendly tone that I now begin to recognize as a national trait. "Relax, it's a free country."

"My friend," I countered, "I've been in a hell of a lot stranger places than this country and I relax when I feel like it. If you're finished with my papers, I'll be on my way."

He snapped my passport shut, but held it in his hand. "Weston," he said, looking me in the eye, "you're a writer. We count on you to use words carefully while you're here. If you come back this way, maybe you'll be able to use that word 'friend' in good faith. We'd like that." He then smiled warmly and put out his hand. Rather to my surprise, I took it, and found a smile on my own face as well.

We drove on, to the Tahoe station of the Ecotopian train system. It turned out to be a rustic affair, constructed of huge timbers. It might pass in America for a monstrous ski chalet. It even had fireplaces in the

---

[2]special suspension of the normal rules

waiting rooms—of which there are several, one a kind of restaurant, one a large, deserted room with a bandstand where dances must be held, and one a small, quiet lounge with leather chairs and a supply of books. The trains, which usually have only two or three cars but run about every hour, come into the basement of the station, and in cold weather huge doors close behind them to keep out the snow and wind.

Special facilities for skiers were evident—storage racks and lockers —but by this time of year the snows have largely melted and there is little skiing. The electric minibuses that shuttle from the station to ski resorts and nearby towns are almost empty.

I went down to my train. It looked more like a wingless airplane than a train. At first I thought I had gotten into an unfinished car— there were no seats! The floor was covered with thick, spongy carpet, and divided into compartments by knee-high partitions; a few passengers were sprawled on large baglike leather cushions that lay scattered about. One elderly man had taken a blanket from a pile at one end of the car, and lay down for a nap. Some of the others, realizing from my confusion that I was a foreigner, showed me where to stow my bag and told me how to obtain refreshments from the steward in the next car. I sat down on one of the pillows, realizing that there would be a good view from the huge windows that came down to about six inches from the floor.

Their sentimentality about nature has even led the Ecotopians to bring greenery into their trains, which are full of hanging ferns and small plants I could not identify. (My companions, however, reeled off their botanical[3] names with <u>assurance</u>.) At the end of the car stood containers rather like trash bins, each with a large letter—M, G, and P. These, I was told, were "recycle bins." It may seem unlikely to Americans, but I observed that during our trip my fellow travelers did without exception dispose of all metal, glass, or paper and plastic refuse in the appropriate bin. That they did so without the embarrassment Americans would experience was my first introduction to the rigid practices of recycling and re-use upon which Ecotopians are said to pride themselves so fiercely.

By the time you notice you are under way in an Ecotopian train, you feel virtually no movement at all. Since it operates by magnetic suspension and propulsion,[4] there is no rumble of wheels or whine or vibration. People talk, there is the clink of glasses and teacups, some passengers wave to friends on the platform. In a moment the train seems literally to be flying along the ground, though it is actually a few inches above a trough-shaped guideway.

My companions told me something about the background of these trains. Apparently the Boeing Company in Seattle, at the time of Independence, had never taken seriously the need to <u>diversify</u> its output from airplanes into other modes of transportation. The world market for new planes had become highly competitive, however, and luckily the Ecotopian government, though its long-range economic

---

[3]relating to botany, the scientific study of plants
[4]lifting up and moving forward

policies called for diversification and decentralization[5] of production in each city and region, took temporary advantage of the Boeing facilities to help build the new national train system. While the Germans and Japanese had pioneered in magnetic-suspension trains with linear motors, Boeing began production on the system only a year after Independence. When I asked how the enormous expense of the system had been financed, my companions laughed. One of them remarked that the cost of the entire roadbed from San Francisco to Seattle was about that of ten SSTs, and he argued that the total social cost per person per mile on their trains was less than that for air transport at any distance under a thousand miles.

I learned from my booklet that the trains normally travel about 360 kilometers per hour on the level. (Use of the metric system is universal in Ecotopia.) You get a fair view of the countryside at this speed, which translates as about 225 miles per hour. And we only attained that speed after about 20 minutes of crawling up and over the formidable[6] eastern slope of the Sierra Nevadas, at what seemed less than 90 miles per hour. Donner Pass looked almost as bleak as it must have to the Donner pioneer party who perished there. We made a stop at Norden and picked up a few late-season skiers—a cheerful bunch, like our skiers, but dressed in raggedy attire, including some very secondhand-looking fur jackets. They carried homemade knapsacks and primitive skis—long, thin, with flimsy old-fashioned bindings. The train then swooped down the long canyons of the Sierra forests, occasionally flashing past a river with its water bubbling blue-black and icy between the rocks. In a few minutes we slid into Auburn. The timetable, which graphically lays out the routes and approximate schedules of a complex network of connecting trains and buses, showed three stops before San Francisco itself. I was glad to notice that we halted for less than 60 seconds, even though people sauntered on and off with typical Ecotopian looseness.

Once we reached the valley floor, I saw little of interest, but my companions still seemed fascinated. They pointed out changes in the fields and forests we passed; in a wooded stretch someone spotted a doe with two fawns, and later a jackrabbit caused great amusement. Soon we entered the hilly country around San Francisco Bay, and shot through a series of tunnels in the grass-covered, breast-shaped green hills. There were now more houses, though rather scattered— many of them seeming to be small farms. The orchards, fields and fences looked healthy and surprisingly well cared for, almost like those of western Europe. Yet how dingy and unprosperous the farm buildings looked, compared to the white-painted farms of Iowa or New England! The Ecotopians must be positively allergic to paint. They build with rock, adobe, weathered boards—apparently almost anything that comes to hand, and they lack the aesthetic[7] sense that would lead them to give such materials a coat of concealing paint.

---

[5]redistribution away from one main center
[6]difficult
[7]having to do with the finer points of beauty and art

They would apparently rather cover a house with vines or bushes than paint it.

The drabness of the countryside was increased by its evident isolation. The roads were narrow and winding, with trees dangerously close to the pavement. No traffic at all seemed to be moving on them. There wasn't a billboard in sight, and not a gas station or telephone booth. It would not be reassuring to be caught in such a region after dark.

An hour and a quarter after we left Tahoe, the train plunged into a tube near the Bay shore, and emerged a few minutes later in the San Francisco main station. In my next column I will describe my first impressions of the city by the Golden Gate—where so many earlier Americans debarked[8] to seek their fortunes in the gold fields.

_____
[8]disembarked

Understanding the Reading

Complete the next three exercises and see how well you understood the excerpt from *Ecotopia*.

Exercise 10.4 Multiple-Choice Questions

Answer the following questions about the reading. Circle the letter of your answer.

TIP: Don't try to answer the questions from memory; go back to the text as often as necessary.

1. Weston's main purpose for visiting Ecotopia is to
   A. spy on its residents.
   B. try to figure out how it can be defeated.
   C. foster understanding between it and the rest of the world.
   D. check out the possibility of moving there himself.

2. Weston's plane had to land at Reno, Nevada, because
   A. it had engine trouble.
   B. Ecotopia has prohibited air and noise pollution in its skies.
   C. Weston wanted to see Lake Tahoe.
   D. Weston wanted to sneak into Ecotopia unnoticed.

3. From context, you can determine that an internal combustion engine (second paragraph on page 218) is
   A. the one most taxis use.
   B. the one most airplanes use.
   C. an engine that burns gasoline.
   D. an engine that runs on efficient, nonpolluting fuel.

4. The phrase "their sentimentality about nature" indicates that
   A. conservation is ridiculed in the "outside" world.
   B. Ecotopians honor and value nature.
   C. Ecotopia was formed primarily to protect nature.
   D. all of the above

5. Weston says the Ecotopians "must be positively allergic to paint" because he
   A. notices that a lot of them are sneezing and coughing.
   B. doesn't understand that they prefer not to use toxic substances just for looks.
   C. notices that most of the cars on the highways are rusty and need paint.
   D. thinks the orchards are as healthy looking as those in Europe.

Exercise 10.5 Short-Answer Questions

Respond to the following questions in one to two complete sentences. Go back to the text, as you did on the multiple choice.

6. The people in Ecotopia are friendly and happy. Why does Weston have a difficult time dealing with that?

   _____

   _____

   _____

7. Weston reports that Ecotopians show no embarrassment about recycling their containers, and are in fact proud of their policy of reuse. Why is citizen pride in this activity important to their society?

   _____

   _____

   _____

8. Why do you suppose one group of skiers wore ragged clothing and carried homemade backpacks and old-fashioned skis?

   _____

   _____

   _____

9. If Ecotopia really existed, would you want to live there? Why or why not?

   _____

   _____

   _____

Exercise 10.6 Extending Your Thinking

Respond to the following question in three to four complete sentences. Use details from the text in your answer.

10. The theme of this unit is "Imagining a World." How does Weston's idea of what the world should be like differ from the typical Ecotopian's?

_____

_____

_____

_____

_____

_____

Reading Strategy Lesson
Exploring Science Fiction and Fantasy

Although science fiction didn't gain popularity until the early twentieth century, long before then authors had been imagining strange worlds, abnormal creatures, and extreme events. Thomas More created a perfect world in *Utopia* in 1515. Characters took imaginary trips to the moon as early as 1634, and Gulliver found himself in an alien world in *Gulliver's Travels* in 1726. *Frankenstein* was published in 1818. Later in the 1800s came Jules Verne's *20,000 Leagues Under the Sea* and H. G. Wells's *The Time Machine* and *The War of the Worlds*.

When science fiction author Isaac Asimov said, in 1952, that science fiction "is concerned with the impact of scientific advance upon human beings," no one had yet shot a satellite into space, and the United States was still almost two decades away from landing on the moon. There was no space shuttle. People were just beginning to buy televisions (with black-and-white pictures and only three channels). No one had heard of computers, CDs, DVDs, MP3s, or the Internet.

As technology continues to advance at an ever-increasing pace, modern science fiction authors continue to ask themselves "Hmmm . . . what if?" It's a great question for all writers, but science fiction and fantasy writers answer it in a different way.

Fairy tales and folktales have been passed down orally for centuries—romantic fantasies about Cinderella, Rapunzel, and Snow White, and scary tales like *Hansel and Gretel*, *Peter Pan*, *Jack and the Beanstalk*, *Little Red Riding Hood*, and *Alice in Wonderland* are fantasies, too. You might be familiar with *The Hobbit*, *The Lord of the Rings* trilogy, *The Borrowers*, and other stories where there are no technological explanations for the characters and their world.

Fantasy differs somewhat from science fiction in that science fiction is often about the future and usually involves futuristic technology, while fantasy may be set in modern, medieval, future, or even prehistoric times. Both science fiction and fantasy can take us to the far past, the far future, and anywhere in between.

Today we see science fiction and fantasy everywhere. It is not just in the library, but at the movies, on television, and in video games. There is a separate Sci-Fi TV channel. Even the special effects in movies are a kind of fantasy: They make things that could not happen seem possible.

Here are some tips to remember when you read or view science fiction or fantasy.

1. Know Your Genre

You read poetry in a different way and for a different purpose than you do a newspaper article. Likewise, science fiction and fantasy must be read or viewed in a certain way. Realize that you are reading something that couldn't happen—at least not yet. Here are some common themes that recur frequently in science fiction and fantasy.

Mostly in Science Fiction	Mostly in Fantasy
alien invasions of Earth or alien visits	kings, knights
space travel or time travel	magic, magicians
repressive governments	castles
takeover of Earth by machines	charming creatures like unicorns and genies, often wise
the world after a destructive nuclear war	trolls, fairies
Earth in the far future	monsters like dragons, giant insects
Earth after environmental devastation	spooky houses and forests
life on another planet	societies made up of animals

2. Abandon Skepticism

Skepticism is doubt. If you want to really enjoy science fiction and fantasy, you have to leave your skepticism behind and agree to enter the world the author has created for you. If this sounds like a contradiction of the first tip, realize that you are willingly and knowingly abandoning your doubt so that you can enjoy the story.

3. Consider the Author's Message

Many science fiction writers are philosophers who tell us about what might or could happen. Early authors of sci-fi told of fantastic voyages into space—something like the space shuttle, whose frequent journeys into space are now taken for granted. Ray Bradbury's *Fahrenheit 451* (written in 1953) paints a world where all forms of media take great care not to offend anyone, where books are burned, and where people watch interactive televisions that take up entire walls while their brains are numbed by comforting drugs. When you read science fiction or fantasy, consider examining some ideas and opinions you may not have reflected much on before.

Exercise 10.7 Practice the Reading Strategy: Know Your Genre

Read the brief description of each story. Then indicate whether it is most likely regular fiction, science fiction, or fantasy by writing FIC, SF, or FAN.

_____ 1. *The Hitchhiker's Guide to the Galaxy* by Douglas Adams. Just before Earth is demolished, Arthur Dent is snatched from the planet and his adventures in the galaxy begin.

_____ 2. *The Postman* by David Brin. After a devastating war, a man travels from group to group telling stories.

_____ 3. *Red Sea* by Diane Tullson. Libby is on a yearlong sailing trip with her parents when disaster strikes. It is up to Libby to reach land and safety on her own.

_____ 4. *The Seeing Stone* by Kevin Crossley-Holland. A young man named Arthur lives in England in the year 1199. His life is changed completely when his friend Merlin gives him a magic stone.

_____ 5. *The Secret Under My Skin* by Janet Elizabeth McNaughton. Blay lives in a rigid society in the twenty-fourth century. She tutors a "bio-indicator," a person who is sensitive to environmental degradation, and joins a group of rebels.

_____ 6. *Redwall* by Brian Jacques. The mice that live at Redwall Abbey enjoy a peaceful life until the rats attack. Matthias Mouse must find the legendary Sword of Martin the Warrior in order to defeat their leader.

_____ 7. *The Giver* by Lois Lowry. Jonas becomes the receiver of memories in the society in which he lives—which proves not to be the perfect place he thought it was.

_____ 8. *Eragon: Inheritance* by Christopher Paolini. Eragon finds a blue stone in the forest and hopes he can sell it to buy food for his family. The stone turns out to be a dragon's egg, and when it hatches, Eragon's life changes forever.

_____ 9. *Zach's Lie* by Roland Smith. Zach is beginning to adjust to the life his family has made under the Witness Protection Program, but the drug cartel against which his father will testify is determined to track them down.

_____ 10. *Watership Down* by Richard Adams. Fiver, a rabbit, has a premonition that the warren where he lives with his family will be destroyed. He convinces them to leave, and they venture out in search of a new home.

Exercise 10.8 Apply the Strategy to Your Own Reading

Following is a list of popular science fiction and fantasy stories. Some have been made into films. Check off the ones you have read or seen. Choose one and write a summary of it (like the ones in the previous exercise). If you have not read any of these books or seen a film version, write a summary of another sci-fi or fantasy story with which you are familiar.

☐ *Tuck Everlasting* by Natalie Babbitt

☐ *Indian in the Cupboard* by Lynne Reid Banks

☐ *The Martian Chronicles* by Ray Bradbury

☐ *When the Tripods Came* by John Christopher

☐ *James and The Giant Peach* by Roald Dahl

☐ *This Star Shall Abide* by Sylvia Louise Engdahl

☐ *Midnight Horse* by Sid Fleischman

☐ *Children of Morrow* by H. M. Hoover

☐ *Hoot* by Carl Hiassen

☐ *Invitation to the Game* by Monica Hughes

☐ *Alien Secrets* by Annette Curtis Klause

☐ *The Dispossessed* by Ursula Le Guin

☐ *The Giver* by Lois Lowry

☐ *A Wrinkle in Time* by Madeleine L'Engle

☐ *Swiftly Tilting Planet* by Madeleine L'Engle

☐ *Mrs. Frisby and the Rats of NIMH* by Robert O'Brien

☐ *Z for Zachariah* by Robert O'Brien

☐ Harry Potter series by J. K. Rowling

☐ *Interstellar Pig* by William Sleator

☐ *The Hobbit* by J. R. R. Tolkien

☐ *The Lord of the Rings* trilogy by J. R. R. Tolkien

☐ *Dragon Steel* by Laurence Yep

Summary of _____:

_____

_____

_____

_____

If you enjoy science fiction and fantasy, take this list and the one in Exercise 10.7 with you the next time you go to the library and check out the ones you haven't read!

Writing Workshop
Using Your Imagination

Both science fiction and fantasy writers must call on their imaginations to create the setting, characters, and events in their stories. They look at what exists. Then they ask "but *what if?*" That is where imagination comes in.

- *What if* that egg in your refrigerator hatches and there's a baby dinosaur jumping around inside when you open the door?

- *What if* those moles that are tearing up your yard are involved in some sort of ancient power struggle?

- *What if* that house on the corner really is haunted?

While "regular" fiction authors use imagination to create stories that are probable, science fiction writers often use imagination to create stories that are possible, even if only very remotely so. Imagination comes in when the writer considers the possibilities he or she will include in the story.

Ernest Callenbach knew that at the time he wrote *Ecotopia*, northern California, Oregon, and Washington were leading the country in environmental awareness and legislation. He asked himself, "What if they joined together, seceded from the U.S., and formed their own country, dedicated to preserving and protecting the natural world? What would life be like in this new place? How would people get around? How would they act? What would they eat? What things would be banned?"

The answers to all of these questions came from Callenbach's imagination.

Exercise 10.9 Practice the Writing Lesson: What If?

Complete the following sentences by stretching your imagination and asking "what if?" The first one has been done for you.

1. You're in your room, working hard to solve your math problems, when
   you suddenly hear a small squeaky voice in the corner saying,
   "The answer to number 7 is 24 percent."

2. You're walking home from the mall with your friends one day, and

   _____

   _____

   _____

3. You're sitting at your computer one evening when you get an instant message that

   _____

   _____

   _____

4. A friend from summer camp gave you a small, beautiful stone at the end of camp. One day when you feel a little lonely for your camp friends, you put the stone in your pocket and

   _____

   _____

   _____

5. You are annoyed that you had to get braces on your teeth, but one day when it's very quiet you realize there is something very special about them. They

   _____

   _____

   _____

Exercise 10.10 Apply the Writing Lesson

Choose one of the situations you created in the previous exercise, or create a new fantasy or science fiction situation of your own. Turn it into a short story. Use your imagination to create the characters. Add details such as what they eat, where they sleep, and who their enemies are. For inspiration, look back at the table of common themes on page 224.

Grammar Mini-Lesson
Reducing Repetition

Ernest Callenbach writes:

> On board the Sierra Express, Tahoe–San Francisco, May 4, I have now entered Ecotopia—the first known American to visit the new country since its Independence, 19 years ago.

He avoids using "Ecotopia" twice, and uses "the new country" instead. This not only creates variety in his sentence; it also gives the reader extra information: Ecotopia is a new country.

In general, it's best not to use the same word or two different forms of the same word in one sentence or in two consecutive sentences. For example:

> We just couldn't believe it had happened. It was unbelievable.

There is no point in stating "It was unbelievable" because you're just repeating what you've already said (We . . . couldn't believe . . .). Use a different word, or give some additional information. For example:

> We just couldn't believe it had happened. It was inconceivable that the television had blown up right before our eyes. Maybe our parents are right. Maybe we shouldn't watch that show!

Exercise 10.11 Practice Reducing Repetition

Replace the italicized repeated word with a suitable synonym. The first one has been done for you.

1. Were you able to see well? I thought it would be hard to view the action from the seat I had, but I was able to *see* everything.
   <u>observe</u>

2. The president obviously was eager for the press conference to end, but the journalists continued to ask questions. Finally he called on a reporter to *ask* the last one. _____

3. She claimed the she was visiting to learn about our club. Was that her true purpose, or did she have some other *purpose* in mind? _____

4. He still has good vision and a keen mind, but his hearing is not as *keen* as it used to be. _____

5. What a fine mind you have! No one else could have imagined a more brilliant idea than yours. I could never have *imagined* it.
   _____

Exercise 10.12 Apply the Lesson to Revise a Paragraph

Read the paragraph and answer the questions that follow.

> Then something inconceivable happened—the umpire reversed his decision. You can easily conceive how this enraged the fans—they just could not stop booing. Though their rage was slow to cool, they eventually quieted down, the stadium slowly returned to normal, and we went on to lose the game. Obviously, the upsetting decision made a deep impression on many of the fans and players. They were deeply troubled by it, and it is still troubling some of them.

1. The word *conceive* repeats a part of *inconceivable*. What word can replace *conceive*?

   _____

2. What can replace *rage* (line 3), which is too much like *enraged* (line 2)?

   _____

3. What can replace *slowly* (line 4), which is too much like *slow* (line 4)?

   _____

4. What can replace *deeply* (line 7), which is too much like *deep* (line 6)?

   _____

5. What can replace *troubling* (line 8), which is too much like *troubled* (line 7)?

   _____

Polish Your Spelling

Troublesome Consonants

A **consonant** is a letter other than the vowels *a*, *e*, *i*, *o*, and *u*. (Sometimes *y* is a consonant, and sometimes it is a vowel.) One of the most common spelling mistakes occurs in words with more than one consonant, especially when they are both to be doubled or when one consonant is doubled and the other is single. We call these "troublesome consonant" words.

Fortunately, you can study these words in groups. The words in each group follow the same pattern.

1. THE 2 + 2 GROUP: DOUBLE-DOUBLE

Every word in this group has a troublesome *doubled* consonant followed by another troublesome *doubled* consonant.

Examples: emba*rr*a*ss*   mi*ss*pe*ll*   po*ss*e*ss*

2. THE 2 + 1 GROUP: DOUBLE-SINGLE

Every word in this group has a troublesome *doubled* consonant followed by another troublesome *single* consonant.

Examples: o*cc*a*s*ion   bu*ll*e*t*in   a*pp*a*r*el

3. THE 1 + 2 GROUP: SINGLE-DOUBLE

Every word in this group has a troublesome *single* consonant followed by another troublesome *doubled* consonant.

Examples: ne*c*e*ss*ary   re*c*o*mm*end   she*r*i*ff*

Exercise 10.13 Practice Spelling Words with Troublesome Consonants

Put each of the following words into its proper group.

buffalo   tariff   Tennessee   aggression   accumulate

satellite   tomorrow   occasional   obsession   beginning

access   apparel   committee   assassinate   vaccination

2 + 2	2 + 1	1 + 2

Chapter Eleven

Prereading Guide
Words to know and ideas to consider before you jump into the reading.

A. Essential Vocabulary

Word	Meaning	Typical Use
defile (*v*) dee-FILE	to pollute or corrupt; contaminate	The wooded pasture was *defiled* by the developers who cut down the trees for the new housing development.
feverish (*adj*) FEEV-ur-ish	agitated or anxious; excited	Mrs. Nichols was *feverish* as she dialed the shopping network, hoping she would not miss out on the Everything Gizmo.
glacier (*n*) GLAY-shur	a large mass of compressed frozen water that formed on land; ice field	As *glaciers* recede, more land becomes visible and there is more water in the oceans.
handiwork (*n*) HAN-dee-wurk	something made by hand; craft	My great grandfather's *handiwork* can still be seen in the hand-turned legs of our dining room table.
headlong (*adj*) HED-long	in a sudden and unexpected manner; headfirst	One minute Pookie was standing there wagging her tail; the next, she had plunged *headlong* into the lake.
immutable (*adj*) ih-MEWT-uh-bul	not subject to variation; changeless	Gravity is an example of one of the *immutable* laws of science.
indifferent (*adj*) in-DIFF-ur-unt	showing little or no concern; uninterested	The squirrels in our yard are *indifferent* to us, not realizing that we fill the bird feeder they raid every day.
miserly (*adj*) MIZE-ur-lee	hoarding money and not generous with it; stingy	Although my uncle has more money than anyone in the family, he is *miserly* when it comes to giving gifts.

Word	Meaning	Typical Use
progeny (*n*) PRAH J-uh-nee	a person's immediate descendants; offspring	My mom says if one of her *progeny* becomes a concert pianist, her dream will be fulfilled.
ruinous (*adj*) ROO-in-us	harmful or damaging; destructive	The strong winds were *ruinous*, toppling trees and ripping off roofs.

B. Vocabulary Practice

Exercise 11.1 Sentence Completion

Using your new vocabulary knowledge, choose the best way to complete the following sentences. Circle the letter of your answer.

1. We should _____; we shouldn't go headlong into it.
   A. just do it
   B. think this through

2. My grandmother does beautiful handiwork. Here is

   _____.
   A. a sweater she made me
   B. her favorite mop

3. I invited him to our party, and he looked indifferent, as if

   _____.
   A. he'd be delighted to come
   B. he was uninterested in joining us

4. Some people feel that _____ defiles the body.
   A. a tattoo
   B. exercise

5. The ruinous _____ of the 1930s produced terrible dust storms that devastated crops.
   A. droughts
   B. rain storms

6. We worked feverishly to finish painting the room because

   _____.
   A. there was no air-conditioning
   B. our guests were arriving in a few hours

7. The Bill of Rights lists civil liberties that most of us consider immutable, or not _____.
   A. subject to change
   B. set in stone

8. Their _____ live everywhere from California to Maine; their progeny are widespread.
   A. second cousins
   B. children

9. "Don't be miserly with that cake," said my dad, "because there is _____."
   A. not much of it
   B. plenty to go around

10. I certainly am glad I was wearing my _____ when we explored the glacier.
    A. new sandals
    B. warm coat

Exercise 11.2 Using Fewer Words

Replace the italicized words with a single word from the following list.

defilement	feverishly	glacier	handiwork	headlong
indifferently	immutable	miser	progeny	ruinous

1. *Corruption and pollution* of rivers by industry was commonplace in America for centuries.

   1._____

2. Before the coach blew the whistle, Jake dove *in a sudden and unexpected manner* into the pool.

   2._____

3. Her eating habits are *harmful and damaging* to her health.

   3._____

4. Inertia, Newton's first law of motion, is *not subject to variation.*

   4._____

5. Despite her limited income, my grandma could never be called a(an) *person who hoards money or is not generous.*

   5._____

6. My grandparents' *immediate descendants* total 14 people.

   6._____

7. When an iceberg falls from a *large mass of compressed frozen water*, the crash and splash are amazing.

   7._____

8. For the craft sale you are supposed to bring *something made by hand* that you did yourself.

   8._____

9. "I don't care one way or the other," she said, *showing no concern.*

   9._____

10. I scanned the room *with agitation and anxiety* to see if I could find the one person I hoped would be there.

    10._____

Exercise 11.3 Synonyms and Antonyms

Fill in the blanks in column A with the required synonyms or antonyms, selecting them from column B. (Remember: A *synonym* is a word *similar* in meaning to another word. An *antonym* is a word *opposite* in meaning to another word.)

	A	B
_____	1. synonym for *ice field*	defile
_____	2. synonym for *craft*	feverish
_____	3. synonym for *destructive*	immutable
_____	4. antonym for *interested*	handiwork
_____	5. synonym for *offspring*	headlong
_____	6. antonym for *generous*	indifferent
_____	7. synonym for *changeless*	glacier
_____	8. antonym for *calm*	miserly
_____	9. synonym for *headfirst*	progeny
_____	10. antonym for *purify*	ruinous

C. Journal Freewrite

Before you begin the reading on the next page, take out a journal or sheet of paper and spend some time responding to the following prompt.

TIP: Don't worry about grammar and spelling; just write what comes to mind. The purpose of freewriting is to explore ideas, not to produce a polished work.

> Some people believe that human beings are on a steady course of using up all the planet's resources—that we will "ruin our own backyard" and no longer be able to survive. What do you see in the future of your world? Why?

Almanac

by Primo Levi

About the Author
**Primo Levi
(1919–1987)** was born in Turin, Italy. He studied to become a chemist, but during World War II was arrested for opposing Mussolini's anti-Semitic Fascist regime. He was deported to Auschwitz, a German concentration camp. Freed in 1945, he returned to Turin and lived in the building his family had occupied for three generations. He managed a paint factory until 1977, when he retired and became a full-time writer. He spent his life trying to deal with the guilt of surviving the Holocaust. He had been spared so the Nazis could use his knowledge of chemistry. His experiences in the concentration camp and in his travels around Europe after the war are often the subject of his memoirs, fiction, and poetry. His cynical view of human beings' effect on the natural world is reflected in "Almanac."

The <u>indifferent</u> rivers
Will keep on flowing to the sea
Or <u>ruinously</u> overflowing dikes,
Ancient <u>handiwork</u> of determined men.
The <u>glaciers</u> will continue to grate,
Smoothing what's under them
Or suddenly fall <u>headlong</u>,
Cutting short fir trees' lives.
The sea, captive between
Two continents, will go on struggling,
Always <u>miserly</u> with its riches.
Sun stars planets and comets
Will continue on their course.
Earth too will fear the <u>immutable</u>
Laws of the universe.
Not us. We, rebellious <u>progeny</u>
With great brainpower, little sense,
Will destroy, <u>defile</u>
Always more <u>feverishly</u>.
Very soon we'll extend the desert
Into the Amazon forests,
Into the living heart of our cities,
Into our very hearts.

Understanding the Reading

Complete the next three exercises and see how well you understood "Almanac."

Exercise 11.4 Multiple-Choice Questions

Answer the following questions about the reading. Circle the letter of your answer.

TIP: Don't try to answer the questions from memory; go back to the text as often as necessary.

1. Lines 1–4 imply that
   A. rivers are different from seas.
   B. nature is a more powerful force than human beings.
   C. our ancestors shouldn't have built dikes.
   D. dikes ruin the landscape.

2. The meaning of *grate* (line 5) can be defined in this context as
   A. scrape.
   B. famous.
   C. large.
   D. good feeling.

3. Lines 5–8 reinforce the idea that
   A. glaciers are ruining the earth.
   B. forests are in danger of being mowed down.
   C. the earth is in a continuous cycle of change.
   D. nature is predictable.

4. Lines 9–11 indicate that the speaker
   A. feels sorry for the sea.
   B. is a disappointed fisherman.
   C. has given up the idea of finding sunken treasure.
   D. thinks the world's oceans are in trouble.

5. The lines "Earth too will fear the immutable/Laws of the universe"
   A. threaten the readers of this poem with personal disaster.
   B. give our planet human qualities.
   C. show that humans have little common sense.
   D. show that Earth is basically cruel.

Exercise 11.5 Short-Answer Questions

Respond to the following questions in one to two complete sentences. Go back to the text, as you did on the multiple choice.

6. The poet says the human beings (". . . we, rebellious progeny") have "great brainpower, little sense." Explain how you think a person can have both.

   _____

   _____

   _____

7. How would you describe Primo Levi's tone in this poem? Which words or phrases best express it?

   _____

   _____

   _____

8. Why do you think the poet included the image of a desert extended "into our very hearts"? What might this metaphor mean?

   _____

   _____

   _____

9. Which line(s) of this poem struck you the most? Why?

   _____

   _____

   _____

Exercise 11.6 Extending Your Thinking

Respond to the following question in three to four complete sentences. Use details from the text in your answer.

10. Is Primo Levi's vision of our planet's future similar to how *you* imagine our future world? Why or why not?

    _____

    _____

    _____

    _____

    _____

Reading Strategy Lesson
Words with More Than One Meaning

One of the more confusing things about the English language is that many of our words have more than one meaning. In the course of reading, you may frequently come across a familiar word that does not seem to make sense in the sentence.

For example:

"The glaciers will continue to *grate*."

If the only meaning you know for *grate* is the noun meaning "a grid or grill covering an opening," then this line could be a mystery to you. If you know that *grate* also means "scrape," the meaning of the line is quite clear. The glaciers scrape the land.

That's not all, though. *Grate* can also mean to annoy or irritate: "That jackhammer is really *grating* on my nerves." Grate can be a sound: The *grate* of her teeth was audible. And of course, if you are making a salad you might want to *grate* some carrots for it. Do you have a fireplace? Then you probably have a *grate* to hold the logs above the bottom.

Here is another example of a phrase from "Almanac" with words that have multiple meanings:

"Sun stars planets and comets"

It isn't difficult to tell which kind of stars the poet refers to here. They are the ones in the skies, of course, along with the sun, planets, and comets. How many other meanings can you think of for the word *star*?

There are *stars* in every field: movies, music, sports, science, academics, and more. Remember the little *gold stars* you got on your chart in grade school because you did well? There are *stars* on the U.S. flag as well as on the flags of some states and other countries. A horse with a white patch on his face is often said to have a *star*. You have probably been told to push the *star key* on a telephone. You might *star* key words in your notes, *star* in a play, be *starry-eyed* with love, or *see stars* if you bump your head. If you've ever read your horoscope, you've checked to see *what's in your stars*. Can you think of any others?

When you run across a familiar word used in an unfamiliar way, you can use context clues to determine its meaning or you can look it up. Either way, the next time you see it used in this second (or third, or fourth) way, you'll recognize which meaning the author intends and your comprehension will improve.

Exercise 11.7 Practice the Reading Strategy

The following words should be familiar to you in at least one sense. In column A, write the first meaning that comes to mind. In column B, write another meaning for the word. The first one has been done for you.

Word	A	B
1. retired	no longer working	not used anymore, like an athlete's number
2. pass		
3. charge		
4. trip		
5. bank		
6. study		
7. file		
8. check		
9. sign		
10. watch		

Exercise 11.8 Apply the Reading Strategy

In each sentence, a familiar word has a meaning that is probably not the first one you think of. On the blank line, write a brief definition or synonym of the italicized word as it is used in the sentence. Try to determine the word's meaning from context, but look it up if you need to.

1. We need to *draft* some preliminary plans for the yearbook.

   _____

2. I think Andrew is trying to *skirt* the question of whether or not he passed the test.

   _____

3. She held him *fast*, as if she would never let him go.

   _____

4. She has a very *dry* sense of humor.

   _____

5. He was the best *center* the basketball team had ever had.

   _____

6. This hot pepper sauce really has a *kick* to it.

   _____

7. Can you read this *copy* once more before we go to press?

_____

8. Visiting the Statue of Liberty was a *peak* experience.

_____

9. The *report* of the cannon was deafening.

_____

10. We had some trouble getting up the steep *grade* because the road was icy.

_____

Writing Workshop
Incorporating Direct Quotations

One way to make your essays more interesting and effective is to use quotations from the story, article, or other selection about which you are writing. Question 7 in Exercise 11.5 asks:

> How would you describe Primo Levi's tone in this poem? Which words or phrases best express it?

This question asks you to give an answer and then find evidence for it. That means you should look for some lines in the poem that you can quote directly. These will be your evidence. An answer to this question might read:

> In "Almanac," Primo Levi's tone is very cynical about the future of the world. Human beings, he says, have "great brain-power, little sense," and "will destroy, defile always more feverishly." The last lines of the poem express Levi's cynical attitude the most chillingly when he describes the human-created desert slowly working its way across the earth and "into our very hearts," leaving them barren.

Keep in mind that it's not enough *just* to quote—you need to explain in your own words what you think the quotation means and how it helps support your argument.

How to Punctuate Quotations

- The title of a poem or short story is enclosed in quotation marks. (If you were quoting from a book you would underline the title if writing by hand, or italicize it if using a computer.)

- The quotation marks go only around material that is directly quoted from the work.

- Information from the work that is used as evidence in an essay question but is not directly quoted should not be enclosed in quotation marks.

Example:

> The last lines of the poem express Levi's cynical attitude the most chillingly when *he describes the human-created desert slowly working its way across the earth* and "into our very hearts," leaving them barren.

The italicized words paraphrase these lines of the poem:

> Very soon we'll extend the desert
> Into the Amazon forests,
> Into the living heart of our cities,

In other words, they restate what the poet said. Since we are not quoting his exact words, no quotation marks are needed.

Exercise 11.9 Practice Punctuating Direct Quotations

Read the following paragraph and insert quotation marks where necessary.

> Glaciers can be dangerous places. They have deep narrow troughs in them called crevasses that you can fall into before you realize what is happening. People who explore glaciers usually do so in groups with everyone roped together in case someone falls into a crevasse. In his poem Almanac, Primo Levi makes glaciers sound like bad news for Earth. He speaks of how they will continue to grate, smoothing what's under them. It's true that large pieces of glaciers calve or break off, but Levi makes this sound like a disaster. For him, they suddenly fall headlong, cutting short fir trees' lives.

Exercise 11.10 Apply the Writing Lesson

Answer the following questions using at least one direct quotation from the poem and one piece of information that is not a direct quotation but still offers evidence for your answer.

In "Almanac," what evidence can you find that Primo Levi has a skeptical view of human beings?

_____

_____

_____

_____

_____

_____

Grammar Mini-Lesson

Using Appositives

An **appositive** is a noun or phrase placed right next to another noun that gives additional information about that noun. Read the following examples. The italicized phrases are appositives.

> Mr. Roberts, *the new principal of our school*, is very strict.

> *Best eaten hot*, pizza is a delicious Italian pie.

> Hallie left the party early, *feeling unwell*.

Punctuating Appositives

An appositive is set off from the rest of the sentence by commas.

- If the appositive is within the sentence, it is set off by two commas, one before it and one after it.

  > Mr. Nigari, *who has a 24-hour emergency service*, fixed the leak quickly.

  > Sunspots, *discovered in the eighteenth century*, are just now beginning to be understood.

- If the appositive comes at the beginning of the sentence, it needs one comma after it.

  > *Not having listened to the directions*, we were soon lost.

  > *Encouraged to talk about their problems*, many teens still won't open up.

- If the appositive comes at the end of the sentence, it needs one comma before it.

  > Michael stayed at the learning lab late, *studying for his Spanish test*.

  > Many common household chemicals are dangerous, *such as bleach and ammonia*.

- No commas are used when the appositive is so closely associated with the noun it explains that the two are pronounced with no pause between them.

  > *My stepdad John took me to see the Lions play.*

  > *My friend Jorge wants to be a teacher.*

Why Use Appositives?

Using appositives can help you add details about the people or things you are describing. They can also help you combine your sentences, and can give your writing a more polished sound and feel. Study these examples to see how you can use appositives to combine sentences:

Kudzu is a creeping vine. It chokes out other plants.

Kudzu, a creeping vine, chokes out other plants.

Primo Levi survived the Holocaust. He spent his life feeling tremendous guilt.

Having survived the Holocaust, Primo Levi spent his life feeling tremendous guilt.

We went to Disney World for vacation. We enjoyed ourselves a lot.

We went to Disney World for vacation, enjoying ourselves a lot.

Annie is my dog. She barks at strangers.

My dog Annie barks at strangers.

Exercise 11.11 Practice Punctuating Appositives

Rewrite each sentence, inserting all necessary punctuation.

1. Slinky my friend's cat chases dragonflies.

   _____

2. I was sent to Room 214 a portable classroom.

   _____

3. Ivan the Terrible was a ruthless dictator.

   _____

4. The hibiscus a tropical plant has beautiful blooms.

   _____

5. Didn't my sister Maria tell you I was back home?

   _____

Exercise 11.12 Practice Using Appositives to Combine Sentences

Use an appositive to combine each pair of sentences into a single sentence.

Example: James rides a motorbike. He is the boy with the red shirt.

James, the boy with the red shirt, rides a motorbike.

1. Gabrielle hurt her knee. She is our best goalie.

   _____

2. Ray Bradbury wrote *Fahrenheit 451*. It's my favorite novel.

   _____

3. The firefighters and volunteers got the forest fire under control. They worked all night.

   _____

4. The next course was lasagna. It was the main dish.

   _____

5. Mahatma Gandhi influenced millions of people. He was a gifted leader.

   _____

6. Next week we will play the Spartans. They are an undefeated team.

   _____

7. Honeybear brushed against my knee. He is my friend's dog.

   _____

8. In Michigan we went to Mackinac Island. There is an old fort on the island.

   _____

9. The string ensemble will probably play something by Bach. He is their favorite composer.

   _____

10. Yoga is a relaxing yet energizing exercise. Many people are studying it.

   _____

Polish Your Spelling

Forming Compound Words

A **compound word** is formed from two or more words joined together.

Note that a compound word usually keeps all the letters of the words from which it is formed.

some + one = someone

team + mate = teammate

none + the + less = nonetheless

English is a constantly evolving language. That means that the spelling of words can change. For instance, *base ball* became *base-ball* and then *baseball*. *Post mark* became *post-mark* and then *post-mark*. That is why you may have seen compound words spelled as two single words or with a hyphen in older books. If you are unsure of how to spell a compound word, consult an up-to-date dictionary.

Exercise 11.13 Practice Spelling Compound Words

One word on each line is spelled incorrectly. Find the misspelled word and write it correctly on the line.

1. salesclerk, roomate, gentlemen   _____

2. doornob, passageway, peacekeeper   _____

3. anyone, hankerchief, toothache   _____

4. homesick, bookeeper, courthouse   _____

5. driveway, nowhere, somone   _____

6. hereafter, teamate, heartbroken   _____

7. heretofore, homade, classmate   _____

8. seasick, businesman, everyone   _____

9. housekeeper, textbook, dumbell   _____

10. timekeeper, extrordinary, rainstorm   _____

Chapter Twelve

Prereading Guide
Words to know and ideas to consider before you jump into the reading.

A. Essential Vocabulary

Word	Meaning	Typical Use
bestow (*v*) be-STOH	to present as an honor; confer	The superintendent *bestowed* a trophy on our coach when our team won the playoff tournament.
devise (*v*) de-VIZE	to formulate or come up with; invent	Bill Gates *devised* a way for people to use computers easily.
enamored (*adj*) ee-NAM-urd	characterized by unreasoning fondness; infatuated	She is totally *enamored* with celebrities, and their pictures cover her bedroom walls.
ferocity (*n*) fur-OSS-ih-tee	fierceness or turbulence; violence	Jada's dog's *ferocity* is all a bluff, but most people still won't go on her property.
intelligible (*adj*) in-TEL-ih-juh-bul	clear and easy to comprehend; understandable	This essay is very *intelligible* and makes a lot of good points.
representation (*n*) rep-re-zen-TAY-shun	a picture, poem, or other work of art; portrayal	Leonardo's *representation* of "The Last Supper" is readily identifiable by millions of people.
reverenced (*adj*) REV-runsd	admired and held in highest esteem; worshipped	Most religions have one higher power who is *reverenced*.
similitude (*n*) sim-ILL-uh-tood	similarity in appearance; counterpart	The law of similarity causes us to link objects in our visual fields that bear *similitude* to one another.
stigma (*n*) STIG-muh	a mark of disgrace or shame; dishonor	He always lived with the *stigma* of being the son of a criminal because he was named after his father.
tedious (*adj*) TEED-ee-us	long and boring; tiresome	Before we can go out, I have the *tedious* task of cleaning up my room.

B. Vocabulary Practice

Exercise 12.1 Sentence Completion

Using your new vocabulary knowledge, choose the best way to complete the following sentences. Circle the letter of your answer.

1. My brothers are enamored with soccer; they _____.
   A. are tired of it
   B. play it all the time

2. The ferocity of the storm _____.
   A. stranded many people
   B. was a light shower in the afternoon

3. This representation of life on the Oregon Trail is done in _____.
   A. oils on canvas
   B. Nebraska

4. People often remark on the similitude between my sister and _____.
   A. her cat
   B. me

5. Early explorers often bestowed _____ on natives to win their friendship.
   A. treaties
   B. gifts

6. Don't stigmatize her for her _____.
   A. unfortunate mistake
   B. vision problems

7. It took me _____ to do my math homework; it was very tedious.
   A. two hours
   B. 20 minutes

8. The star of this movie is practically reverenced by _____.
   A. her admirers
   B. those who criticize her

9. I suggest you devise _____ to help you catch up on your homework.
   A. a friend
   B. a plan

10. His ideas are good, but his _____ is not intelligible.
    A. thought
    B. writing

Exercise 12.2 Using Fewer Words

Replace the italicized words with a single word from the following list.

bestow   devise   enamored   ferocity   intelligible

reverence   representations   similitude   stigma   tedious

1. I like to spend weekends looking at *pictures and other works of art* in museums and galleries.

    1._____

2. He gave a(an) *clear and easy to comprehend* explanation of his absence.

    2._____

3. The people spoke with *admiration and high esteem* about their spiritual leader.

    3._____

4. I found the lecture on the theory of relativity *long and boring*.

    4._____

5. We want to *present as an honor* a large bouquet of roses on the director of our play.

    5._____

6. There is a certain *similarity in appearance* between a computer desktop and a well-organized office.

    6._____

7. We need to *formulate or come up with* an outline of how we are going to conduct our club meetings.

    7._____

8. There was once a *mark of disgrace* associated with women who enjoyed sports, but that has fortunately passed.

    8._____

9. The *fierceness and turbulence* of her verbal attack was completely unexpected.

    9._____

10. I am *characterized by unreasoning fondness* with my new pug, Max.

    10._____

Exercise 12.3 Synonyms and Antonyms

Fill in the blanks in column A with the required synonyms or antonyms, selecting them from column B. (Remember: A *synonym* is a word *similar* in meaning to another word. An *antonym* is a word *opposite* in meaning to another word.)

	A	B
_____	1. antonym for *interesting*	bestow
_____	2. synonym for *invent*	enamored
_____	3. synonym for *portrayal*	intelligible
_____	4. antonym for *gentleness*	reverenced
_____	5. synonym for *infatuated*	representation
_____	6. synonym for *confer*	devise
_____	7. synonym for *worshipped*	ferocity
_____	8. synonym for *dishonor*	similitude
_____	9. antonym for *difference*	stigma
_____	10. synonym for *understandable*	tedious

C. Journal Freewrite

Before you begin the reading on the next page, take out a journal or sheet of paper and spend some time responding to the following prompt.

TIP: Don't worry about grammar and spelling; just write what comes to mind. The purpose of freewriting is to explore ideas, not to produce a polished work.

> How do different forms of art—paintings, drawings, photographs, sculptures, etc.—tell stories or express ideas differently?

Letter from Overseas

by Thomas Hart Benton

About the Artist
Thomas Hart Benton (1889–1975) was born in Missouri. In his teens, he worked as a newspaper cartoonist. Then he studied art and began a career as a painter. He became known as a regionalist—he painted mostly scenes of ordinary life in the Midwest.

Reader's Tip: This reading is not a written text but a visual one, a lithograph. *Lithography is a process of making prints with a flat metal surface that is treated to hold more ink in some areas than others, depending on the picture. This picture belongs to a genre known as* narrative art *because it has some elements of a narration, or story. As you "read" or study it, look at all of the details and try to imagine a possible story to go with the picture. Keep in mind the title,* Letter from Overseas, *and the date, 1943. Other words to know are* foreground *(the part of the picture closest to you) and* background *(the part that is farthest away).*

Understanding the Visual Text

Complete the following three exercises on *Letter from Overseas*.

Exercise 12.4 Multiple-Choice Questions

Answer the following questions about the lithograph. Circle the letter of your answer.

TIP: Don't try to answer the questions from memory; go back to the picture as often as necessary.

1. The time of day depicted in this picture is most likely
   A. very early in the morning.
   B. in the middle of the night.
   C. during the afternoon.
   D. either early evening or early morning.

2. All of the following are clues the letter is likely important to the girl *except*
   A. she didn't bother to close the mailbox.
   B. she doesn't get a lot of mail.
   C. someone in the background seems to be delivering messages.
   D. she brought a lantern to read it right at the mailbox.

3. Which word does *not* help describe the mood of the scene?
   A. urgent
   B. carefree
   C. hopeful
   D. uncertain

4. Benton's purpose for creating the lithograph was most likely to
   A. inform viewers about the war.
   B. entertain us with a haunting nighttime scene.
   C. tell a compelling story.
   D. depict a poor girl's life in a rural town.

Exercise 12.5 Short-Answer Questions

Respond to the following questions in one to two complete sentences. Go back to the lithograph, as you did on the multiple choice.

5. In 1943, people rarely made long-distance phone calls. No one had cell phones, computers, or televisions, and many people did not even have electricity. Think about these conditions and then draw a conclusion about the importance of the letter the girl is reading.

_____

_____

_____

6. Judging from the title and the time period of this piece, from whom might the letter be?

_____

_____

_____

7. Multiple-choice question 3 asked you to think about mood. Describe the mood in your own words, with evidence.

_____

_____

_____

Exercise 12.6 Extending Your Thinking

Respond to the following question in three to four complete sentences. Use details from the picture in your answer.

8. The theme of this unit is "Imagining a World." Because this lithograph is narrative art, it invites you to imagine the story behind the picture. Some questions you might ask as you look at the picture are, "Whom is the letter from?" "What does it say?" "Is this a young girl hiding the letter from her parents?" "Or is she a grown, married woman?" "What did she do just before she arrived at the mailbox?" "What will she do when she finishes reading the letter?" Study the picture with these questions in mind and write a summary of the story you imagine.

_____

_____

_____

_____

_____

_____

Journal Freewrite

Before you begin the second selection, take out a journal or sheet of paper and spend some time responding to a new prompt.

Suppose you read a poem about the experience of galloping across the countryside on a gorgeous horse. You also have a photograph of someone doing this action. Which form, the poem or the photograph, would you find more powerful? How does the format affect how you feel about or appreciate the moment depicted? Why?

from Notebooks

by Leonardo da Vinci

About the Author
Leonardo da Vinci
(1452–1519) lived in Italy during the Renaissance, a "golden age" when art and science flourished. He is still recognized as one of the greatest geniuses of all time. His interests were extremely diverse: He was an artist, an architect, an engineer, and a scientist. He designed weapons, forts, churches, and bridges. He drew detailed pictures of the human anatomy and wrote essays about the elements of mechanics, art, and science. He even sketched plans for a "flying machine" and a submarine—which would not become realities for four hundred years. In addition, he was a superlative artist, best known for the *Mona Lisa* and *The Last Supper*. His *Notebooks* are collections of his loose papers and notes that were put together after his death.

Reader's Tip: This selection may seem difficult the first time through. It might help you to first skim it. Then, go back and do a slower reading, rephrasing what the author has written and using the think-aloud technique to help you understand the main points of the essay.

How painting surpasses all human works by reason of the subtle possibilities which it contains.

The eye, which is called the window of the soul, is the principal means by which the central sense can most completely and abundantly appreciate the infinite works of nature; and the ear is the second, which acquires dignity by hearing the things the eye has seen. If you, historians, or poets, or mathematicians had not seen things with your eyes you could not report them in writing. And if you, poet, tell a story with your pen, the painter with his brush can tell it more easily, with simpler completeness and less <u>tedious</u> to understand. And if you call painting dumb poetry, the painter may call poetry blind painting. Now which is the worse defect—to be blind or dumb? Though the poet is as free as the painter in the invention of his fictions[1] they are not so satisfactory to men as paintings; for, though poetry is able to describe forms, actions, and places in words, the painter deals with the actual <u>similitude</u> of the forms, in order to represent them. Now tell me which is the nearer to the actual man: the name of man or the image of the man? The name of man differs in different countries, but his form is never changed but by death.

And if the poet satisfies the senses by means of the ear, the painter does so by the eye—the worthier sense; but I will say no more of this but that, if a good painter represents the fury of a battle, and if a poet describes one, and they are both together put before the public, you will see where most of the spectators will stop, to which they will pay most attention, on which they will <u>bestow</u> most praise, and which will satisfy

---

[1]imaginary representations of life, in words for the poet and in pictures for the painter

them best. Undoubtedly painting, being by a long way the more intelligible and beautiful, will please most. Write up the name of God in some spot and set up His image opposite and you will see which will be most reverenced.

Painting comprehends in itself [2] all the forms of nature, while you have nothing but words, which are not universal as form is, and if you have the effects of the representation, we have the representation of the effects. Take a poet who describes the beauty of a lady to her lover and a painter who represents her and you will see to which nature guides the enamored critic. Certainly the proof should be allowed to rest on the verdict of experience.

You have ranked painting among the mechanical arts but, in truth, if painters were as apt at praising their own works in writing as you are, it would not lie under the stigma of so base a name. If you call it mechanical because it is, in the first place, manual, and that it is the hand which produces what is to be found in the imagination, you too writers, who set down manually with the pen what is devised in your mind. And if you say it is mechanical because it is done for money, who falls into this error—if error it can be called—more than you? If you lecture in the schools do you not go to whoever pays you most? Do you do any work without pay? Still, I do not say this as blaming such views, for every form of labor looks for its reward. And if a poet should say: "I will invent a fiction with a great purpose," the painter can do the same, as Apelles painted Calumny.[3]

If you were to say that poetry is more eternal, I say the works of a coppersmith are more eternal still, for time preserves them longer than your works or ours; nevertheless they have not much imagination. And a picture, if painted on copper with enamel colors may be yet more permanent. We, by our arts may be called the grandsons of God. If poetry deals with moral philosophy, painting deals with natural philosophy. Poetry describes the action of the mind; painting considers what the mind may effect by the motions [of the body]. If poetry can terrify people by hideous fictions, painting can do as much by depicting the same things in action. Supposing that a poet applies himself to represent beauty, ferocity, or a base,[4] a foul or a monstrous thing, as against a painter, he may in his ways bring forth a variety of forms; but will the painter not satisfy more? Are there not pictures to be seen, so like the actual things, that they deceive men and animals?

---

[2] includes
[3] Apelles was a Greek painter who lived in the fourth century B.C. A jealous rival accused him of conspiracy, but Apelles was proved innocent. Out of revenge, he painted *Calumny*, which means "malicious lies and slander." The painting shows an innocent man being dragged before the king by figures representing Calumny, Malice, Fraud, Evil, Ignorance, and Suspicion. Off to the side are Remorse and Truth.
[4] immoral

Understanding the Reading

Complete the next three exercises and see how well you understood the excerpt from Leonardo's *Notebooks*.

Exercise 12.7 Multiple-Choice Questions

Answer the following questions about the reading. Circle the letter of your answer.

TIP: Don't try to answer the questions from memory; go back to the text as often as necessary.

1. What audience do you think Leonardo da Vinci had in mind for this essay?
    A. his art students
    B. poets
    C. architects
    D. mathematicians

2. Leonardo wrote that man's "form is never changed but by death" to point out that
    A. people speak different languages in different countries.
    B. poetry describes words and actions.
    C. painters need protection.
    D. visual forms like painting are understood everywhere and at all times.

3. What evidence does Leonardo give for his argument that the eye is a "worthier sense" than the ear?
    A. People are more attracted to visual images than to written ones.
    B. Most people can't read, so they are more impressed by pictures.
    C. Painting is more intelligible and beautiful.
    D. People are more interested in real battles than they are in poetry.

4. Leonardo says that both poetry and painting can be seen as "manual" because
    A. you can learn to do both at vocational school.
    B. neither one requires much imagination.
    C. painters use paint, poets use pens, and both use imagination.
    D. neither one pays very well.

Exercise 12.8 Short-Answer Questions

Respond to the following questions in one to two complete sentences. Go back to the text, as you did on the multiple choice.

5. Why do you think Leonardo da Vinci felt it was important or necessary to write this essay?

_____

_____

_____

6. What do you think Leonardo means by "Poetry describes the action of the mind; painting considers what the mind may effect by the motions [of the body]"?

_____

_____

_____

7. Do you agree with his opinion that painting is a better form of art than poetry? Why or why not?

_____

_____

_____

Exercise 12.9 Extending Your Thinking

Respond to the following question in three to four complete sentences.

8. If you read a poem or story about the girl in *Letter from Overseas* receiving the letter, rather than seeing the lithograph about it, how would it affect you differently?

_____

_____

_____

_____

_____

_____

Reading Strategy Lesson
"Reading" a Visual Text: Visual Literacy and Narrative Art

Visual Literacy

When we use the word *literacy*, we are usually referring to the ability to read and write. More and more, though, we are getting our information about the world from **visuals**. A visual can be just about anything that you look at: a cartoon, a weather map, pictures in print and on the Internet, graphs and maps, and paintings and photographs.

Leonardo da Vinci asks: "Are there not pictures to be seen, so like the actual things, that they deceive men and animals?" He would probably be amazed to see just how true that is in the twenty-first century with virtual reality technology, computer graphics, and even an average computer's photo-editing software.

When you looked at *Letter from Overseas*, you weren't just looking at a picture. You were looking at a "slice of life" from the mid-twentieth century. Benton may have been inspired by a real person and a real event, or the idea may have simply occurred to him, but his picture represents the emotion almost anyone feels when receiving a letter from someone important.

Likewise, the visuals that surround you every day are communicating meaning. You may mute the TV during commercials, yet the message still gets through because of the images you see on the screen. Music videos often narrate the stories that go with the songs. Political strategists like to catch opponents at their worst moments and use those pictures in negative advertising, while their own candidates are photographed at their very best. The paparazzi—photographers who relentlessly follow movie stars and other celebrities—shoot hundreds of pictures a day, hoping that one might make the front of a supermarket tabloid.

The Elements of Visuals

As we've said, there are many different types of visuals, but all share certain elements. First is what you see: circles, lines, shapes, and colors, with various shades and hues of those colors (even if the colors are black and white). Then there are things you see without necessarily realizing it, such as **light** and **shadow**. In addition to making visuals accurate, light and shadow create different moods. **Scale** is a way of showing objects in a visual in relation to one another. Sometimes scale is intentionally used to emphasize one thing over another. A final element of a visual is the viewer's **emotional response**, which might be very strong, nonexistent, or anywhere in between.

In *Letter from Overseas*, Benton used shades of black and white to create mood and to emphasize the important parts of his picture. He used **scale** to emphasize the woman in the foreground. The person and the car up on the hill are shadowy and seem less important.

Narrative Art

Narrative art suggests a story to its viewers. Since artists began drawing on cave walls, stories have documented human history.

Historical painting is a certain type of narrative art. Historical paintings depict scenes from events with which the viewer is probably already familiar. For example:

> *Washington Crossing the Delaware* by Emanuel Leutze
>
> *Daniel Boone Escorting Settlers Through the Cumberland Gap* by George Bingham
>
> *The Midnight Ride of Paul Revere* by Grant Wood

From the titles, you can probably imagine what the paintings look like. You can type in the titles as Internet search terms and view these paintings to see how close you came in your imagination to how they really look.

Genre painting is another type of narrative art. Genre painting shows scenes from everyday life. The people, animals, and scenes are common to many people. *Letter from Overseas* is an example of this type of narrative art. Some other examples are Eastman Johnson's *The Tea Party*, which shows a little girl sitting at a small table with her dolls and her tea set. In Martin Lewis's *Boss of the Block*, a large woman in an apron stands on the sidewalk looking down the street. Somehow the viewer just *knows* that the children on this street don't take any chances on disobeying this woman.

Exercise 12.10 Practice the Reading Strategy: Using Your Visual Imagination

Look at the following titles and imagine what is depicted in them. These are all real pictures from the genre form of narrative art. Write a brief description of what you would expect to see. (Don't just restate the title.) Then perform an Internet search to view the actual pictures and see how close you came.

1. *Doctor and Doll* by Norman Rockwell

I imagine this picture shows _____

_____

It actually shows _____

_____

2. *The Storybook* by Charles W. Hawthorne

I imagine this picture shows _____

_____

It actually shows _____

_____

3. *The Eavesdropper* by Eastman Johnson

I imagine this picture shows _____

_____

It actually shows _____

_____

4. *The Gulf Stream* by Winslow Homer

I imagine this picture shows _____

_____

It actually shows _____

_____

5. *Children Playing on the Beach* by Mary Cassatt

I imagine this picture shows _____

_____

It actually shows _____

_____

Exercise 12.11 Improving Your Visual Literacy

For the next few days, observe how often you are influenced by visuals. Then choose an example of narrative art that you find in a magazine, in a newspaper, or on the Internet, or you can even use a picture you take or draw yourself. It should be a picture that "tells a story." Prepare at least three questions about your visual that you can discuss with your class.

Writing Workshop

Avoiding Clichés

What Is a Cliché? (pronounced klee-SHAY)

We are all familiar with trite expressions, also called clichés, because we hear them constantly. When you hear or see the beginning of a cliché, you already know what the rest of it will be. For example, when you hear "Last but . . .," you can already fill in ". . . not least." If a friend is telling you a story, and says "Beyond the shadow of . . .," you automatically fill in ". . . a doubt."

When Leonardo da Vinci compared painting and poetry, he made a number of points to try to prove that his position was correct, and he expressed them in unique ways. For example, he wrote, "Write up the name of God in some spot and set up His image opposite and you will see which will be most reverenced." He found his own way of expressing the idea that "a picture is worth a thousand words."

Like lack of variety in sentence structure, writing that lacks uniqueness and is riddled with clichés is not likely to interest your reader for long. Clichés are so "expected" that you don't really hear them when you are listening or reading. Using vivid, unexpected phrases when you write makes your ideas seem fresh and keeps your reader involved with what you are trying to communicate.

Recognizing Clichés

To replace clichés, you must first recognize them. While there are thousands of clichés and trite expressions, here is a list to help you identify some of the most common ones.

hard as nails	at the drop of a hat
on the road to recovery	the ladder of success
raining cats and dogs	no problem
the bottom line	time to kill
at the crack of dawn	time and time again
been there, done that	hook, line, and sinker
nutty as a fruitcake	needless to say
off the beaten track	fame and fortune
I'd give my right arm	have a nice day

Exercise 12.12 Practice Recognizing Clichés

For each item, see if you can fill in the remainder of the cliché.

1. He's on a _____.

2. Hold your _____.

3. Don't throw the baby out with _____.

4. It's not what it's cracked _____.

5. A little bird _____.

6. Throw caution to the _____.

7. He's sharp as a _____.

8. I had them eating out of _____.

9. A penny for _____.

10. Has the cat got your _____?

Replacing Clichés

Looking back at Exercise 12.12, what new phrases could be used to replace the worn-out ones? That's where your imagination and creativity come in.

Example:
Instead of "He's on a roll," you might write, "He is amazingly, incredibly successful no matter what he does."

The next exercise has you practice creating fresh replacements for overused clichés.

Exercise 12.13 Apply the Writing Lesson to Improve Sentences

Rewrite each sentence, eliminating the cliché.

1. He's as wise as an old owl.

   _____

2. It looks like it's about to pour cats and dogs.

   _____

3. Jobs are scarce as hen's teeth in this town.

   _____

4. Time heals all wounds.

   _____

5. It looks like we're all in the same boat.

   _____

6. Don't make a mountain out of a molehill.

   _____

7. It's as plain as the nose on your face.

   _____

8. He really read us the riot act.

   _____

9. We're not going to sweep this under the rug.

   _____

10. She's got her head in the clouds.

    _____

Grammar Mini-Lesson
Commonly Misused Words

You've learned that many words have more than one meaning and that you can improve your reading comprehension by recognizing the meaning an author intends. Likewise, there are words whose meanings are often confused. You can improve your writing by being careful to use these words correctly.

One of the best ways to learn which words and phrases are correct is to notice them when you are reading or listening to a well-educated speaker (or one who has a good speechwriter!). For now, study the following table (continued on page 266) and then complete the exercises to practice and reinforce what you learn.

Commonly Misused Words	
accept, except	To *accept* is to agree to something or to receive something. *Except* means something is left out. *Except* can also be used in place of "but."
advice, advise	You *advise* someone. What you give him or her is *advice.*
a lot	This is two words. Do not spell it as one (alot).
allusion, illusion	An *allusion* is a reference to something. An *illusion* is a figment of your imagination.
among, between	*Among* refers to a group of three or more ("among the students in our class"). *Between* refers to two people or two groups ("between you and me").
beside, besides	*Beside* means "at the side of." *Besides* means "in addition to."
fewer, less	*Fewer* describes things that can be counted. (There are fewer than five shirts in my closet.) *Less* is used when referring to a quantity or degree of something. (I like him less and less.)
formerly, formally	*Formerly* means "before" or "previously." *Formally* means in a formal way. (Formerly people could not dress formally for weddings if they had only one set of clothes.)
further, farther	Use *farther* when comparing distances and *further* for anything else. (Brady can kick the ball farther than he ever has before. Now if only he would worry more about furthering his education.)

Commonly Misused Words	
hopefully	When you write, "Hopefully, the author will write another book soon," you're saying the author is full of hope. Instead, say, "I hope the author writes another book soon."
imply, infer	You *infer* something from what you read or hear. The writer or speaker is *implying* what you are *inferring.*
irregardless	Don't use this. Just use "regardless," or you will be writing the opposite of what you really mean.
proceed, precede	*Proceed* means "to go forward." *Precede* means "to go ahead of." (The faculty preceded the students as they all proceeded into the auditorium for graduation.)
that, which, who	Use *that* and *which* to refer to people or things, and *who* to refer only to people.
whether, weather	*Whether* is the word to use in phrases like "whether or not." *Weather* refers to things like rain, sunshine, and temperature.

Exercise 12.14 Practice Using the Correct Word

For each sentence, write in the correct word on the blank line.

1. I'd like to ask your (advise, advice) _____ about something.

2. What is the (whether, weather) _____ going to be like today?

3. (Hopefully, I hope) _____ we'll be able to go to the beach.

4. I'm not sure what you are trying to (imply, infer) _____.

5. (Regardless, Irregardless) _____, I'm not going out with him.

6. I like that boy (which, who) _____ sits behind me in math class.

7. (Proceed, precede) _____ with caution.

8. Writers are masters of (allusion, illusion) _____.

9. Don't worry, we never dress (formerly, formally) _____ when we go out.

10. There are (fewer, less) _____ calories in an apple than there are in a candy bar.

Exercise 12.15 Apply the Grammar Lesson to Edit a Paragraph

Read the following paragraph. Cross out each misused word and write in the correct one above it.

Allot of the time I have no idea what is going on in algebra class. I don't know weather I will ever get it. I precede to do the problems and hand in my homework. I keep thinking I'll get farther ahead that way even if my answers are wrong. Hopefully that will be enough so I will at least get an average grade, irregardless of my test scores. The teacher that we have is very nice. Just among the two of us, she inferred she would help me after school. I have no allusions that I'm a math whiz, but I would like to understand algebra better, so I think I will ask her to help me.

Polish Your Spelling
100 Spelling Demons

Nearly everyone has difficulty spelling certain words in the English language. That is why there is only one winner in the National Spelling Bee! The 100 words on the following list are among the most commonly misspelled words. Read the list. Then complete Exercise 12.16.

accidentally	accommodate	achieve	acknowledge
acquire	aerial	aggravate	appropriate
argument	assassin	athlete	bachelor
because	beginning	benefited	bureau
business	category	chaos	chief
colleagues	commemorate	commission	commitment
committee	comparative	compatible	competent
conscious	correspondence	courteous	criticism
desperate	deterrent	disappoint	disastrous
dissatisfied	efficient	eight	embarrass
environment	equipped	especially	essential

exception	exercise	extraordinary	fascinate
February	foreign	forty	friends
gauge	government	guardian	harass
height	history	hypocrisy	illiterate
illuminate	immediately	immigrant	incidentally
independent	Internet	irrelevant	irreparable
irresistible	judgment	knowledge	livelihood
maintenance	medicine	miniature	necessary
negotiable	neighbor	noticeable	occasional
occurrence	omission	parallel	privilege
rhythm	scholastic	scissors	seize
separate	strategy	tendency	truly
twelfth	unconscious	usually	valuable
view	Wednesday	weird	withhold

Exercise 12.16 Personal Spelling Demons

Go back over the list of spelling demons and circle the 20 words
with which you think you have the most trouble. Have a partner
read the words to you while you write them on a separate sheet of
paper. Then change places and test your partner. When you have
both finished, check your paper with the list to see how well you
did. Rewrite any words you missed and make them part of your
personal spelling list.

Unit Four Review

Vocabulary Review

A. Match each word with its definition.

	DEFINITION	WORD
_____	1. regarding government relations	a. handiwork
_____	2. clear and easy to comprehend	b. representation
_____	3. mass of compressed frozen water	c. investigative
_____	4. mark of disgrace or shame	d. reverenced
_____	5. harmful or destructive	e. intelligible
_____	6. a picture, poem, or work of art	f. glacier
_____	7. a person's immediate descendants	g. diplomatic
_____	8. relating to finding facts	h. stigma
_____	9. held in highest esteem	i. ruinous
_____	10. something made by hand	j. progeny

B. Match each word with its synonym.

	SYNONYM	WORD
_____	11. confer	a. tedious
_____	12. headfirst	b. enamored
_____	13. changeless	c. insinuate
_____	14. expand	d. portal
_____	15. tiresome	e. bestow
_____	16. gateway	f. immutable
_____	17. unheard-of	g. diversify
_____	18. infatuated	h. devise
_____	19. imply	i. unprecedented
_____	20. invent	j. headlong

C. Match each word with its antonym.

	ANTONYM	WORD
_____	21. uncertainty	a. candid
_____	22. purify	b. deter
_____	23. interested	c. feverish
_____	24. friendliness	d. ferocity
_____	25. difference	e. miserly
_____	26. gentleness	f. similitude
_____	27. encourage	g. antagonism
_____	28. generous	h. defile
_____	29. calm	i. indifferent
_____	30. rehearsed	j. assurance

Grammar Review

Each of the following sentences *may* or *may not* contain an error in a word or phrase that is underlined. Circle the letter of the error or, if there is no error, mark D.

1. *Future Shock* Alvin Toffler's amazing book, appeared in 1970.
                 A   B   C
   No change
      D

2. It was a controversial book in which Toffler was basically
                      A   B
saying to the world, "Wake up and smell the coffee."
  B   C
No change
     D

3. Toffler's definition of future shock was defined as a feeling that
                          A   B
there has been "too much change in too short a period of
                  C
time." No change
        D

4. He predicted that people would not be able to except the
        A   B
ever-increasing amount of technological and social change that
                            C
would become part of their everyday lives. No change
                                           D

5. <u>Toffler's premise</u> was that major social <u>problems would</u> result
            A   B

   from <u>"information overload" another</u> term he coined.
                       C

   <u>No change</u>
     D

6. Toffler <u>alluded to</u> some of the things <u>we take for granted</u>, like
           A   B

   home computers being <u>as common as Grandma at bingo</u>.
                             C

   <u>No change</u>
     D

7. He <u>maintained that, people</u> would become overwhelmed
               A

   <u>with the stress of trying</u> to deal with <u>lives that would be</u>
           B   C

   <u>changed</u> so quickly. <u>No change</u>
     C   D

8. *Future Shock,* <u>with</u> sales of over six million copies <u>and still</u>
            A   B

   <u>counting</u>, is still a fascinating book <u>to read today</u>. <u>No change</u>
     B   C   D

9. Many people would <u>agree that</u> Toffler accurately predicted the
                     A

   <u>results of technological</u> advances on our <u>society and</u> that future
           B   C

   shock is now a reality. <u>No change</u>
                     D

10. Many others would <u>say that</u> Toffler was <u>off his rocker</u> because
                   A   B

    he couldn't see <u>all the good things</u> that technological progress
                  C

    would bring to the world. <u>No change</u>
                        D

Spelling Review

Circle the misspelled word in each group. Write it correctly on the line.

1. embarrass, aparrel, recommend   _____

2. necesary, bulletin, occasion   _____

3. aggression, accumulate, assassanate   _____

4. satelite, buffalo, tomorrow   _____

5. bookkeeper, houskeeper, timekeeper _____

6. passageway, roomate, everyone _____

7. homemade, teammate, extrordinary _____

8. fascinate, rhythm, aquire _____

9. conscious, ommission, commitment _____

10. parallel, scissors, privelige _____

Writing Review

Choose one of the following topics. Plan your essay. Write your first draft. Then revise and edit your draft, and write your final essay. Be sure to identify your audience, purpose, and task before you begin planning.

Identify the three different genres used by the authors and artist in this unit. Compare and contrast the messages each one conveys. Which is the most entertaining? Which requires the most thought? Which two people would be the most likely to agree with one another?

OR

Each day you are surrounded by visual media: TV, movies, advertising, video games, signs and billboards with huge photos, and graffiti. Choose one of the media listed (or another to which you are frequently exposed) and analyze how it influences your emotions and/or actions.

SPEAK/LISTEN

A Call to Action

Ernest Callenbach's message about the future may be that human beings will have to learn to live simpler lives that are more in balance with the environment. Choose a nature-related issue that is currently in the news. It might be drilling somewhere for oil, or removing certain animals from the endangered species list. Research the issue and take a position. Find information to support your stance and refute (disprove) the opposition's view. Prepare a persuasive speech and read it to your class.

 EXPLORE

"Reading" a Picture

Choose one of the artists listed in Exercise 12.10. Research his or her life and visit an online museum to view more of the artist's work. Print out a picture you particularly like. Write a paragraph about the sensory messages of the picture. What do you see, hear, feel, touch, taste? If the picture is narrative art, what story do you think is behind it? If you prefer, you can write a poem to accompany the picture. (For an example, read Longfellow's *Midnight Ride of Paul Revere*, a poem that goes well with Grant Wood's painting by the same name.)

 WRITE

Continuing the Story

Think about Thomas Hart Benton's lithograph, *Letter from Overseas*. Write the letter the girl received, as well as her reply. Don't be afraid to use your imagination!
OR
Continue Weston's journal about Ecotopia with another entry about the time he spent there.

CONNECT

A Real Renaissance Man

In his *Notebooks*, Leonardo da Vinci concentrated on five main areas of thought: art, science, math, architecture, and human anatomy. Work in groups of five and assign each person one of these areas. Each person should research Leonardo's contribution to that area and write at least one paragraph summarizing his or her findings (include a copy of a sketch, painting, or other visual related to the topic, if possible). Share your discoveries with your other group members and then with the full class.

Acknowledgments

Grateful acknowledgment is made to the following sources for having granted permission to reprint copyrighted materials. Every effort has been made to obtain permission to use previously published materials. Any errors or omissions are unintentional.

"Loretta and Alexander." Excerpt from MOTHERS AND OTHER STRANGERS, copyright © 1996 by Budge Wilson, reprinted by permission of Harcourt, Inc. Page 7.

From HAPPY ALL THE TIME by Laurie Colwin, copyright © 1971, 1974, 1978 by Laurie Colwin. Used by permission of Alfred A. Knopf, a division of Random House, Inc. Page 31.

"Young Love: The Good, the Bad and the Educational." By Winifred Gallagher. Copyright © 2001 by the New York Times Co. Reprinted with permission. Page 52.

From MY FORBIDDEN FACE by Latifa. Translation by Linda Coverdale. Copyright © 2001 Éditions Anne Carrière. Reprinted by Permission of Miramax Books. Page 81.

"Diner" by Mary L. Dennis. Copyright © 2006 by Mary L. Dennis. Page 184.

From THE DEATH AND LIFE OF GREAT AMERICAN CITIES by Jane Jacobs, copyright © 1961 by Jane Jacobs. Used by permission of Random House, Inc. Page 101.

"Prologue," copyright © 1952 by Ralph Ellison, from INVISIBLE MAN by Ralph Ellison. Used by permission of Random House, Inc. Page 123.

From A VIEW FROM THE BRIDGE by Arthur Miller, copyright © 1955, 1957, renewed © 1983, 1985 by Arthur Miller. Used by permission of Viking Penguin, a division of Penguin Group (USA) Inc. Page 126.

From *Notes of a Native Son* by James Baldwin. Copyright © 1955, renewed 1983, by James Baldwin. Reprinted by permission of Beacon Press, Boston. Page 151.

From LETTERS TO A YOUNG POET by Rainer Maria Rilke, translated by Stephen Mitchell, copyright © 1984 by Stephen Mitchell. Used by permission of Random House, Inc. Page 171.

From "Interview with Amy Tan" by Jami Edwards. Used by permission of Bookreporter.com. Page 191.

From ECOTOPIA by Ernest Callenbach, copyright © 1975 by Ernest Callenbach. Used by permission of Bantam Books, a division of Random House, Inc. Page 217.

"Almanac" from COLLECTED POEMS by Primo Levi, translated by Ruth Feldman and Brian Swann. English translation copyright © 1988 by Ruth Feldman and Brian Swann. Reprinted by permission of Faber and Faber, Inc. an affiliate of Farrar, Straus and Giroux, LLC. Page 237.

Photo Credits

William Shakespeare © Stock Montage/Getty Images. Page 49.

James Baldwin © Peter Turnley/CORBIS. Page 151.

Amy Tan © Lawrence Lucier/Getty Images. Page 191.

Thomas Hart Benton © Alfred Eisenstaedt/Getty Images. Page 253.

Thomas Hart Benton, LETTER FROM OVERSEAS, Gift of John Nichols Estabrook and Dorothy Coogan Estabrook, Image © Board of Trustees, National Gallery of Art, Washington. Page 253.

Leonardo da Vinci © Time Life Pictures/Getty Images. Page 256.

Vocabulary Index

Subject Index

question-answer relation-
ships on multiple-
choice tests, 196–198
thinking aloud, 35–36
visual literacy, 259–260
words with more than one
meaning, 240
Repetition, reducing, 229
Restatements in defining
word, 14
Rhyme schemes, 51
"Right there" answers, finding, 196–197, 198
Rilke, Rainer Maria, 171

S

Scale, 260
Scanning, 198
Science fiction, 223–225
Semicolons, in forming com-
pound sentences, 41
Sentence combining, 40–41
Sentences
adjectives in, 22
adverbs in, 21–22
breaking down long, 56
complete, 21
complex, 64–65
compound, 40–41, 92
compound-complex, 92–93
topic, 133–134
transition, 158–160
Shadow, 260
Shakespeare, William, 49
Similes, 179
Simple predicate, 56, 57
Simple subject, 56, 57
Singular subject, 114
Singular verb, 114
Skepticism, abandoning, 224
Skimming, 198
"Sonnet 29" (Shakespeare),
49
Sonnets, rhyme scheme of, 51
Spelling
adding suffixes to words
ending in -y, 24
base words and deriva-
tives, 43–44
changing adjectives to
adverbs, 94–95
changing nouns into adjectives, 67
changing verbs into nouns,
138

changing verbs to adjec-
tives, 116
compound words, 247
homonyms, 163–164
ie or *ei*, 186
100 spelling demons,
267–268
troublesome consonants,
230–231
using -*able* and -*ible*,
203–204
Spider maps, 39, 90, 91
Subject, 21
plural, 114
simple, 56, 57
singular, 114
Subject-verb agreement,
113–114
Subordinating conjunctions,
64
Suffixes
adding, to words ending in
-*y*, 24
defined, 24
Synonyms, 6, 30, 48, 80, 100,
122, 150, 170, 190, 216,
236, 252

T

Tan, Amy, 191
Task, identifying, 18–19, 35
Tense, 184–185
Thesis statements, 110–111
formulating good, 110–111
"Think and search" questions,
197, 198
Thinking aloud, 35–36,
180–181
Third person point of view
limited, 87
omniscient, 86–87
Topic sentences, 133–134
Transitions, 158–160
to compare like ideas,
160
to contrast ideas, 160
to emphasize, 160
to enumerate, 160
to link thoughts, 160
to show cause and effect,
160
to show sequence, 160
to summarize, 160
Transition sentences,
158–160

V

Verbs, 21
active, 161–162
changing
to adjectives, 116
into nouns, 138
passive, 161–162
plural, 114
singular, 114
tense of, 184–185
View from the Bridge, A (Miller),
126–129
Viewpoints, 87–88
Visual literacy, 259–260
Visuals, 260
elements of, 260
Voice
active, 161–162
passive, 161–162

W

Wilson, Budge, 7
Words
compound, 247
focusing on most impor-
tant, 56, 57
misused, 265–266
with more than one mean-
ing, 240
Word-within-a-word clues, 15,
43
Writing workshops
avoiding clichés, 262–264
creating poetry, 183–184
identifying audience,
17–18, 35
identifying purpose, 18, 35
identifying task, 18–19, 35
incorporating direct quotations, 242–243
personal narratives, 90–91
planning stage, 37–40
producing first draft,
59–63
thesis statements, 110–111
topic sentences, 133–134
transitions in, 158–160
using imagination, 227

Y

"Young Love: The Good, the
Bad and the
Educational"
(Gallagher), 52–53